Short Story Anthology Project

*Un*usual
Circumstances

Pocol Press

Stories compiled and edited by J. Thomas Hetrick
Twenty five stories. Twenty five authors.

POCOL PRESS

Published in the United States of
America by Pocol Press.
6023 Pocol Drive
Clifton, Virginia 20124
http://www.pocolpress.com

Copyright © by J. Thomas Hetrick

Publisher's Cataloguing-in-Publication

Unusual circumstances : short fiction from around the
    globe / stories compiled and edited by J. Thomas
    Hetrick. -- 1st ed.
      p. cm. -- (Short story anthology project)
      ISBN 978-1-929763-03-0
      ISBN: 1-929763-03-4

    1. Short stories.   I. Hetrick, J. Thomas,
1957-

PN6120.2.U58 1999   808.83'1
                     QB199-901832

Editor's Comments

Decades ago, my father, Joseph S. Hetrick (1932-1998), gave me a gift more wonderful than any bicycle, electric train, chemistry set, or Flexible Flyer. That gift was the love of reading.

Our family moved a lot (courtesy of the United States Army), and home was where our books were. We seemingly followed these books and magazines everywhere, stuffing them inside their cases and piling them upon the floor. No specific genres dominated, just writing devoted to a widening variety of topics. Clever mysteries mingled with ancient histories. Volumes of poetry shared a shelf with books about the secret, inner mechanisms of clocks. The weight of our *National Geographic* collections strained the floors. My mother often railed at her husband to "Get rid of some of that junk!" Instead of discouraging him, her admonishments strengthened dad's resolve. He'd smile and say, "We simply need to get a bigger place, dear." Of course, as soon as we got more space, he'd fill it up with more books.

Being young, impressionable, and ravenous about reading, I attempted to devour every word. I'd swallow up subjects (and predicates) at the dinner table, before school, after school, and late at night, illuminating my world with a penlight when I should have been sleeping. When caught, my mother would chide me to close my eyes. "Tomorrow's a school day," she'd say. Dad left me alone, no doubt because he too, snuggled up with books long past bedtime.

All of the material selected for this volume contains insights into what we call "the human condition." These stories examine age-old issues of love, hatred, fear, loneliness, revenge, unbridled happiness, delusions of grandeur, depression, sexuality, and hope. The editor at Pocol Press extends his congratulations and appreciation to each contributor.

This work was made possible by the technical assistance of Steven Riddle, Sue Fuerst, and Lewis G. Green, Sr. Other editorial assistance was provided by Nimota Aruna, Sam George, Asheia Hayden-Ahaghotu, and Michael Lamarra.

-J. Thomas Hetrick
Compiler, Editor
Clifton, VA
Dec 1999

6

Unusual Circumstances
Table of Contents

Author	*Story*	*Page*

I do not know whether I was then a man dreaming I was a butterfly, or whether I am now a butterfly dreaming I am a man.

-H. A. Giles, *Chuang Tse*, ch. 2.

The Hour Glass
Sue W. Fuerst

Aunt Daisy's button box was more than just a container for clothing fasteners. Over the years, it had taken on the air of a family archive, the storage place for small things of importance. During my visits to her, now spinning out in her last days in the nursing home, I frequently turned to it as a source of conversation. Aunt Daisy's memories were sharp and clear, although she sometimes stirred in a mischievous dash of fantasy just to see if I was listening.

"What's this one, Aunt Daisy?" I said, handing her a small, flat, roughened object. "I don't remember seeing it before."

Her eyes bright, Aunt Daisy turned the piece in her hand several times before answering. "I haven't told this story to anyone because I can't explain the end. Maybe I *should* tell it, though; maybe someone else can figure it out."

"The things I'm about to tell you happened at a time in my life when I was trudging through a 'desert place'," Aunt Daisy began, " one of those long, bare, thirsty stretches when my main activity seemed to be putting one foot in front of the other. One weary day I dropped in on a friend who was recovering from an exhausting series of major surgeries. Judy and I had been through episodes of the best and the worst in each other's lives. We knew each other's secrets, and we laughed and cried at the same things.

"After we had exchanged the usual pleasantries, Judy turned to me and said, 'Who are you today? What's going on?' I shrugged and cobbled together a vague explanation that I felt hemmed in by my personal life, disappointed in my job, and generally frustrated and defeated.

"One of the reasons that Judy is so precious to me," Aunt Daisy went on, "is that she doesn't soothe with blandishments. After hearing me out, she was quiet for a time and then faced me again to say, 'If you had one hour in which you could do anything you wanted, what would you do?' Now it was my turn for quiet as I tumbled the possibilities over and over in my mind, then came to rest with the answer. 'I'd spend it looking for sea glass at Marblehead,' I replied.

"At first I thought Judy hadn't heard me, she sat unmoving for so long. When I was just about to tell her about Marblehead again, she stirred and pointed at a small table across the room. 'Pull open that little drawer,' she said, 'and hand me the box inside.'

"The box was about four inches square and quite heavy. Judy raised the hinged lid and rummaged among numerous small, clinking objects until she found a tiny slip of paper. 'Take this,' she said. 'Maybe you'll find what you need.' Then she lowered the lid with a firmness that closed not only the box, but also the subject.

"Several days later I ran across the slip of paper again. On leaving Judy that day she handed me a book she wanted to share, and as I picked up my things to go, I had tucked the slip inside the cover and forgotten it. Now that I had time to examine the slip more closely, I saw that it was just an address: 5343 103rd Street, N.W. 'Oh, no,' I thought, 'it's downtown.' Reluctance to go anywhere in the city almost made me toss the paper into the trash, but something nudged me; the least I could do was see if I could get there by subway. A check of the map showed a subway stop very close to the address, and in answer to a sudden impulse I gathered my coat and purse and set out for the station.

"During the hour-long ride from the suburbs into the heart of the city, I studied my map. Its makers must have struggled with 103rd, for the street was so short that there was scarcely room for a label. Riding up the subway escalator, I checked the map again and when sure of my bearings at the surface, set off through a rather dubious part of town. After several circlings and nearly giving up, I found 103rd Street tucked at an angle, hardly more than a narrow alley between two unnumbered streets, the logic of its naming unclear.

"The street was so short that only four tiny, dingy stores lined the way—a men's hat shop, a furrier, one that sold cigars and newspapers, and one labeled '5343' in old-fashioned, curly-cue numerals that had once been gold. The windows were dark and grimy, and as I tried the door, it opened stiffly, as though seldom used.

"As my eyes adjusted to the gloom, I saw a sort of faded elegance in what had been an apothecary. The ancient shelves and counters of the shop were crowded with more than just tinctures and pills, however. Ranks and rows of jars, baskets, trays, boxes, barrels, bags, stacks, and bins marched in orderly chaos around the walls of the tiny store, under, over, behind, and against any surface that would hold them. From behind the counter a ladder rose, and at the top of the ladder were two very long denim-clad legs ending in sturdy tan work boots. Startled by the opening door, the boots jerked and the ladder trembled as their owner descended. Everything about the man was tall, from his high, narrow forehead and startled shock of hair to his long, thin arms and slender fingers.

"The shopkeeper blinked at me through thick lenses, and I realized that I had no idea what to do next. I looked around the shop again, hoping for some inspiration, and then stepped to the counter and offered my now-limp slip of paper with the flat explanation, 'I was given this address.' The words sounded small and hollow even to me, but the man nodded as though he understood. 'Where?' he said. Confused, I began a rambling explanation, but he cut me off with a duck of his head and then fixed me with his gaze. Again he said, 'Where? Where is it you want to go?'

"'Feeling a bit foolish, I answered, 'The beach glass cove in Marblehead, Massachusetts.' He ducked his head again in acknowledgment and turned away, bony fingers already questing. Suddenly he turned back to ask, 'An hour?' At my nod, he picked up a small bucket and began puttering among his stores. Now and then his long, white fingers would pluck something to be added to the bucket; occasional long pauses were interspersed with dartings and mutterings as the collection grew. Then, apparently satisfied, he approached the counter again and upended the bucket into an old grocery produce scale which hung from the ceiling. Watching the dial, he reached a long arm under the counter for one more ingredient, then nodded and smiled in satisfaction. 'Now!' he said. 'We'll have you on your way in no time!'

Moving quickly, he gathered the scale's contents, sniffed them deeply, and then disappeared briefly into a back room. I listened with growing curiosity to what might have been a blender, followed by brief hammering, and then stared when the man returned to hand me a small glass bottle tightly stoppered with a cork. 'That'll be fifty cents, please,' he said. Amused and mystified, I rummaged for change in my pocket. As the old cash register clanged, he smiled cheerily. 'When you're ready,' he said, 'just pull the cork.' Then he turned as though he had forgotten me, muttered something to himself, and began to reascend his ladder. 'Just a minute!' I said, 'I don't understand! What kind of a shop is this? What's in this bottle?' His response as he turned away was kind, but final: 'Just pull the cork when you're ready to go.'

"My feet took me outside into the watery February sunshine, where I took a deep breath and shook my head, trying to dispel the feeling of unreality. I considered going back in, demanding an explanation, but the memory of the little shop's stuffy atmosphere and the dismissal of its keeper made me hesitate. As I stood in indecision, I realized that the wind had turned cold and a thin rain was falling.

"Coffee was what I needed, hot coffee and a few minutes to think all of this through. A glance at my watch told me there was plenty of time. Rounding the corner, I was surrounded by the hustle of 3:00 p.m. downtown. From across the street, however, wafted the unmistakable fragrance of Starbuck's coffee, and feeling blessed, I hurried to enter the warm haven. Nearly empty at this mid-point in the afternoon, the coffee shop was the perfect retreat. Holding a steaming cup redolent of cinnamon and rich with cream, I snuggled into a corner booth to examine my strange purchase.

"Close inspection revealed a small, five-sided glass bottle about four inches high. Holding it to the light, I could see tiny bubbles caught in the glass, but I couldn't see through to the contents inside. Its color was difficult to describe, a sort of brownish-gray, but as I turned the bottle the light flashed topaz along the beveled edges. Engraved or etched on the bottom were tiny markings that could have been scratches, and the neck was graceful and narrow. The brand-new cork was firmly wedged.

"'Pull the cork when you're ready to go.' The simplicity of the words mocked the questions they raised. Who was the man? What kind of shop had I visited? What did he mean? What was in the bottle? And most of all, *go where*? Again, I held the bottle to the light; then, with a shrug and one firm twist, shut my eyes and pulled the cork.

"The first sensation was the softness of the air against my cheek; then an involuntary deep breath filled my lungs with decidedly un-coffeeshop-like air. My ears heard a gentle splash, and I opened my eyes to see a harbor, boats rocking at anchor, swells of green water, a rocky strand. My left hand held the bottle, my right held the cork, and I was standing in the early summer morning in the cove at Marblehead.

"My feet crunched on pebbles, and looking down, I saw a beautiful piece of beach glass between my booted toes. The size of a quarter, the pale aquamarine shape had been scoured by the rocks and the waves, all sharp edges smoothed, its surface etched frosty by salt and sand. I leaned to pick it up and saw another, amber-colored, at the edge of the water. Then I saw a third, bottle-green this time, half buried. Walking to the rocky wall of the cove, I carefully placed the bottle and its cork in a snug niche and turned to the hunt. The beachcomber's rhythm took over; walk a few steps, eyes sweeping the sand, lean to grasp a treasure, into the pocket, a glance up into the sky and around the horizon, a few more steps. It was a good beach glass day, and I was finding some real beauties, each a different shade from the last. As usual, most were white, green, or amber, but there were occasional finds tinted yellow, one pinkish, a mauve, many variations on green, and several bits of red glass that winked like rubies. There were even a few pieces of what I called "beach pottery," the smoothed fragments of china or porcelain or stoneware, sometimes with a scrap of flowers or scrollwork border faintly showing.

"Up and down the tiny cove, back and forth, my sense of peace grew with the weight of beach glass in my pocket. Now the sun was overhead, and I began to play the old game: just one more piece, then one more after that, then just two more because the last one had been so truly beautiful. From one side of the cove to the other I walked, sometimes searching among the litter of shells and seaweed that marked the high-tide line, then returning to the water's edge to scuff the pebbles and overturn small rocks. As my collection grew, however, so did the old excitement: would I find any pieces that were blue? That had always been the measure of a beach-glass expedition, almost a superstition: if I found a deep-blue piece, then it would be a Good Day. Several blue pieces foretold a happy week ahead; once, I had found a dozen and wondered what old blue bottle had died to influence the rest of that summer.

"Although the sea was calm, I kept an eye on the waves, having more than once in the past been soaked to the knees by a wave stronger than its brothers. As I once again neared the niche where I had placed the bottle and cork, I decided to pause in my favorite place, a sun-warmed rock just made for sitting. I turned out the contents of my pockets and sorted my finds; a really extraordinary collection. When I got home, I would add them to my aquarium, or better yet, put them in a bottle of their own, covered with water to bring out their beauty. They would glow like pastel jewels when the sun shown through.

"Now and then I looked up from my sorting to see the sea birds creaking and wheeling overhead, watch a sailboat leave its berth, or squint at the round white clouds bumping and merging out to sea. Out of habit, I scanned the top of the cliffs as I had in the years when Jones, the finest little dog the universe has ever known, had shared my beach glass days. To my shock, I saw again the tiny black figure waiting for my glance to trigger her race down the rocky path along the cliff to the beach below. Reaching the sand, she fled straight towards me, young again, her slim poodle body stretched full out, ears swept back like flags in a gale. Within three feet of my astonished stare, she abruptly swerved, as she always did, and instead headed for the water's edge, pretending to sniff a pebble or nose a pile of foam. Having achieved nonchalance, she dropped pretense and came to sit quietly by my side, favoring me with a quick lick and her beloved, lopsided grin. 'Little girl,' I whispered, finally daring to reach out for her small form. 'You're here, too? How can this be?' I caught her up to smell her fur, to hold again her slim legs, feel the warmth of her, her weight so perfect for holding.

"What was this, then? Heaven? Bewildered but happy, I sat with Jones on my lap and concentrated on the joy and wonder all around. It had to be some kind of magic bottle; the man an alchemist or an angel or someone from a dimension where miracles were dispensed like free samples. Closing my eyes, I pictured the coffee shop, my hand holding the tightly-stoppered bottle to the light, heard the pop! as I pulled the cork free—then here, the warm sun, the soft breeze from the water, the shells and glass, little Jones alive again. Long I sat, lulled by the sound of the waves, the quiet of the beach, my hair stirred by occasional passing sprites of breeze. Jones lay contentedly in my arms, the beach glass collection dried in the sun, the sun sank lower in the sky. Between mental yawns, my mind asked, 'What is this?' but each time the question had less urgency.

"The only thing I understood was that I had somehow been given a day of peace in a place of beauty with a companion so precious that the combination melted and ran like warm honey. The bottle had something to do with it, of that I was convinced. Suddenly rousing myself I stood, with Jones still in my arms, and walked to where the bottle stood in its niche in the rocks. Realizing that her nap was over, Jones struggled to be put down and I stooped to set her on the sand. She gave one sharp bark and headed for the water's edge, running for sheer happiness and full of youth. I turned again to the bottle and reached for it, sure now that it held magic. If I corked it up carefully, the day might be mine to enjoy again and again.

"As I grasped the bottle, a small rogue wave sneaked silently up the beach and slapped the back of my knees. I staggered against a barnacle-roughened boulder, lost my balance, and sat down abruptly in the water. The bottle slipped from my hand; I watched in slow motion as it fell to the beach and struck a rock, the fine glass shattering into small fragments. I scrambled to my feet but as I leaned down towards the ruin, I saw a cobalt-blue piece of beach glass half the size of my hand nestled among the brown-gray shards. It was absolutely the finest piece of blue that I had ever found. As I seized the prize, I heard Jones give her sharp, happy bark, and I smelled coffee. The breeze died, and I no longer tasted the sea.

"I opened my eyes to find that nothing had changed. The walls of the coffee shop were around me again, and the February rain tapped dully on the window. My mug of coffee, grown cold, was still before me; other customers sat in the booths around me, talking quietly. I glanced at my watch—four o'clock— was it possible that I had slept for an hour? What a dream I had had! It had been so real—the warm sun, the bottle, the smell of the sea, the collection of glass, little Jones. I glanced around the shop guiltily—had I snored? No one seemed to take any notice, so I rose from the table to gather my things for the trip home. As I opened my hand, however, something fell to the table. My breath caught as I reached for it: a cobalt-blue piece of beach glass half the size of my hand, a few grains of sand clinging to it still."

"That's all, Aunt Daisy?" I said. She remained silent, her eyes turned to look out of the window. Surely there was more! "What did you do then?" I asked insistently. "Did you go back to the little store and ask the man? What about the bottle?"

"I told you, I don't understand the end myself," said my aunt. "The day was late; I felt more tired than I ever had in my life, and all I could think of was the long ride home. I told myself that I would go back to the little shop on another day, that I would solve the mystery once and for all. But somehow, days led to weeks; other things became important; and when I finally did return to the area one late spring afternoon, 103rd Street was not to be found. I asked several people, but after enduring puzzled looks and mistrusting stares, I finally gave up. The coffee shop was there, all right, but it was somehow ordinary, less fragrant, more crowded. The neighborhood I had visited was gone, along with the map I had used to find it. Everything about that winter day had most likely been only a dream.

Aunt Daisy paused again, and when she spoke, it was barely above a whisper.

"Only one thing was left to endanger my certainty. . ."

She stopped speaking and opened her hand. Nestled in her palm was a shape of cobalt blue, smoothed by the waves, frosted by the salt and sand.

Back to Back
Jessica Slater

There are splinters of it, the death of her, like glass shattered through my head. My mother is lying on the tiled kitchen floor in a puddle of bright blood. On the bench lies the discarded knife and the onion she was chopping: fine slices and a curved unleafing chunk, juice still glistening on the board. There must be onion tears, damp, now crystallizing, on her cooling cheek. Onions never failed to make her cry.

I can't measure time. Just still life. Still life with onions. (Unsigned.)

"Jen, I need to see you."
"What's up?"
"Are you busy? Can I come round?"
"Well, I was working, but if it's important..."
"Thanks. I really appreciate it. I'll be there in half an hour okay?"
"But what's..?"
The line is already dead.

I am waiting to cross the road. A young woman stands on the other pavement and it occurs to me that we are at once identical and opposite. She faces this side of the world and wants to be where I am. I face that side and want to be where she is. My 'here' is her 'there'. Same map but different lands.

The traffic clears. We traverse the same strip of road and then our worlds are back to back, sliding further and further apart.

"Do you love me?" I ask when the door opens, shifting my feet on the steps.

"Yes!" she laughs, hair flopping across her face like curtains. "Come in, silly."

I grasp her hand and pull her to me, out into the cold air, smothering her so she can barely breathe. She doesn't see my eyes squeezed tight like fists. She pulls away and looks at me. I think she looks suspicious. Perplexed, at least.

"What's wrong?" she asks.

I stare back in silence, hardly seeing her.

"Come on, let's go inside."

She drags me after her like a reluctant child. My head sags with the realization that I don't know how to deal with this and hadn't expected things to feel so half perfectly normal and half completely crazy rather than some smooth mixture of the two. Everything seems double-edged. Both sharp and dull.

"Do you want some tea?"

I nod. Fucking tea. I want to laugh. My mother's lying dead in her kitchen and here I am about to have tea. How fucking English.

I hear the radio on and my mother humming along. I'm not wearing shoes so she doesn't hear me coming into the kitchen. I stand for a moment without speaking, watching her.

"What're you making?" I ask and she jumps, visibly, my voice startling her.

She looks at me, not with relief but with tense agitation: "Please don't do that, dear, you know it terrifies me!"

Her response jars me so I am stunned and then something snaps and I shout: "But I didn't do anything! I've never done anything, but you're always terrified!"

Her eyes freeze on me as if I'm the one holding the knife.

"I can't stand this anymore! What do I have to do? I just talk to you and you jump out of your skin! It's ridiculous! It wasn't me!"

I am exasperated.

She is silent, shaking, the knife twitching in her hand. She has no intention of reasoning with me. She is probably preparing to defend herself. Her mind, calculating the distance, the speed, her reaction time. I stand still, closing my eyes and trying to calm myself but I can't. Even against the screen of my closed lids I see fear dragging at her eyes as they stare through me, her face taut as a fishing line.

Cut. Cut, slack and fall. I've dreamed it before. The slow motion dull thud and then the silence, broken only by the tick of things done.

My mother brings me a plate of leftover moussaka, heated up in the microwave. She's not eating. It's late.

"How was college today?"

"Oh, all right."

I wish she would just leave me to eat. But the kitchen is her territory. She sits sideways at the table, her body facing away from me, her shoulders hunched, only her words thrown carefully in my direction like raw meat to lions. I watch her profile. The slight hollow where her cheek and jaw connect. I imagine her insides like a system of cogs that clunk and grate together under her skin. Her thoughts, sharp, pointed like spears, like the defensive quills of a porcupine. I wonder if she knows I know. Maybe she can sense it somehow. I wanted to say something but now I can't imagine how the words will escape when they've been locked up for so long. There is nothing for us to go back to after we have hugged and laughed and cried with relief that finally it's all out in the open because it's instilled in me, in the way my blood jumps through me, hers always running from his.

"I called by to see Uncle David on the way home. We had a good talk," I say.

"Oh, that's nice. How is he?" she asks.

"Fine, I guess. Just a bit tired. He's been working a lot. We talked more about you, actually."

I pause. She is simply curious: "Oh?"

"Well, about my father."

I watch the impact of the reference. It gives me a rush even though I should detest him. The thing is, she's blamed me for so long I can't help but feel a strange sympathy.

She is startled. Alert. I feel her pulse quicken. I don't look away, but follow her recoiling eyes, shrinking deep, deep inside her until her face is just a cave with two pinpricks of torchlight.

"But there's nothing to say about him," she says, her voice a terse fidget of air.

"No, of course not," I sigh, pushing my plate away in frustration and getting up out of my seat. "Of course not."

"I need to know. I don't think I can deal with it anymore and believe me, not knowing doesn't prevent my imagination from concocting things."

I can be so direct with him, which makes life with her seem unreal in contrast except it is my life and even if she's crazy she's still my mother. But I mean what I'm saying. It's becoming unbearable. Somehow my getting older seems to have made it worse rather than better. Just the last few weeks she's been flaking before my eyes. Every time I look at her another muscle freezes in her face. My uncle is calmer than I expect. We have discussed it before and he has always remained firm about it not being his business to tell me if she doesn't want me to know. But now he seems resigned to it. He is quiet, stroking the tablecloth with long smooth strokes, and then looks up and says:

"She was raped. No words ever passed between them. She learned his name at the trial, but she refused even to look at him."

Boom (fact) boom, like a pistol!

"Christ!" I've imagined it, of course, the worst possibility - but I always reasoned that she would never have kept me, under such circumstances. I'd end up thinking, hoping, that even if he'd been bad to her, there must have been some love in it somewhere. Some vague redemption.

In the pause I am both a wiry scream and a hollow silence.

"But why did she keep me?" I ask, eventually.

"She was against abortion. It must have been one of the hardest decisions she ever made," he replies and the next pause utters all the rest that we haven't the heart to say.

I have always imagined that she saw his face in mine. She refused even to look at him. The words throb in my mind. He never had a face. Until I was born. I don't just remind her of him. I am him. I really am just a ghost.

I feel a hatred for him that I can barely contain. And yet, all the years of despising her, of detesting her weakness, her fear, above all her inability to love me, mould into a mute congratulation of the act. Trickling comprehension mingles with disgust. Like the twisting battle of their genes inside me.

Cut. Cut, slack and fall.

The radio is unbearable. I can't find the switch to turn it off so I pull out the plug. It crackles and goes silent.

Now I look at her.

I find her, as in life, rather pathetic. She has fallen awkwardly. Her neck, messy with blood, twists strangely so she looks like a puppet, crumpled, strings loose and confused without gravity, head a little misplaced. Unfortunate that she should carry such tension through to her death when it burdened her more than enough in life.

There is less blood than I would have imagined.

Strands knot: I am alive. She gave birth to me, alone in her mother's house. I am here, alone with her as she lies dead on the tiled floor. I can't even cry.

Jen brings the tea and settles herself on the armchair opposite me, her arms wrapped around her knees and her thick striped socks as if it's story time and she's waiting for me to begin.

"I've just killed her," I say at last.

"What are you talking about?"

"My mother. She's dead. I mean, I killed her."

Tea is spilling. Now the fusion begins. Normality will shiver and shake and spill and be forced to acknowledge that things aren't right.

"Oh my God! You're not serious... Oh my God!"

Having expressed horror, she has no idea how to respond. I have no idea how she should respond. So we are left in a strangely calm silence as if our batteries have faded.

I feel almost relaxed, more functional at least, now that our thoughts are approximately aligned.

I don't really want to talk. I want to hold her, to be held. I get up and move towards her but she shrinks back, despite herself, into the armchair.

And then, at last, I begin to cry. I look into her eyes, locking them, promising her, promising her, and crying. Hard, hot tears. She is crying too.

Finally she gets up from the chair and takes my hand. Our eyes squeeze tight like fists.

I can't measure time.

Just still life.

Jamaica Breakdown
Steven Riddle

That was all part of it too. When you stayed up too late drinking and fell asleep with the television on but no sound, so you could hear your wife snoring in the other room. You could feel sorry for yourself, or you could do something, and so you pass out.

The only thing you can remember about the subway station is that it was dark, and there was something wrong with the man at the other end of the platform, and you needed to use a bathroom, but you didn't dare. You think that you were there to catch the Long Island Express home, but you don't know why you're there without your mother or father, and it seems that you are on the way home from Philadelphia. There are a lot of other people in the station, other kids, and some adults, and you don't know why you're scared by the man at the end of the platform, or why you feel all alone. And this is as close to Jamaica as you'll ever come.

And you know that if you could get there everything would be all right. That if you could make it there the sea and the beaches and the nightlife and everything would be all right. Your wife would be as young as she was when you married her, and she would be in love with you. You would be younger and able to love her back. There would be children and champagne and dancing. And knowing that you spend another night in the other room with a bottle, and you don't even turn on the set.

Once it was the novel you were going to write. And then the song, and the book of poems. You were going to save the entire Amazonian rain forest on the proceeds of your book of poetry. Then you were going to invent something, you didn't know what. Then it was the money you were going to inherit from your uncle who went bankrupt right before he died of a heart attack. And now it's weekly sinking your money into the lottery. Trudging in behind all the other people in the line who have a system, and who play the numbers. And you don't even have enough hope to play a system. You just let the computer pick them, and you don't even check the tickets, because you know it isn't going to happen, but you've got to do it anyway because it fills the empty spaces where everything else used to be.

That in itself is worth another night with the bottle and listening to the old lady snore, and wondering whether she was dreaming the same things.

How did you get here? Where are you? You're too old and too fat, and you aren't even what anyone, except some teenager, might call old and fat. But you know that this is the end of the line, and you're going to be here for quite a while cause the train doesn't stop by all that often, and you're nowhere near the station when it does.

So you didn't go to M.I.T. when you had the chance. You didn't go to Harvard or to Yale. But you suspect, even if you did you'd still be in the same place waiting. It isn't in your past but in your present, you can't even operate in the real world anymore. You think that it would be so much better to have a real job, like in construction, rather than sitting behind a desk writing up portfolios for ambassadors' wives on who they are, how many children they have, and what are taboo topics for discussion. Sitting there and thinking the phone on the desks whirs and lights up, purring and blinking at you, waiting politely, but insistently for an answer. You pick it up.

"Ansley speaking."

"Bob, what are you doing tonight? A couple of us are going out, maybe bowl a couple, drink a couple, maybe pick up some chicks, you want to come?"

Larry Sarban calling again, knowing that there's no way in hell you'd dare try it, not with Lucille. It's bad enough living with her, but at least she was there. What would it be like with no one?

You smile into the phone and say, "Love to Larry. When should Lucille and I be at your place."

He laughs and puts down the phone. You can get back to work. Even as you mark up a couple of words, running that blue pencil down its thin line he is at your side.

"Hey, Bob. Lunch time, let's take a break, you look like you could use one."

"Sure, Larry. Just let me go wash my hands." And you go into the washroom and look at a person who seems to be a total stranger. And you're just glad that you don't have easy access to the junk. Something like that in the agency and you're out. You run your hands through your hair to straighten it and wash your hands. You step outside where Larry's waiting and say, "So where are we going?"

"Your choice Bob. Seems like you're the one who needs the break."

You admit to yourself that it's good to get away from that desk. It's good to take a break and you don't want to just spend it anywhere. So you say, "Let's go to Montego Bay." It's just down the street and maybe enough of a break.

But Larry says, "Jamaica? You paying?" And you laugh even though it's not that funny. But it is.

Over lunch Larry says, "So you're not the engineer you always thought you'd be, is that so bad?"

And you can't tell him it's worse than he can even imagine, because he's five years younger and he has a girlfriend who belongs in centerfolds and he wears suits that look hand-tailored, and there's nothing in the world he wants that he won't have. Even that smile with perfectly even teeth shows it. You're angry and sad all at once, and you have nothing to say to this man who can't see past his own reflection in the mirror behind you.

But he surprises you and says, "So what's wrong? It's something more than just a job, nothing could get you down that much."

You take a gulp of beer to push down the block that has risen up in your throat and you say, "You can't even guess the half of it."

"Lucille stepping out on her old man?"

It never occurred to you, and as soon as you hear it you know that it's sheer nonsense, because she's tied just as tight and as fast to you as you are to her, and for the same reasons. You both live in a little self-made hell that you won't tell the other one about. So what is it all about? You know it's going to take more than lunchtime to figure that one out.

You get home at ten after six, and even though it's late spring, with the curtains drawn it may as well be three in the morning. You toss your jacket into the chair by the door and head for the kitchen, although you're tempted to stop by the bar on the way. The phone rings and you answer it.   "Honey, it's me. I'm going to be home a little late tonight. We're closing out a couple of accounts, and I can't get away until I show Jules how to do it."

"When should I expect you?"

"Don't wait dinner. I could be real late. She doesn't seem to be picking it up real easy."

"Okay, be careful on the way home."

"I will. Bye."

"Bye." And you hang up the phone, and decide it doesn't matter if you stop by the bar after all. It's been a hard day, and you need to slow down fast and there's no better way than hitting a wall, hard.

Tonight it's something special, because even though you finish a bottle and it must be two in the morning you have not passed out. The front door opens and Lucille comes in. She takes off her shoes downstairs and comes up quietly into the room. You close your eyes and the room spins away. You hope that you don't throw up, but you don't really care.

The Ambassador to Liberia wants to know what the chief exports of Ghana and the Ivory Coast are and needs the information this morning because he is going to lunch with ministers this afternoon. You are looking it up in your World Fact Book when the phone rings. You punch the button and pick up the receiver, "Ansley here."

"Bob," it's Lucille's voice, " I was hoping you'd be at your desk."

"Yes?"

"It looks like I may be late again. But Jules wants you to stop by and go out with us to celebrate this account."

"What time?"

"You mean you want to?"

"Sure, why not."

"Hold on a second." Lucille puts the phone down and is gone. You look back at your file for the Ambassador, and thumb through some of the stack of paper on your desk, looking for the most recent factsheet on Ghana. She's back and you don't catch the beginning of what she says. " ... about eight o'clock."

"That sounds good." But it doesn't because it means you can't spend the night alone with a friend-in-a-glass, and you can't even visit because you might kill someone picking them up. "I'll see you then."

And even Lucille notices and says, " Is something wrong Bob?"

"No, why do you think that?"

"Oh, I don't know. I thought you might be coming down with a bug."

"No, I'm fine. See you tonight."

"Bye."

And you bite your lip and turn back to the file for the Ambassador. And what you'd like to do more than anything else is grind that fucking file under your heel. Just tear out the pages and burn them under that lazy-ass bastard's nose. But you can't do that, not now.

You drive the car like you play a pinball machine, bouncing lane to lane and hoping that the machine doesn't tilt before you get to where you're going, but not really caring if it does. And the thought crosses your mind that you are one self-pitying self-involved bastard. If you cared about anything but yourself you wouldn't be here. And that's truth. But you don't indulge in truth. It's a luxury few can afford. So you turn off the thought and slide into the exit lane on the beltway.

You pull up in front of the building and there are Lucille and Jules standing just inside the front doors of the building. It is raining.

They run to the car. You flip the electric switch to unlock the doors. The two curbside doors jerk open and Lucille spills into the front laughing, and Jules into the back. You have not met Jules, and Lucille says, after she is finished laughing and gasping, "Jules Davenport, this is my husband Bob." And Lucille leans over and gives you a peck on the cheek. The only kiss you've gotten in a month, and a display of property more than love. Lucille says, "Jules is new, we hired her on about three months ago."

"I know," you say in a voice you hope is neutral. And Lucille looks at you with that warning look that you know means, "Don't make trouble."

But it's already too late. And you're halfway to your flight.

So you reach the restaurant, which is owned by Jules's father, and at which you are going to be treated to dinner. You let the ladies out in front, and after Jules has closed her door Lucille ducks back in as though she forgot her purse and says in a hiss, "Don't make trouble. I don't need trouble."

And you smile your sweetest and say, "Neither of us do." And you know that you're halfway down the runway already, and there isn't anything that can stop you. And you want to stop, but you can't. Lucille clutches her purse with knuckles that are white. That's just too bad. You notice that there's more than a little white on your knuckles as you drive into the garage.

You join them at a table, far from the bar, and an overdressed waiter asks you what you'd like to drink. And what you'd like to drink is a double boiler-maker followed by something strong. But what you order is a gin and tonic. Jules and Lucille are already drinking their drinks, and Lucille's lips are drawn tight as a gash. Jules looks around like she hasn't been in the place before, her head going every direction before she looks at you, her teeth lighting the way for many poor sailors to find home. You don't know why, just the day, and the fact that you want to be in Jamaica, but you want to take the shine out of just one of those teeth. You grin, but your eyes are sharp and cold.

Jules says, "Lucille has been showing me how to close out accounts."

You nod your head and the waiter returns with your drink, which you start to drink too fast. You look at the menu.

Jules says, "We haven't had a chance to do a lot of talking. What do you do?"

And you want to say, "Drink myself into a stupor every night watching television without the sound, and sometimes make love to my right hand, why do you ask." But it's too early in the evening to bring out the big guns so you say, "I edit government documents, and write resumes and summaries for the State Department."

"Oh, that sounds interesting."

About as interesting as a cave to a claustrophobe. The waiter is back and you order another gin and tonic and think that you haven't gotten smashed on perfume before. And it's time to order dinner. There's nothing on the menu that you want. But you order the prime rib because it's the most expensive and Jules's dad would foot the bill and you could leave it on your plate.

And you think to yourself that it would be a whole lot easier if you knew what you were angry about. But you don't, and it doesn't matter.

Lucille says, " The Watner account ..." and you can't even hear the end of the sentence. You pick up your second drink and drain it. Almost as soon as you put the empty glass down the waiter is there to take your order for another. He knows a mark when he sees one.

Lucille looks at you while she talks to Jules. And your eyes lock so that she stammers and lifts a napkin to her mouth and excuses herself. And it's round one to the good guys.

As she goes to the ladies room you think about Jamaica, and how the money you made from your book and your new diet and your exercise machine and the lottery got you there to sun on the beach. And you grit your teeth and smile at Jules who smiles back uncertainly. She hasn't known you long enough to know, but she can tell there's probably something wrong.

And that's just fine with you because the water around Jamaica is filled with sharks, and you have to be mighty careful where you're swimming even when you're one of them.

And Lucille is back, Jamaica is gone. You have a headache and you down your drink, hoping you can smash it with a big enough hammer. Lucille will have to drive home tonight, with you in the back seat. And part of you feels ashamed, and part of you just wants to get back to the sandy beaches and the waters filled with sharks. Because the sharks don't matter if you never go in the water. And you only go to Jamaica to sit on the beach and look out at the water.

The waiter passes by again, and you think you'll order another drink. And Lucille looks at you again, but this time you think you see something else, and the hammer hits you in the head and the headache is gone. Jamaica is gone.

Suddenly the room is filled with Lucille whose eyes are not angry, but maybe sad and whose frown is not foreboding, but trembling. And you think that maybe there is room for the two of you there on the beach.

You remember little of your night at the restaurant. You wake up in your own bed beside Lucille. You roll over and touch her shoulder to wake her. She mumbles. You think maybe you should kiss her, but you haven't in such a long time you can't. And you say, "What say you and me go to Jamaica."

And she turns over and looks you straight in the eye and says, "Have you gone out of your mind..." and you don't hear what she says anymore because you are already gone. Only this time you may be out in the water, and the sharks may be there, but they don't matter in the tropical sunshine. All that matters is that you have reached the end of the line, and you don't know how you got there. You decide that it will be a ticket for one, one way.

Dead Aim
Bryan Steven Follins

Jesse Green had begun his nightly check of e-mail. There were 26 new messages in the mailbox. One message had an attachment. The title of the message read: One Hundred Different Ways to Cheat On Your Spouse. A mile-wide grin spread across Green's face, as he rapidly scrolled down to the e-mail. Cynthia, his wife, would not be in for another hour, so he was going to enjoy reading THIS MESSAGE.

Green opened the e-mail.

It read: "Here are some foolproof methods to help you establish an airtight plan on how to cheat on your spouse. This demo is free, so you do not have to worry about pulling out your credit card. Feel free to click on the attachment."

A wider grin crossed Jesse's face.

He clicked on the attachment.

The screen turned black.

Next, a pulsating white circle appeared in the middle of the monitor. The circle became larger and larger.

Then a voice said: "The first step to cheating on your spouse is to blind them."

At this point the light pulse flashed ten times brighter than the sun, and Green was blinded.

Then the voice said: "The second step is to make them deaf."

Now, a high-pitched whistling sound erupted from the file. Green grabbed his ears. The whistling became louder and louder, and then, silence.

Jesse realized he could no longer see or hear. He panicked and tried to stand up, and he tripped on his chair. He fell to the floor, and lay there in a state of total shock.

Then the voice said: "Now that they can neither see nor hear, there is nothing they can do to stop you."

Now there was a grinding noise on the computer. A message flashed across the screen saying: "System hardware failure." The screen went blank, and Jesse was blank.

While all of this was going on, Cynthia had entered the room. She was feeling proud. Her newly developed e-mail virus had worked.

She had to get changed, for she had a date an hour later.

Destiny's Touch
Jason Andreas

Destiny.
What is destiny?
I suppose Destiny is something that touches each and every one of us. It's not something you can see, hear or feel, but it's there all the same. Quietly controlling us. It maps out our entire lives from beginning to end, occasionally throwing in a couple of unexpected twists for good measure. It knows all that will happen in our futures, good, bad or indifferent. Everything, from the greatest triumph to the smallest breath.

Sometimes I wonder, though, if destiny is all it's cracked up to be. I mean, surely nothing can have that amount of control. Or does that just mean that we're all prisoners in ourselves, living with an illusion of freedom, but nothing more than an illusion? Haven't you ever experienced something in your life, even just one little event, which you just couldn't fathom out or explain? There you are then, that's what you call destiny.

You may wonder where I'm going with this. Matter of fact, so do I. I suppose now would be a good time to introduce myself. My name's Casey, I'm a seventeen-year old kid from the outskirts of Castleville. It's only a small town, but I'm happy here. I live with my folks still, but me and my friend Bobby are going to get an apartment together soon. We'll get around to it eventually. Anyway, I'm talking about destiny because that's the only explanation I have for what happened to me last summer. It was one of the aforementioned inexplicable events, which contrived to change my life, and the lives of those around me, forever. My tale begins in June 1999, the first day of our summer holidays.

It was one of those lazy summer days that you can only dream of. The noonday sun was beating down from the cloudless sky, and there wasn't even a hint of a breeze. Most of the residents of Castleville had converged on their local parks to work on their tan, or just to avoid work. My family and friends were no different. We sat there, in the park, just talking and laughing with each other. The world was at peace, and we were content. My friend Sarah Cannon was there, along with Bobby and Jenny. You may wonder why I gave Sarah's second name, and not those of Bobby and Jenny. Well, simple reason is that I was in love with her. She didn't know it, of course, and I wasn't about to tell her. Why?

She was too good for me. Sarah was stunningly beautiful. She had no end of romantic offers (and some not-so romantic ones, too); most of which were from guys a lot better looking than me, and wealthier too. She could have had her pick of any guy in Castleville, without exception. We had been close friends for about five years by this time, and she hadn't shown any interest in me whatsoever, so I didn't think there was much of a point in pressing the matter.

The sun was really intense by afternoon, so we all decided to go down to the lake in the middle of the park in an attempt to cool off. That's when we met the stranger.

He was the only person at the lake, which was really strange considering the oppressive heat. He was sitting on a boulder, facing away from us and over the lake. He was playing a violin of some kind; his bow caressing the strings, moving backwards and forwards slowly. The music was sad, really melancholy. It was the kind of sound, which enters your head, and makes you start to think about how wrong the world is. Imagine pure depression converted into music, and you're on the right track. Jenny started to cry softly, and it took all my willpower to keep from joining her. Sarah and Bobby's eyes were also beginning to leak gently. Sarah, apprehensive, began to approach him. I wanted to reach out and stop her, but I couldn't seem to move. I felt like a spectator in my own body, helplessly watching as the love of my life moved towards the somber stranger.

"He..hello?" she called out softly, as if not wanting to break his concentration. "Hello? Er...excuse me...I...um."

The music abruptly stopped and the stranger turned deliberately from his perch. I almost screamed when I saw his face. Or, to be more precise, his eyes. They were like two black holes in his face, they were so dark, and when they fixed upon mine, his eyes seemed to glow with a soft, bluish light. He turned to look at Sarah, regarding her with some curiosity before he spoke.

"Greetings to you, young Sarah," he said. His voice sounded soft and level, almost like a loud whisper. Then I realized what I'd missed. He knew her name.

Sarah must have also noticed this, because after what seemed like hours, she said, "You know my name."

It wasn't a question, but a statement, but it begged for clarification.

"I know lots of things, Sarah."

His eyes flicked over to me again.

"I have seen eagles fall from the top of mountains. I have watched as lions have hunted down wildebeest. I have seen death, chaos and destruction. I know too much, your names are merely the surface of what I can tell you."

By this time, you could virtually taste the fear in our hearts. I looked over at Bobby and he looked back with a resigned and tired expression on his face. I looked at Jenny, who appeared close to tears. She seemed like she was on the verge of collapse. Then I looked at Sarah, and I wished I hadn't. Her expression was not one of fear, or even caution. Instead, she looked enthralled. She stared at the man with something approaching adoration on her face. That scared me more than anything.

"Who are you?" I managed to blurt out. I felt like those eyes were tearing at my very soul as he returned my gaze.

"That is a very good question, Casey. A very good question. I have many names, but I can truthfully say that I *am* every one of them? I think not. If truth be told, I have no names at all, merely descriptions. Most of which are not very accurate, but they serve their purpose adequately, I suppose."

Bobby took a tentative step forward. "Are you the Devil?" The question was asked carefully, with no trace of emotion, positive or negative, whatsoever.

"Some would like to think so, Robert. But no, I am not Lucifer, nor do I serve him. If truth be told, I am one of his sworn enemies."

"What, an angel?" Bobby's eyes grew wide as he asked his next question.

"No. I am not of that realm, I am of the mortal plain, just as you are."

At that point I realized that I had regained control of my body, and I wasted no time in taking advantage of the situation. I screamed at Bobby and Jenny to run, grabbed Sarah by the hand, and dragged her away. I then fled myself, with Sarah following close behind. I risked a look back. The stranger did not seem bothered with our retreat. He merely turned away and resumed his playing. His sorrowful violin strains followed us all the way home.

We all ran straight back to my house. My folks must have still been at the park, because the place was empty. We ended up in my room and sat around, each nursing his or her own thoughts about what had just transpired. After an hour of silence, without even looking at one another, finally Jenny broke the ice. She'd been silent through the whole encounter.

"Who the hell was that?"

"*What* the hell? More like." I answered. Bobby nodded mutely. Sarah stayed silent. Bobby must have picked up on this.

"Sarah, what in God's name happened to *you* back there? If Casey hadn't dragged you away, you'd probably be making love to that thing by now, judging by the way you were looking at him!"

Sarah just looked at Bobby and bit her lip.

"I don't know what happened to me. I couldn't help myself. There was just something about him, it just... I mean, it was like I was being pulled in, I just, I just, I..."

Sarah broke down in tears and curled up into a ball. I scowled at Bobby and took Sarah in my arms. I tried to soothe her sobbing, but it took a long time before she calmed down. She was quite clearly terrified at her reaction to the (for want of a better word) man. Jenny turned on Bobby, too.

"What the hell was that for, Bobby? Haven't you got any sense? You think she wanted to go to that, that, thing out of her own free will? Look at her, she's close to cracking up and all you can do is attack her! You make me sick, Bobby Mitchell! Sick!"

Jenny stood up and stormed out of the room, slamming the door behind her so hard that it almost came off its hinges. Bobby just looked on in astonishment. I knew exactly how he was feeling. No one had ever heard Jenny raise her voice before. She was such a quiet, gentle girl. Of course, you can guess what my first thought was then, but I quickly dismissed it. We were all just a little stressed after our encounter, and we'd probably be able to think better in the morning. I voiced this opinion to Bobby, who wholeheartedly agreed. He said his goodbyes and left, promising to call me first thing the next morning. It was just me and Sarah now, alone in my room. She was lying hushed in my arms, breathing softly. At first I thought she was asleep, but then she turned to look up at me.

"Casey," she whispered, "Casey, I'm so sorry. I don't know what he did to me back there, but I couldn't control myself."

"It's okay, Sarah," I answered, "I understand. I'm here for you. You can stay in my room if you want, I'll crash on the couch."

She snuggled up to me then.

"Thank you, Casey. You don't know how much I appreciate you. I love you, you're the best friend I have."

"I love you too, Sarah." I answered, just a little too sincerely. Thankfully, she didn't seem to notice. "Come on, you'd better go to bed, you've had a rough day."

"Casey, don't move, let's just stay like this. I need to be close to someone just now. Please."

The pleading in her voice almost drove me to tears. Choking them back, I reassured her that it was fine. "Thanks, Casey. I won't forget this."

"A check will do fine, Sarah. You can make it payable to Casey Keller plc."

She laughed softly.

"All right, Casey, I'll contact the bank in the morning."

She moved a little to get comfortable, then quickly fell asleep. I stayed awake all night, watching her, keeping her safe. I though that maybe everything would be OK after all.

I felt very close to Sarah that night; not just physically, but emotionally and spiritually too. Bobby and Jenny both knew how I felt about Sarah, but they were good enough to keep it a secret. I would never have been able to look her in the face again if she knew, and that sense of closeness and togetherness would never have occurred. She may not have loved me then, but I knew we had the next best thing.

The next morning, we didn't know quite how to act. All sorts of little undertones and subtleties cropped into everything Sarah and I said or did. I figured that it was a mixture of embarrassment on her part and longing on mine, with the weird stranger's shadow hanging over us at all times. After Sarah had made her excuses and left, I resolved to find the stranger and discover exactly who he was and why he was here. I wasn't going to take any of the others along though, especially not Sarah, after the way she'd reacted the first time around. I didn't want her to ever have to go through that again. Ever. Later that day, after telling everyone that I had to go and visit my Aunt in the neighbouring city, I set out again for the lake.

Once again, though not as surprising this time, I found the lakeside to be completely empty. Totally empty, without one human soul. Not even the stranger was there. I felt glad. Despite my feverish anger at this stranger that I had worked myself up into, I didn't quite know exactly what I'd do if we crossed paths again. I started to look around, paying close attention to the rock upon which he'd sat the previous day. It looked much, much older than the surrounding boulders, like it'd been there since the dawn of time. I knew this to be odd, since the town shipped them in when they were building the houses. The rocks added 'texture' to the lakeside. I don't know if rocks can rot, but this looked as close to deterioration as possible. I just didn't understand it, so I decided to move on. I turned to walk back the way I came and almost walked into him, the man I'd come searching for - the stranger that both captivated and terrified in one fell swoop. He brushed past me and sat down on what I had come to think of as 'his' rock. He didn't seem to have his violin today, which kind of relieved me, because I didn't fancy hearing that music again.

"Casey, you intrigue me..." he began in his hushed monotone. "Not many people seek me, especially of your age. There are things I know of you that I wish I did not, such as your love for the other girl, for that is yours to know alone, but there are also things I do wish to know, and cannot, such is the way of things."

I stared at him, more confused than scared.

"How did you know I was in love with her?"

He sighed, gently, almost inaudibly.

"My young fellow, it is foremost on your mind at all times. Your love for her crowds all other thoughts to the back of your mind. I am surprised that she herself has not noticed, for she has good sight."

"Sight?" I questioned.

"She can see things as they are, not as other think they should be. That is why she approached me yesterday. She knew I meant her no harm, and she was intrigued."

"She told me she couldn't help herself, it –"

"Yes, I know what she told you last night. Such are the problems with life. Instinct so often scares you into your little warm burrows, preventing you from evolving to the next level of your existence. Technology is, of course, to blame, but humans must find that out for themselves. I cannot tell them what to do, for this is not my place."

I was interested now. I mean, he didn't seem to want to hurt me. I got the impression that if he did, there would be no way I could stop him. So, I decided to go with the flow, as it were, and find out as much as I could about him.

"Who are you? I asked you yesterday, but you didn't answer me properly..."

"No, I will admit that I withheld the knowledge from the four of you. I had a reason for this. Your friends Jennifer and Robert don't have the mental strength to understand. It would have damaged them if I had told them, and that was not my wish. Even your true love, although she has good sight, may not have been able to take the information. You however, are strong enough, a rarity in humanity. If I tell you, you must never reveal my true identity to your friends, for it will cause them nothing but harm. Do you understand me, young Casey?"

"Yes, sir."

I don't know where the 'sir' came from, but this stranger had such presence, such power, that it was a natural reaction.

"Good. Then I shall explain to you." He paused momentarily, then began his speech.

"From the beginning of time, since life first existed, my being was required. My job is to take away the hurt, to end the suffering, and to heal the pain. Humanity remains the only species I have ever come across which has thought of me as more person than event. Humanity gave me a solid form, and a mind to go with it. They were not precisely correct, of course, for it was beyond their reasoning to make me look like one of their own. They would generally represent me as a shadowy figure, or an animated skeleton, because terror is easier to deal with if it is easy to recognize. For reasons which even I cannot explain, they associate my function with a farming implement - a scythe, I believe it's called. That part I find most peculiar."

"Wait a minute," I stammered. "Are you trying to tell me that you, sitting here in front of me, are *Death*? The Grim Reaper?"

The figure nodded.

"Yes, although as I stated previously, I have no idea where the 'Reaper' part came from."

A kind of, almost insane calmness came over me at that point, and I felt a chill right down my spine.

"You're here for Sarah, aren't you?"

Death nodded, almost sadly, it appeared.

"Why? What's to happen to her?"

Death turned to stare into my eyes - I felt like he was examining my soul. He transfixed his gaze at me like that for what seemed like forever. I stared right back, not daring to look away. What I saw in his eyes was pain. Fear, pain, and sadness. And then it dawned on me. This was suddenly all so clear. Humanity had given him a body. They had given him a mind. Yet, worst of all, humanity gave him a conscience. This figure sitting before me had seen the death of every single person, animal, and thing to have ever existed. He had no one to share his suffering with, no counsellors or friends, just himself, for all time.

"Ah, my young friend, you can see it, can't you? You know how it is to be me."

I could only nod simply; the force of the realization had left me dumbstruck. "And now I take yet another, a mere child, with family and friends who love her, a whole life unfulfilled."

"No! You can't!"

I don't know where the words came from. My subconscious had taken over for a brief moment.

"Please, you can't. You can't!"

He reached over and placed his hand upon my shoulder. His eyes were glowing again, a dull, yet powerful blue.

"My young friend. Your love's time has come. There is not much you can do."

"There must be something! Anything!"

I began to sob loudly and beat the rock I was sitting upon with my fists.

"It's just not fair!" I wailed.

"No. With that, I do agree."

"Is there anything I can do? Anything at all?" I pleaded.

"I feel your awful pain, child. I regret this, for I should have never allowed this meeting. It was a lapse on my part. I was wrong."

"Well, do something to make it right!"

He shook his head sadly.

"The price for such things is too great. I cannot."

I could have sworn at that point that a tear had began to form in his eye. It was difficult to tell for sure, but there was definitely something.

"I have tried before, to save a child, but the price, the price..."

His voice had changed now, instead of the structured monotone from before, there was a sadness and deep regret which tore at my heart. Somewhere in the past, he had tried *something*, and that had resulted in great pain to him. Even with my developing mind, I could see that.

"Tell me." I said gently. "What is the price?"

His answer was strangulated, as if he truly didn't even wish to think of it.

"For one to be saved," he began, "For one to be saved, seven must take their place. Seven lives for one - the price is too great."

"Which seven?" I trembled as I spoke.

"That is the worst of the price. I cannot know who the seven are until their lives are snuffed. I once tried to save a little girl. She was five of your years old... One of the seven was the girl's mother... I watched, helpless, as for the next twenty years the saved girl's father's abuse drove her to madness until she took her own life... There was nothing I could do to save her from that. In the end, she would have been better off on the other side. I could do nothing. Nothing. I cannot allow that to happen again... I am sorry."

We just sat there without conversing for the next couple of hours, each to his own thoughts. At one point I began to wonder what was happening to all the people who were dying during our meeting. "Who did they meet?" I asked him. He told me that he was omnipresent, everywhere at once. That was another torture he had to endure. That was why he was forced to watch the destiny of the child he had saved. We lapsed into another long silence. I suddenly thought of something.

"Is the legend true about you?"

I was inadvertently shouting. The hope rising within me had sent my adrenaline through the roof.

"I am sorry, but I do not know what you mean," said the Grim Reaper.

"The game! Can I challenge you for her life?"

Death smiled lachrymosely and slowly nodded his head.

"Yes, but the stakes are high. Your life for hers, for that is the way of such things."

"Fine. Without her, my life isn't worth living anyway. So, what's the game? How do we play?"

Death looked at me with his big, blue, dull sockets for eyes.

"The game is chance, my young friend, nothing more. For chance is universally recognized."

He pulled a blank cube from his pocket and touched it gently. The sides suddenly bore two sets of pictures - one were angels, the other devils. There were three of each, as he explained the rules to me.

"I think that you are smart enough to recognize the rules. If the angel faces upwards, the girl's life is yours."

I noticed that his voice had reverted to his original monotone. This was obviously business.

"If the devil faces up, both her life and yours are forfeited. You have one last chance to change your mind before I roll."

"Never. Not if you promised me the world."

Death nodded. He and I both stood up and faced each other with a small gap between us. Death looked down at me. He raised his hand, then suddenly dropped the dice. What happened next, I'm still not sure about, although I have my suspicions. As the dice tumbled over and over and came to a stop, a devil appeared on the top face. I opened my mouth to scream in frustration, but then blinked. The face now depicted an angel! I rubbed my eyes and gazed at the die and yes, it was an angel. Stunned, I looked up at Death, but he was suddenly gone. When I looked down again at my good fortune, the cube had disappeared, too!

I slumped down to the grass and lay there, unable to figure out what to do. Only hours later could I summon the courage to return home.

To this day, I can't be sure what really happened. Did Death roll a devil or did I just imagine it? Did Death do something? Out of pity, maybe, or hope? Honestly, I'm not even sure that I even met him, for none of my friends have ever mentioned the stranger since. Still, Sarah and I have been going out for nearly a year now, and life is calm and content. Sometimes, when we're out walking by the lake I get the impression that there's someone behind me, but there never is. I guess I'll never really know what happened, but like I said, I do have my suspicions...

Corridors
Terri J. Barczak

The metal cart, piled high with yellowing books and wrinkled magazines, wailed as Joseph pushed it down the passageway. He kicked at the loose wheel to unlock it from the undercarriage. Now free, it spun like a leaf carried by the winds of a Black Sea storm. It threatened to slip off, but at least the squealing stopped.

A single drop of sweat trickled down the back of his neck. A headache roared between his eyes. He paused in front of a cell to rub his temples with fingers deformed by a pipe in last year's spring riot. No longer could they close completely to grip the hand of a child. The cellblock baked its occupants like a smokehouse. Fans attached to the ceiling turned slowly, serving to mock the residents rather than actually circulate the humid, tangy sweat-laced air.

The pain momentarily subsided. "I am weary of this menial work. This life."

He spoke softly, so softly that no one heard. The fewer prisoners who knew who he was, the better. The squealing of the wheel always put his nerves on edge. He patted his blue denim shirt pocket for an aspirin. His fingers brushed over the tag sewn into the material. It was labeled USR904-33A, his official name for the last five years at Claragrad State Penitentiary. He found a small packet, ripped it open and emptied the aspirins into his mouth, relishing the bitterness.

Noise aggravated his headaches. The Claragrad physician, Hendrik Telsin, had examined Joseph when the headaches had first started over a year ago. Nothing was found. The tests showed no neurological or spinal damage from the fights or from the punishment delivered by the prison guards for Joseph's "infractions."

"Comrade Stalin," said a man with a nasal voice. "Come. Join me over here."

He waved his ashen hand weakly and smiled. His standard orange jumpsuit hung on him like sagging, wrinkled skin.

"Tell me again how you once ruled the fair lands south of here and how the young upstart Trotsky keeps you locked up to protect himself from your coup attempts."

Joseph glanced at the older inmate and sneered at his pathetic attempt to irritate him. If a field burning from exploding shells, blazing in the night could not frighten him, how could a few words possibly affect him? He could leave this prison any time he wanted. Joseph knew that. He was just waiting until the political situation became a bit more stable.

Joseph shoved a magazine wrapped in brown paper at the slack-jawed man. "This day finds you with good fortune, Comrade Kerchenko. My memory fails me. I recall so little of the Union's history. Rest assured though, I remember everything that transpires in here."

The man swallowed, visibly disturbed and fearful. Joseph turned, hiding his smile and continued down the passageway with its cement floors and artificially bright yellow corridors. The square cells held their men in silence. They wrapped them in a dampness smelling of urine and cigarettes. Joseph paused and sat on a bench attached to the prison wall. The headache drained him. Frequent rests were necessary in order to finish his rounds.

The smell of wet cement, drenched from the morning hose-down, surrounded him and reminded him of how the sidewalks outside his house in Moscow smelled after a warm summer rain.

His heart raced as he recalled how they marched in step for hours, he and his young friend, Colonel Martinov Serloskovo, creating plans to expand Soviet control over the Balkans and Poland. He tried to remember their conversations, the smell of the cigar that was his favorite, the sound of horses galloping in the fields. He missed Martinov. Since he entered prison, Joseph hadn't seen his old friend. He feared the worst. Martinov had enemies too.

Instead of the stony, weathered face of Martinov, his lost confidant, a female face appeared in Joseph's mind. Her proud aquiline nose and high cheeks startled him with their loveliness. He shook his head to chase away the image of her bathing in water spread with a carpet of rose petals. It confused him. Recently his mind had begun to wander.

He frowned and tried to recall the second Great War and the occupation forces from the summer of 1945, when he last walked with Martinov at his side. He would have to tell Dr. Telsin about these strange thoughts and images. Telsin would give him some powder to take away the invasive images of the blonde woman and her pink dress that flowed like a cloud of mist around her.

As he sat in the corridor, more disturbing images came unbidden to his mind. The woman with red lips, the color and sweetness of strawberries. He shivered. How could he possibly know that? She was beautiful. He admitted that to himself. It was like a memory. He and this woman followed a brick path past a sign labeled Piedmont Park. They held hands and laughed. There were hundreds of people around, none of them in uniform. Joseph felt his body break out in a cold sweat. His breath came in short gasps. There was tightness in his chest. A moment passed and his body relaxed as the image faded.

Not fully recovered from his headache, he longed to rest. Not for the first time, he wondered if the guards weren't drugging his food. He stood. It was time to talk to the commandant. Using the wall for a brace, he strode toward the commandant's office.

He would explain, if not demand, that Dr. Telsin do something to give him relief. For the last year these inexplicable images invaded him, torturing him with visions of this woman and that dreamland of green valleys and fields of corn that he had never seen. For a time, Joseph believed he had pushed these invasive images away. But the visions of a land of peace, where a woman loved him, always returned. Her smile, her perfume, and the feel of her long blonde hair as he combed it at night.

He was shown a seat at a table in the outer office, away from the weapons. He smiled, a sharp turn of his lips, well aware how careful they were with him. A dangerous man. As he waited the pain returned. He ground his palms into his eyes, trying to force the images from his mind. Why did she keep returning? Were the images connected to his headaches? What punishment was this? How could he drive her from his thoughts?

"Joe." A woman's voice whispered next to his ear.

Joseph jerked his head up and searched the room for her. He saw nothing but the other inmates leering at him through the window in the door, enjoying his misery. But it was her voice. The woman from his mind. He recognized her honeyed voice.

"Joe, try and hear me." The woman spoke softly. Her voice cracked as if she struggled not to cry. "Remember, when we married-- the church in Virginia--the spring rains that soaked all the guests. Remember how everyone laughed in surprise?"

Joseph shook his head, trying to banish her voice. He reminded himself of why he was imprisoned. The wrong he did to Martinov. How he failed to lead by example.

"Joe, please come back. I want you to come home. Martin, your son, is fine. Just a few scars. They'll go away as he grows up."

Joseph shook his head from side to side. He didn't have a son. Martinov couldn't possibly need him. He was a master tactician who could take care of himself. He needed no one. Martinov didn't need someone as irresponsible as Joseph, who neglected his duties and got them both thrown in prison.

"The fire, it wasn't your fault. A short in the house's wiring. That's what did it." The woman's voice was pleading. Crying now, she took his hand. For the first time, Joseph felt her clasp his hand. His imagination was becoming so powerful. It frightened him.

"Joe, he needs his father. Martin needs you. Please come back."

"I can't," he whispered. "I failed him."

He dropped his head, cupping his face with fire-scarred hands. They trembled and filled with his tears. The woman's hands rested upon his shoulders and he felt her kisses on his neck. Wet drops landed on his neck as she joined him in his sorrow.

The distant sound of a man's voice echoed in the background. The doctor.

"He heard you. It's a start Mrs. Stallen. He took a big step today. Residents deal with loss differently. Hopefully, he will leave that world where he punishes himself and rejoin you and your son. Be patient."

Low Water Crossings
Paul Perry

Ben had seen some strange things during his fifteen years of drifting around the country, from a naked woman strolling along the shoulder of IH 10, fifteen miles or so west of Houston, to an escapee elephant thundering down a sidewalk in downtown Atlanta. But now, on this bright, hot summer day, as he walked along a farm road halfway between Marble Falls, Texas, and Austin, he saw something even stranger, or so it seemed to him. He saw a man in a wheelchair traveling down the middle of that road; a man with no legs and wild hair and a beard the color of rust and thick arms working like pistons to send the wheelchair careening, fairly flying along that nearly deserted road.

Ben had heard a whining sound, noticeable among the peaceful country sounds--birds singing and the breeze rustling the leaves of the trees lining each side of the road--and he had turned and there the wheelchair came, headed straight toward him, and Ben, who always acted first and thought later, stepped out in front of him and held up his hands. The man glared at him and kept coming, and Ben barely managed to leap out of the way. He fell in a heap on the side of the road but his blanket roll saved him from injury, although he did get the breath knocked out of him.

"Hey!" He stood up, shouted, shoved his blanket roll under his arm and went trotting after the man. The man didn't slow down so Ben had to run all out to catch up with him, and then he had to run alongside him, breathing hard, trying to talk while he struggled for breath. "Where you going?" he managed to get out.

The man turned to look wild-eyed up at Ben. "Atlantic Ocean," the man yelled. "Now get the hell away from me."

Ben thought about stopping and standing there, waiting 'til a car or truck came along then hitch a ride on to Austin, get to a shelter in time to get a bed, a meal, a shower, but he found--as he had often found in his thirty-three years--that his legs didn't do what his head told them to do. He started following the man.

At first Ben tried to keep up but the man was moving fast, slapping at the wheels of his wheelchair with firm strokes of his thick hands, so after a while Ben settled into the stride that he used when he was in a walking mood, his thick-soled shoes reaching out in a measured rhythm that could eat up the miles.

Still, the man moved farther and farther ahead but he seemed to be slowing some, seemed to be tiring, and sure enough, when the bank of clouds on the western horizon started to turn to glowing shades of orange and pink, Ben began to close the gap. When the sun was gone and the fields on each side of the farm road were filling with purple shadows, Ben was close enough to hear the whisper of the wheelchair's tires on the road's surface, hear the grunt of the man as he slapped at the spinning wheels. Ben speeded up until he was a few feet behind the wheelchair.

"What do you want?" the man called out to him. He was puffing with each stroke, his voice strained.

"I thought I'd travel along with you a ways."

"What the hell for?"

"Well, I figured I could use some company. I got some meat spread and some crackers, got a big bottle of water. We could eat a bit, get some sleep. I could build us a little fire."

The man kept pumping away. "I want to make another mile," he said.

"Okay," Ben said, and settled into a pace that kept him alongside the wheelchair.

It was completely dark when the man in the wheelchair finally slowed then rolled over to a grassy area near the side of the road. He sat there for a while, breathing hard, then reached into one of the satchels that hung on each side of his wheelchair and removed a bottle of water and drank deeply.

"Well," he said, sighing, "I guess it is time for a rest. But I got to get going early in the morning."

Ben dropped his blanket roll and gathered sticks and dry brush for a fire. There was a full moon just coming up and it afforded enough light so that Ben was able to see well enough to get the dry brush to smoldering.

"I'll use a little of my water to make us some coffee," Ben said. "I got some instant and a little pan I use."

He thought the man would offer some of his water but he didn't, instead he maneuvered his wheelchair into some bushes and didn't come out for ten minutes or so. Finally Ben called out to him; "You okay back there?"

The man moved out of the bushes and over by the fire. He opened his other satchel and removed a plastic jar. "I got jerky," he said. "That's all I need."

Ben shrugged. "Okay. But I'm going to make myself some cracker and Spam spread sandwiches." He hesitated then said, "My name's Ben. Maybe you could tell me yours."

The man was bent forward, rubbing tiredly at his face. Finally, he straightened up and said in a low voice, "Henry. My name's Henry."

After he'd finished eating, Ben drank from his water bottle then looked over at the man named Henry. "You didn't eat much," he said.

"I don't need much."

Ben studied him curiously. "How do you sleep?"

"Right where I am."

"In the wheelchair? Don't you want to stretch out?"

"Why?"

Ben shrugged. "It just seems more comfortable." After a pause he said, "So how come you're going to the Atlantic Ocean?"

The man was a still, dark form in the shadows cast by tree branches overhead. After a pause he said, "It's just something I'm meant to do."

"Yeah? How come?"

The man didn't answer but stretched his arms overhead and yawned deeply. "I'm going to sleep," he said. "I got to get started before sunup."

Ben didn't go to sleep right away, which was unusual for him. He usually stretched out on his blanket, closed his eyes, and fell asleep. But he kept thinking about the man and kept looking over to where he was huddled in a blanket of his own, one he'd pulled from one of his satchels. Why was the man so anxious to get to the Atlantic Ocean? Why was it something he was meant to do?

Finally, Ben drifted off to sleep, but in his dreams he saw the man's rust-red hair flying in the wind and heard the hum of the wheelchair's tires on the roadway.

Ben was awakened by a clap of thunder that shook the ground beneath him. He sat up, his heart pounding, just as lightning flashed and struck something nearby with a fearsome crack. Feeling dazed, Ben got to his feet, realizing now that it was raining, raining hard. He bent and picked up his blanket and tarp, pulled them around him, and turned to see in another flash of lightning that Henry was also awake. The wheelchair man had dug a yellow poncho out of one of his satchels and pulled it over his head.

"Where the hell did this storm come from?" Ben yelled, bending to pick up his backpack and tuck it under his arm.

"The wind came up a couple of hours ago," Henry yelled back. "You slept through a lot of it." He was pushing things into his satchels. "It'll be dawn pretty soon. I need to get going."

Ben struggled through a driving rain to stand beside Henry while peering down at him. "Hell, you can't go anywhere in this stuff."

"Well, I can't just sit here and wait it out. Anyway, I'll be moving with the wind. I got to go."

He started pushing his wheelchair toward the road, having trouble because the dirt had turned to mud. When Ben tried to help him, Henry said sharply, "Leave me alone." When he was up on the road he started pushing himself along.

Ben hesitated, looking up at the trees they had slept under, trees that afforded some shelter from the driving rain. But, when Henry was several yards down the road, Ben stepped out on the roadway. "Hey!" he yelled. "There's low water crossings on down the way a bit. You'll get yourself drowned."

Henry kept pushing, picking up speed. Ben sighed, pulled his tarp and blanket tighter about himself, got a better grip on his backpack, and went after him.

Although it was still some time before dawn, the lightning came so frequently, it was like the roadway was lit by flashing brightness, and the thunder rolled and pounded constantly, while the rain seemed to come down even harder and the wind pushed and shoved them forward. Ben was often off-balance and several times was almost thrown to his knees by the power of the gusts, but the wind seemed to be pushing the man in the wheelchair steadily forward, so that Ben had to half run, half stagger to keep close to him. Then there came the sound of the rushing water.

"Hey!" he called out to Henry, "I think we're coming up on one of those low water crossings."

Henry turned and called out, "It's up ahead. It don't look too deep. I can make it across."

Then Ben saw the water. There was a dip in the road and at the foot of that dip, there was a torrent of dark water, although, as Henry said, it didn't look very deep. But even as Ben watched it, it seemed to grow deeper.

"It's going to be tricky in the wheelchair. I'll push you across."

"No," Henry said, edging closer to the rushing water. "I can do it on my own."

Ben thought about arguing but he had heard the firmness in Henry's voice. Also, he could see the speed of the rushing water, see that it was getting deeper even as they talked. Before he could say anything else, Henry had edged forward and was carefully moving into the water.

"You're crazy," Ben called out to him. "What the hell's your hurry? Why are you doing this?"

Henry turned and looked back at him.

"I don't have much time, and this is something I've got to do," he said, above the rumble of the thunder and the howling of the wind. Then he moved deeper, until the water was over the wheels of the wheelchair.

Ben moved forward until the water was up to his knees, felt then the power of it, and stopped. He stood there and watched the wheelchair move deeper. Ben saw the glisten of the yellow poncho in the flash of the lightning and then there was a long moment of darkness. In another flash of lightning, Ben saw the wheelchair being pushed by the water. Another flash revealed the gleam of the yellow poncho and Henry's arms pumping furiously beneath it. As Ben watched, entranced, he saw the wheelchair stop and then start edging toward the far side of the crossing. The wheelchair moved slowly against the rush of the water but it moved inexorably toward the roadway on the other side. Quickly, it was up onto the roadway, then around a curve, and then gone.

Ben stood there for a long time. He stood until the rain slowed and the lightning stopped flashing and turned into an occasional flickering pulsing, and the sky overhead turned slowly into a dull gray, and the water finally began to recede. When the water had grown shallow, Ben started across but halfway to the other side he turned and came back and waited until the water was no more than a trickle. Then, carefully, he made his way across.

He stopped on the other side, stood there for a moment looking back at the low water crossing, then set off up the road. He muttered once to himself, "Supposed to happen, huh? What the hell does that mean?" As he resumed his walk toward Austin, still wrapped in his tarp and blanket, Ben walked slower than usual even though the sky overhead was brightening. As he moved along, Ben thought about his own life, wondering what low water crossing awaited him down the road.

Now Playing Right Field
Jack De Vries

The other night I visited my fountain of youth.

It's in a box of my favorite stuff that's been sentenced to the attic—now that my house is furnished in a style that befits a proud father of two daughters, married to a lovely wife.

In other words, anything that bounces or shoe with cleats is banished to the basement or attic. We need room for dollhouses, glass statues, and flowery stuff.

But back to my fountain of youth. I opened the box and there it was—my first baseman's mitt. It's tan, beat-up, and flat—a real thing of beauty. I reached my hand inside and drifted back to 1967.

I first saw my mitt when I was nine. It was hanging on a hook in the old Two Guys store in Totowa where Home Depot is today. I was with my grandfather. The mitt cost $9, and I had $7.47 stuffed in my pocket.

My grandfather, who knew zilch about baseball, spotted me the $1.53 on faith, and I walked out wearing the glove. It was made by an unknown company called "Big League," and about as long as my forearm. I slept with it that night.

I wasn't a first baseman but planned to become one. If my hero Mickey Mantle were moving to first because of his bad legs, then I'd also make the sacrifice. But when kids started to whip the ball at my shins, I retreated to the outfield. Let Mickey deal with the low throws.

My next mitt was a Dick McAuliffe model. It was a small infielder's glove that I bought because my friend Gary had the same mitt. The way he'd broken it in sold me. The glove was dark and soft, and wearing it was like having a large webbed hand. Gary had soaked it in Crisco Oil to get it that way.

The autograph on the mitt became important as I got older. One Christmas in the 1970s, my father gave me a "Sammy Ellis" model. Sammy Ellis—was he kidding? Ellis had one good year in 1965 going 22-10 and went 12-19 the next. I continued using my old glove and kept Sammy home. At least McAuliffe was a decent player.

In 1984, I helped start a softball team and began using a basket-size Wilson A2000.

And soon after, I discovered the true power of a baseball glove.

Playing softball means exercise, camaraderie, friendship—and untold aggravation when someone doesn't show up. Such was the case one Sunday morning when we learned Paul, our third baseman, had overslept. He was 15 minutes away and if he didn't arrive by then, there'd be no game.

I took my dilemma to Uncle Sal, our first base coach and a former player—with the emphasis on former. My uncle was 78 at the time.

"Uncle Sal," I asked, "can you go into right field and stand there so we don't forfeit the game?"

Uncle Sal was also the same man who was nearly killed earlier that season when he was run over by a player making a wide turn at first going to second.

"Sure!"

"If a ball comes," I warned, with visions of having to explain to my mother how Uncle Sal died chasing a fly ball, "let it go, let the center fielder get it. Here," I said, handing him a mitt, "put this on."

When the glove went on, Uncle Sal's eyes glazed over. He smiled and pounded his fist into the pocket. Years melted away before my eyes. He turned back into the kid shagging balls behind the Doherty Silk Mill on his lunch break.

"Don't get hurt," I said.

"Okay, okay," he replied, not having heard a word I said.

He walked toward right field, calling for a throw from one of the infielders. My God, he was warming up! The other team, knowing our predicament (and being aptly unsympathetic), watched, planning to hit every ball to right.

Now my uncle was jogging—yes, jogging to the outfield. "Sal the Kid" was ready. The umpire asked if I was sure about this.

My uncle was—because the glove was working its magic.

Before I could answer, Paul's truck pulled up. We waved Sal in, took off his glove, and the spell was broken. Within minutes, he turned back into a first base coach—but looking a lot happier.

In about 35 years, if you see a senior citizen walking around wearing a tan first baseman's mitt, you'll know why.

Tell me not to get hurt.

First appeared in the *Herald & News* in Passaic, New Jersey, Sunday, August 29, 1999.

Fragile Lost
Merryn Spencer

You'd like to think you're a woman. In the scene of early morning, he is leaving the girl you are. Packs up, and he doesn't look at you, so you button your eyes against his known form. But you feel worthy of your scrape of skin on his fleshed desire. You stare at him with red, whitewashed eyes of induced affection. It does not happen. You have known so well the bringing of raw joy under you in waving gasps. He heated your trembling body so no one could see you both together; so he passed the time with the entwining of fresh limbs. Often, it's all you think about, being with him. The fire of his release is half the experience; so you can ask him, the man lying beside the child. His actions made you shiver at the somehow eulogistic mistake. Memories: the two of you watching each other, spellbound in the half moonlight. You stared life in the eyes with each drawn breath for breath. Silent words filtered through the thickwarmed air. Your feelings became all shambled and swollen together like torn mesh in slivered linen.

You'd like to tell him that only with him have you lived. Now you have to try and forget the pleasure. And you allow yourself to swallow pain each second moment in an effort to block out the sorrow twisted inside you. Blocking a soul crying for brief release. All, living together inside make the mind so crowded. All coming together in one shortened bandwidth. He does not know the fragile woman who bursts angrily crying and sighing. She has lived a life of brief pleasure - only once discovered, now shortly silenced. He is leaving you. Alternately, in your own sight, your watchful thinking corrodes and voices which dip in their trembling are set straight. Set like wicks in candlelight in the gaped furrowed structure of intimacy. There is a gasping noise, a degradation of conversation. The child speaks: I am young. My young body is less than a life; I try to be a woman. I do not succeed. Instead, I have become attached to a simple guest. I can stretch out my inexperience on the palm of my hand and know something is there. The response time quickens. The pulse tricks you into thinking that you reached for him, his intention protruding, your limbs grasped inside a carnal frenzy. The act becomes something like attempted paradise. Watching anxiously for the unfinished ending - we cannot be together, but must be content with a simple flesh tryst. A simple, gasping mass, she can feel your being, vacuolated in the dimness. A part of me has yet to find out from what point in time you are adult.

From when is the invisible line crossed, a slight shift in terms
and you are over childhood, over those feelings of contradiction and
being inside white glass? The constraint surrounds you, the child is
remanded to being eternally grateful. Growing is coming to terms with
how to react to this Religion, when a man rubs your swelling woman's
thighs, following the ripple of flesh across the nerve. The advice offered
from a reality, into the images we create as one, we lie from ourselves in
the culture of ourselves around. But the woman does not want help.
She does not want help to forget the unlimited grasping of two beings
together climbing inside each other with lust. When love, paid back in
kind, expresses some deep meaning several contributors find they have
not lost worth. Several, the same ones kindle a fire - how does this
matter in one's eyes? Symbolism becomes fruitless and aptitudes of two
beings come together for a time. The man continues to pack and she
stings her eyes with repressed emotion. He tries to say something but
finds he cannot, and the childwoman moves to reach for him against her
conscience. You touch his hand in a simple way. It is the only way you
know. Somehow the human rubber stings, and you know the eyes
turned into yours by the stained mark they wear. Then comes the power
of the male beside you. Trying to ignore desire, you, the woman, know
the brittle plastid power. Yet you enjoy it. Somewhere the concept is
held between desire's disfigured fingers. It is a crime to tell, the truths
still stay in place: yet female
adults lie. The woman remains, with her partner, a soulful child to
please. It is only entering this world fresh from childhood do you realize
this lie. Takes away in chunks and strips from the bereaved longing -
the false words float in the human milk, clinking with the fragile, ebbing
memories. Pressing his mouth to hers in adulation of farewell; you are
too young to own. Teeth folded thick with unworded whisperings of
love. The thickened smelltaste reminds you of life.

Good-Bye, Marie
M.E. McDonald

THE OFFICE

It's the end of a long, tiring day and Marie is anxious to get home. She clears her desk of the project that has occupied her afternoon and reaches for her jacket and handbag.

She knocks on her boss' door and opens it.

"I'm leaving now, Barry. Have a good evening," she says.

"Right. You too, Marie." He appears flustered.

"Anything wrong, Barry?"

"No, no. I'm just tired," he answers.

"Well, good night, then. See you tomorrow."

"Yes, good night."

Marie works as a secretary. She likes her job, but isn't fond of her boss. She suspects that he's been skimming company funds. He often talks about his big new house, gifts he's given his wife, his diamond ring, and his expensive new car. She knows he doesn't earn enough for all he claims to have, though it's been only a few years since he was wearing cheap suits and out-of-style ties.

As she's leaving the office, it's starting to rain. She goes back for her umbrella and sees her boss through the open door, packing bundles of money and securities into his briefcase. She doesn't want him to see her, but she drops the umbrella and he hears the clatter as it falls. He calls her and pretends nothing is unusual, but she hesitates and he realizes she knows what he's doing.

"Come in, Marie," he says, walking towards her. "Did you forget something?"

"I, I forgot my umbrella. It's raining," she stammers.

Barry has a strange look on his face – a combination of fear and anger. Before she can scream or run away, he hits her, sending her reeling across the room. Swiftly, he removes his tie and wraps it about her neck, twisting it like a tourniquet. He holds it tight for several minutes and lets her limp body fall to the floor.

He goes into the outer office and looks out into the hall. After a while, he comes back, picks her up, and puts her over his shoulder. The freight elevator is down the hall. He carries her quickly toward it and waits impatiently for it to come up to this floor. When it arrives, he pushes the button for the garage. Once there, he looks around carefully to see if anyone is about. Satisfied, he removes the keys from his pocket and opens the trunk of the car. A couple of folding beach chairs and a jack are in his way. He pushes the chairs back and throws the jack over to the side of the trunk, where it hits a bottle and smashes it. He dumps Marie's body in the trunk and closes it.

THE ALLEY

She becomes aware that it's dark and she's on the ground. It's dirty and smells of garbage and urine. She's not in pain, but she can't seem to move. She lies there for a long time. She's a little uncomfortable, but is really not afraid. A cat comes over to her and sniffs, then jumps over her and is out of sight. After a while, a dog comes by and barks at her. He keeps barking and someone yells, "Shut up," but the barking continues and it seems like hours before someone comes to quiet him. A car! Thank goodness. Now she'll get the help she needs. A bright light shines on her and she tries to call out, but no sound comes forth.

"Dave, she's dead. Call it in," he says.

What does he mean? I'm not dead. I just can't move, but I can hear him. They'll take me to the hospital and find out I'm still alive – I just can't move or talk.

Shocked, she realizes she can hear what the policeman is thinking. He wishes they had gone for coffee and let some other car answer this call. He's afraid the paperwork will take all day and it's almost time to quit for the night.

More police arrive and there is a cacophony of conversations and people yelling out of windows. She hears a siren in the distance and then it comes closer.

"The Medical Examiner is here," someone says.

He'll know, she thinks, *Then he'll take me to the hospital and I'll be all right.*

A while later, a photographer appears. The photographer starts shooting pictures of her and she wishes she could stand up and comb her hair. She'll hate these pictures – she just knows she will.

"It looks like strangulation. I'll know more after the autopsy," the M.E. says. 'This one looks pretty cut and dried – poor little chick,' he thinks.

Autopsy! They only autopsy dead people and I'm not dead.

She's lifted onto some plastic – she can hear it rustle as they place her upon it. Then the sound of a zipper – it comes up over her face.

It's dark in here. Dear Lord! I'm in a body bag! Even the Coroner thinks I'm dead. What will I do? I can't move or call out.

How will they know? I read a story like this once. It was a case of narcolepsy. That's it. They'll see me breathing before it's all over. But, what if they don't?

Strange. She doesn't know why, but she isn't in a panic. She's…concerned. That's all.

She feels the bump as the stretcher is placed in the wagon. The engine starts and she feels the motion of the wagon as it moves along the road – sometimes smoothly and sometimes with the roughness of broken streets.

The driver and his assistant are talking about going to the track on Saturday. They're laughing about the time one of their friends won three hundred and thirty dollars and lost the ticket to collect on it.

Finally, the wagon stops and the two men get out. She hears one of them saying something about getting a cup of coffee.

"No," says the other, "Let's get this unloaded first."

The very idea! I'm not a "this." Be careful. I'm not a sack of beans, you know.

A wheel on the gurney squeaks as they push it along a hall. When it stops, she can feel them lift her onto a hard surface, then hears their footsteps as they walk away. A moment later a door slams.

This is another fine mess you've gotten me into, Stanley, she thinks. What now? Her right hand is stuck behind her. *Maybe if I really try hard I can move and someone will see.* But there was no one to see any movement – even if she could have moved.

THE CORONER'S OFFICE

Bang! A door slams open and she hears footsteps. A voice she recognizes as the Coroner's says that there was a new one during the night.

"It looks like murder, Mike. Strangulation. D'Angelo got me out of bed at 3 a.m. and there was this pretty little thing lying in an alley – just dumped there on all kinds of garbage."

Zip. Two men are standing over her looking serious.

"She really is a pretty little thing. I don't get it, Doc, why would anyone want to do such a thing? If he wanted to kill her, he could at least have left her in a decent place. Why a filthy alley?"

Hey, I'm not dead. Can't you see that?

The one called Mike is undressing her.

Hey, don't do that! Stop it!

But, he continues. He hasn't heard her. She's got to find some way of communicating with these people.

The M.E. adjusts the microphone over the table and puts on his glasses. He takes a sample of blood and picks some broken glass out of her hair with tweezers and puts it in a small plastic bag and hands it to Mike.

"This is case number J-10566, an unidentified Caucasian woman about twenty-four years of age; five feet, three inches tall; weighing approximately one hundred twenty-two pounds; auburn hair; brown eyes.

"Judging by the lividity, she died somewhere else and was dumped in the alley later," he says. "Look at this, Mike. The esophagus is crushed and there's this red mark around her neck. It wasn't done by a rope or cord – probably with a piece of clothing like a scarf or a tie. There are tiny strands of red filament from the cloth; bag this, will you, Mike? And look at this bruise along the jawline; there's a cut on the right side of the bruise, probably made by a ring. This girl was punched first and then strangled. I would say the approximate time of death was between five and six o'clock last night."

He seems to have a picture of what happened, but he still doesn't know I'm alive. What kind of a doctor is he?

Suddenly, she hears the sound of metal instruments on a metal tray.

They're going to cut me open – and with no anesthesia! I don't like this one bit. I've got to show them I'm alive.

"Don't you hate cutting up a young girl like this? Somehow, it doesn't seem so bad if it's somebody who's been sick a long time or an old guy who drank himself to death – but a pretty young girl…"

"It's the only way we might be able to get a clue as to who she was and possibly who killed her. Hand me that scalpel, will you, Mike?"

She could feel pressure on her chest and stomach, but strangely, no pain.

It's something like sitting in a dentist's chair and being worked on after having been given Novocain. After a while, you get bored with what's going on and you start thinking about other things.

It's beginning to come back to her now.

Polly and I went to lunch at the little pizza place on the corner after we cashed our checks at the bank. We talked about Jean's wedding and Jacqueline's promotion and I told her my suspicions about my boss… That's it! He's the one who knocked me out! Tonight, I saw him taking money out of the safe and putting it in his briefcase. And he saw me!

When we returned to the office after lunch, Polly got off the elevator at the fifth floor and I continued on up to the eighth, where my office is. When I got to my desk, I could hear Barry Miller talking on the phone. I couldn't hear what he was saying. He sounded excited, but I couldn't tell whether he was angry or happy. After he hung up, he was going out to lunch and came through my office. He was surprised when he saw me and asked how long I had been back. I thought it was a strange question at the time, because I was due back from lunch, but I realized he didn't want me to have heard the conversation, so I told him I had just gotten back. He seemed to relax then.

He was gone most of the afternoon. I guess it was about four o'clock when he got back to the office. Then he closed the door to his office and didn't open it until I knocked on it to tell him I was leaving. I don't think he closed it again...

"That's it, Mike. Put her in the fridge and get started on the lab work, O.K.? I have a meeting downtown with Lieutenant D'Angelo."

"O.K. Chief."

Sure, Chief, he thinks, *Leave the dirty work to me while you go off and have a few beers with D'Angelo. One of these days I'm going to apply for a job with a pharmaceutical company and really make a few bucks.*

She feels him move her onto a gurney – the one with the squeaky wheel – and cover her with a sheet or blanket or something, then push her into a cooler area. She hears him walk a short distance away.

Autopsies always make me thirsty. I guess I'll have a Pepsi, he thinks as he walks past her again and into another room. He comes back shortly and she hears a drawer slide open. He moves her onto another surface and she feels the drawer slide closed.

It's cold in here. And dark. They've got me in one of those drawers where they put dead bodies. First thing you know, they'll be calling me a "stiff." Why can't I make myself understood by them? Well, at least my hand isn't stuck behind me any more.

THE VIEWING ROOM

She's on another gurney, being wheeled along a corridor. It stops and Mike pulls the sheet from her face.

"That's my baby!" she hears her mother cry.

Mom! Mom! I'm not dead! Why can't you hear me? Can't you tell that I'm still alive!

Her mother is sobbing now on Buddy's shoulder. She's not looking at Marie any more. Buddy leads her away gently.

What's the matter with him? We grew up together and did

everything together. He and I were always very close. Why can't Buddy tell that I'm not dead?

She feels like crying, but tears will not come. She feels grief at seeing her mother and brother leaving her so sadly. She wishes she could comfort them – tell them she's alive and really quite comfortable.

Slowly, very slowly, she begins to realize that perhaps she really is dead. After a few moments, she hears a new voice.

"You're on a journey, Marie. In a while, you will shed your outer self and you will be coming to your new life."

Who are you? Where will I go? I don't know the way. I don't want to go. I want to stay here. Answer me. Who are you?

But, there is no answer, no sound, only Mike wheeling her back to the drawer.

THE FUNERAL HOME PREPARATION ROOM

"I can put a scarf around her neck, but that bruise on her jaw is going to be hard to cover up. I'm glad she had her makeup on; it makes it easier for me to match it up. After her 'bath' I'll get to work on her hair. Did anyone bring an outfit for her?"

"Yes, her brother dropped off an outfit. He said it was her favorite dress, but the shoes don't match. Oh, well, who's going to see them anyway?"

"Poor little doll! Why would anyone want to hurt her? I'll do a special job on her makeup – that'll make her folks feel better."

Oh, sure. Mom and Buddy will feel just fine when they see my makeup looks good. Now, now, Marie. Don't be sarcastic. The woman is only trying to be kind and Mom would feel awful if she had to look at the bruise again.

I guess Polly and the other girls in the office know all about this already. The place is probably buzzing. I wonder what kind of stories are going around. There'll be a lot of speculation, but only Polly will know a little about it. I wonder if she'll put two and two together and realize what happened. There's really no reason for her to think of that. On the other hand, Polly is no dummy and she does think things over. I wonder if she'll go to the police. And, if she does, will they pay any attention to her and investigate Barry Miller. They probably won't have anything to go on except Polly's word.

"Time for your 'bath,' little one. Lord, Everett, it should be a bubble bath instead of this stuff. After all these years, you'd think I'd be used to this, but it always gets to me when it's a young one."

"I try not to think about it, Greta. You'll drive yourself crazy if you let it get to you. We all gotta go sometime, ya know."

"I know, but it seems a shame that there are so many good things she'll never experience."

"But so many troubles she'll never have, either. Come on, I'll give you a hand with her. Into the bath you go, little one."

THE FUNERAL HOME – GETTING READY

Good. Buddy brought the rust-colored dress that I like so much. Mom probably picked it out. She knows how much I like it.

"Come on, Everett, her family will be here in forty-five minutes and the flowers are already starting to arrive. You did nice work on her makeup, Greta. I didn't think you'd be able to cover that bruise completely, especially with the gash in it, but you did a fine job. Now, let's get her out on the floor."

"We're ready, Mr. McCaffrey. We'll have her all set up shortly."

She feels herself, once again being wheeled along a corridor, then a little bump, then quietly – probably on carpet. She smells the flowers and a hint of formaldehyde. It reminds her of when her father died. She had had the odor of the mortuary in her nostrils for weeks afterward.

The one called Everett does something behind her and props her up a little. She feels comfortable enough and she's glad they've stopped fussing over her. Now she only has to lie here and wait for Mom and Buddy to come and see her for the last time.

Maybe Polly will come, too. She'd like that. If only she had some way of telling Polly to think about their conversation at lunch that day…

THE WAKE

She hears her mother's voice, though she can't hear what she's saying. Buddy's voice is deep and she can hear him better. He's telling her to come over to the casket and say a prayer for Marie before the people start coming. Her mother is crying and Marie hears her coming closer to the casket.

"Oh, my baby! Why did they do this to you? Why did they take you away from me?

She sobs uncontrollably and leans over the casket to put her arms around her child. The funeral director rushes over to Buddy and says softly, "Make her get off the casket. It could tip over and that would be devastating for her."

Buddy gently pulls his mother away and leads her to a chair. She continues to sob in his arms.

This is worse than I thought possible. Mom is really broken up and Buddy is crying, too. I wish I could go over to them and tell them it's all right. This is so painful! My heart is breaking for them.

Her Aunt Elenor and Uncle Peter from New Jersey are the first to arrive. As usual, Uncle Peter wants to take over from Buddy.

"Have you set up the procession of the limousines? I think Elenor and I should ride with your mother and you should ride with your Aunt Elizabeth and Uncle Frank in the second car. That way, the family will be represented in the first two cars."

"No, Uncle Peter, Aunt Elizabeth is Marie's godmother and I'm her brother, so Aunt Elizabeth and Uncle Frank and I will ride with mother in the first car and you and Aunt Elenor and the Orwells will ride in the second one."

Uncle Peter is flustered and angry, but seems to be trying to keep it under control.

Great going, Buddy! I've always wanted to tell the officious old coot off and you've done it for me. Right in front of me. He did the same thing at dad's funeral and took everyone off guard. I'm glad you didn't let him take over mine.

MY FUNERAL! This is the first time I've thought of it as that. Why don't I feel scared? I feel a little apprehensive – it's like stepping off a train in a foreign country where you don't know anyone. I don't know what's next.

"Elenor, come over to the casket with me," Uncle Peter growls. She follows him obediently and as they settle themselves on the kneeler, he hisses to her, "That brat. Did you see the way he deliberately took over? Didn't my sister ever teach him any manners?"

"Well, Pete, after all, it is his sister's funeral. He has a right..."

"Oh sure. Take his side against me. I might have known."

Elenor says a prayer and Peter kneels next to her, thinking, *I hate all this stuff. This is the last funeral I'll attend. It's too bad about Marie, but that brother of hers is off my list.*

I'll bet Buddy would be really upset about that, Marie smiles to herself. *I think I hear the Orwells. I haven't seen them since Dad's funeral. She'll start crying when she sees Mom and get her started all over again.*

They're her aunt and uncle on her father's side of the family, but they have always been referred to as "the Orwells." They're a matched set. She's a crier and he's a sympathizer.

When her Aunt Elenor and Uncle Peter leave the kneeler, the Orwells kneel down. "Look at that poor little darling. She's been through so much, and at such a young age," she whines and then resumes her boo-hooing. Her husband, ever her supporter, puts his arms around her to comfort her once more.

They get up and walk back to a row of chairs and sit down.

There's quiet conversation for a little while, and then Polly comes in. She walks over to Marie's mother and offers her condolences, then turns to the casket. At her first sight of Marie, her face crumples and tears roll down her cheeks.

Marie, Marie, my best friend, I'll miss you so much. When we had lunch together the other day, I didn't know it would be the last time I'd see you alive. How could I know? If I had, I would have told you how much I love you, instead of talking about Jean's stupid wedding or Jacqueline's promotion. Everything seems to have changed in the last few days. I'm walking around in a daze and there are all kinds of theories going around the office about what happened to you. Now that I think of it, Jacqueline has come up with several ideas. Her favorite one is about you being mugged, but she's also talking about a jealous boyfriend of yours that you may have dumped or maybe that you witnessed a murder or something. Barry Miller and she have gotten pretty tight in the last few days. She's always in his office.

How I wish you could hear and talk to me. I really want to know what happened to you. Polly was still crying.

Polly! Look at me and think about our last lunch conversation! Think about what I told you about Barry – that I suspected him of embezzling company funds. I DID witness something! I saw him taking money and bonds from the safe and putting them in his briefcase. I believe he was going to abscond with them. Polly, please, think about what we talked about.

Marie feels desperate to communicate with Polly. Her friend is obviously distraught over losing her.

But Polly doesn't hear Marie. It makes her feel better to keep talking to Marie silently. *I got a call from the police, this morning. I have to go to the police station after I leave here and talk to a Lieutenant D'Angelo. I don't think they know anything yet. I don't know how I can help them either. All I can think about is that last day we had lunch together in the pizza place.*

THAT'S IT! Polly, that's it. Think about that. Think about what I told you. Don't forget to mention it to the police. Maybe they'll be able to piece it together and get Barry Miller.

Well, Marie, I've got to leave now, but I'll be back this evening to say my final farewell to you. I love you, dear friend.

Polly walks away, stopping to say only a few more words to Buddy. *I love you too, Polly. You're the best friend I ever had.*

Several of her friends come by and stop for a few minutes, look at her, say a prayer or two and some only say their good-byes. A few more relatives show up and do the same. She wonders where Aunt Elizabeth and Uncle Frank are. She knows they will come.

Jacqueline comes into the room with "Bare-y", as she calls him.

My goodness, thinks Marie, *They really are getting tight. Funny that Polly should mention that when she was so upset.*

Barry walks over to Marie's mother and says in a loud voice, "She was a wonderful girl. The best secretary I ever had. I'll never be able to find another one like her."

You hypocrite. How do you have the gall to come here and talk like that to my mother, when you know what you did to me?

"Come, Bare-y, let's go say good-bye to little Marie," Jacqueline says, taking Barry by the arm.

They walk over to the casket and stand beside it.

Well, Marie, thinks Barry, *you can't tell anyone, now, what you saw. What happened to you was your own fault. If you had just gone home as you were supposed to, you'd still be alive. Now Jacqueline and I will have to wait a few months before we can leave. You really messed things up for us.* A wry smile crosses Barry's lips as he thinks, *But we'll have the last laugh when we arrive in Mexico with a bagful of cash and negotiable bonds.*

Jacqueline, leaning a little toward the casket, thinks, *You stupid broad, me and Bare-y were all set to take off for Mexico. When you screwed everything up for us, we couldn't leave. It would be too much of a coincidence if you were found murdered and me and Bare-y disappeared with the money and bonds at the same time. Now we have to wait a few months. I could kill you myself, if you weren't dead already.*

"She looks so peaceful and natural, doesn't she Bare-y? I hope I look as good as that when I pass away."

"Shut up, Jacqueline," he hisses. "At least pretend to be a little sad, will you?"

She shoots him a dirty look and walks out of the room. After a moment or two, Barry Miller follows her.

"Pardon me, folks, we're going to close for a couple of hours so that the family can get something to eat and a little rest. We'll be open again at seven o'clock."

The funeral director herds the mourners out of the room, while Buddy and Mom take a last look at Marie before leaving for dinner.

Well, Marie thinks when she's left alone, *This has been quite a day. You really get to know what people think of you in a situation like this. What am I saying? There is no other situation like this!*

And that was a surprise about Jacqueline and Barry Miller. I always thought his wife was number one in his life. I wonder if his wife knows about Jacqueline, yet. She's a nice woman; I hate to see her get hurt. Besides his infidelity, there will be the scandal, the gossip, and the trial – if they ever catch him, that is.

Poor Mom is taking this very badly. Buddy is holding up pretty well, but I guess he has to, for Mom's sake. She's been talking about getting a part-time job for a while, I hope he makes her do it.

"Marie, time is running out." She hears that strange voice again.

Who are you? Why don't you answer me?

"Very soon, you'll be coming with me and leaving your body behind."

I don't understand any of this. I can hear and see people and even understand their thoughts. Although I feel no pain, I can feel movement and, until this morning, temperature changes. I can hear you, too, but I don't know who you are or why you're taking me away.

"Marie, by now you know that you have died. Your awareness of heat and cold has already left you and your emotions are in low key. Your other senses will begin to leave you very shortly and when they have gone, your spirit, which is your "self," will come with me. You will know more about that in a little while.

You still haven't told me who you are. But again, there is no answer.

THE END OF THE WAKE

She hears the doors open. The funeral director is telling Everett to straighten out the rows of chairs. "They'll be coming back soon," he says. She hears the chairs hitting each other, as they are moving about. Her sight is going, just as the voice said it would, and she doesn't smell the flowers or the embalming fluid any more. Soon she would hear her mother and Buddy for the last time. She hoped Polly would keep her word and come back again. Aunt Elizabeth and Uncle Frank still haven't arrived and she feels a mild disappointment. Any other time she would be deeply hurt, but the voice was right again; her emotions are diminishing.

Buddy and Mom are first in again, followed soon after by Polly. She sits with mom and Buddy and they talk in low tones. Polly is doing most of the talking.

Aunt Elizabeth and Uncle Frank arrive. Marie hears them talking to Mom and Buddy. Mom introduces them to Polly and there is more conversation she can't quite hear. Again, Polly is doing most of the talking.

Come over here, Polly, and let me in on what happened at the police station. But Polly is still talking to her family.

After a few minutes, Aunt Elizabeth comes over and kneels down beside Marie. She makes the Sign of the Cross and says a fervent prayer for Marie and her family.

My darling niece, how I'll miss your sweet smile and the cheerful letters you send me. I'm shocked and crushed that someone could do this to you. We'll stay close to your mother and Buddy for a while to help them through this terrible time. A tear spills down Elizabeth's cheek.

Good old Aunt Elizabeth. She's so loving and sincere. She's been so good to me all my life.

As Aunt Elizabeth leaves her side, Marie hears Polly's thoughts.

I told you I'd come back and tell you what went on. I spoke to Lieutenant D'Angelo – by the way, his name is Bill and we went for coffee – I told him about our last lunch together. He wanted to know everything we talked about. At first, I only remembered about Jean's wedding and Jacqueline's promotion, then I remembered what you had told me about your suspicions.

Good girl, Polly! I knew you could do it!

Well, he already had the autopsy report, so he knew the time of your death and he knew that someone with a ring had punched you before strangling you. He had spoken to Barry before he spoke to me and noticed the big ring on his finger. He knew you were transported to that alley, but you weren't killed there. He knew that there were strands of red filament from a silk cloth – probably a tie. There were little fragments of glass in your hair, but he doesn't know yet, where they came from. All these put together make Barry a prime suspect, so he's going to see a judge this afternoon to get a search warrant to search Barry's office and his car.

Polly, you angel, if I could get up, I'd kiss you.

Polly kneels down and says a last prayer before she leaves.

Another parade of friends and relatives come by that evening and finally everyone is gone and Marie is alone again.

"You're happy that your death has been explained." It was the voice again.

THE FUNERAL

Faithful as ever, Polly is at the funeral home before they leave for the service the next morning.

Bill D'Angelo called me last night. He's got the search warrant and will search the office and Barry's car this morning, Polly thought.

As she was standing beside the casket, Barry Miller came up beside her. "Too bad, Polly. You'll miss your friend," he said.

Polly had difficulty controlling herself as she said, "Yes, I will."

"You never really expect something like this will happen to someone you know, do you?"

"No, you don't," she answered.

Just then, Lieutenant D'Angelo put his hand on Barry's shoulder.

"Barry Miller, You're under arrest for the murder of Marie Schroeder. You have a right to remain silent. You are entitled to legal counsel. Anything you say…"

"But, did they find anything that will convict him?" Polly whispered to another detective who had entered with Lt. D'Angelo.

"They did. When he was making room in the trunk of his car for Marie, he smashed a bottle with a wrench in the trunk. That's where the glass in her hair came from."

THE JOURNEY

I'm very tired and I can't see at all any more. It's even getting difficult to hear. When are you taking me away? Marie asked the voice.

"Here we go, " the voice said. "Take my hand."

Hindsight
Patty Colombe

The burning glare of the morning sunlight pierced his eyelids. Ben turned to get up from the bed but found himself nearly immobilized. Both his arms and legs were bound to the four-post bed.

He grinned to himself. Allyson must have been reading 'How to spice up your sex life magazines again.

Ben turned his head as far as his bonds would allow and scanned the room. Allyson was nowhere to be seen.

"Allyson," he called out in singsong. " I'm up in more ways than one."

No response. Everything was quiet as a tomb.

"Allyson, I can't keep this up forever. Allyson!"

After ten minutes, the singsong had left his voice. His bladder felt like it was ready to burst and this game was losing its cuteness.

The red LED of the clock radio taunted him, letting him know he had been there alone for forty-five minutes. He studied his shackles. There were four sets of handcuffs. Each was covered in a foam material and a layer of sheepskin was covering that. It looked as though it was applied as an after thought.

On the bedside table to his left, Ben saw a glass half filled with a cloudy liquid. Next to it was a pill crusher, an open bottle of aspirin, two large syringes and a thin, long tube. His stomach started to knot. What could Allyson have in mind? His bladder spasmed and he urinated on himself. Ben's patience was wearing thin. Self degradation wasn't a turn on for him.

Ben woke with a start. Sunlight no longer streamed through the window as night took over. The clock radio glowed eight forty five p.m. His whole body ached from the bondage and he was cold from the stale urine.

"What's going on?" He shouted to anyone, no one. The tomb echoed his question and then it drifted away. His mind raced. This wasn't Allyson, it couldn't be. Someone was playing a sick joke on him. But who would bother to go through so much trouble to piss him off?

"Ryan. " Ben shouted triumphantly. He had set Ryan up a few months ago, just before his wedding. They had went out for a few drinks and an informal bachelor party. Ben made sure Ryan got smashed. He paid a stripper at the party to pose nude with Ryan while he took pictures. He couriered the pictures to Ryan's fiancée Liddy an hour before the wedding. How was he supposed to know Liddy didn't have a sense of humor?

The wedding was cancelled that day. After three months, Liddy still hadn't spoken to Ryan.

But didn't he fix that? He explained everything to Liddy and even set it up so she could talk to the stripper. Could Ryan still hold him responsible if Liddy still refused to talk to him? He should be thankful he saved him from such an uptight bitch. And if memory served him right, she wasn't much fun in bed either.

And Ben knew exactly what Ryan had in mind. He would show up in a few hours and take pictures of him bound and gagging from the stink of foul urine.

"If Ryan thinks he's pulled one over on me, just wait 'til I get outta here. He's gonna be real sorry he fucked with me," Ben yelled hysterically to the empty house.

"But how did he get in?" he continued to talk to the emptiness.

"He must have waited for Allyson to leave... then jimmied one of the windows," he mused. "Yeah, that must be it."

And where was Allyson?

The slam of the front door startled Ben. The clock radio beamed twelve thirty a.m. He was sore, cold, and hungry. He hoped it was Allyson.

"Allyson," he yelled in a shaky voice.

"Allyson!" his voice began to rise." For fuck sake Allyson, answer me!"

Footsteps sounded on the stairs and stopped at the bedroom. It took several minutes for Ben to realize it wasn't Allyson. It had to be Ryan.

"Ryan! Hey man, it was only a joke. I tried to fix it for you. It's not my fault she wouldn't listen."

Silence.

"Okay, a joke's a joke. you got me back good. Now come on in and let me go. I'm starved, I need a shower and a dump. Come on man," Ben was pleading now. "This isn't funny anymore."

The doorknob rattled then began to slowly turn. The door opened a crack. A shaft of light sliced the darkness. Ben blinked to adjust his eyes.

"I can smell you Ryan. Get in here!"

The silence was as sharp as the light. The door creaked open another few inches. Ben could make out a silhouette. It looked too small to be Ryan.

In one quick motion, the door swung all the way framing a small shadow.

"Hi, baby," droned a deep, throaty voice.

Ben felt his blood turn icy.

"Liddy!" It came out as a croak.

"Who were you expectin' sugar? The tooth fairy?"

"Why'd you do this? Is it the joke I played on Ryan?"

"Actually, you did me a favor. I don't want Ryan. I've met someone else who is much more....interesting."

"But why are you doing this to me?"

"Well, it's the only way."

"What are you talking about?"

"Ben, you're no good for Allyson. You lie. You fuck around on her. And now she knows."

Ben broke out into a sweat. "H-how?" he stammered.

Liddy took a video tape from her coat." You don't mind if I pop this in do you?" She turned to the VCR and turned the power on. "This'll explain everything," she drawled as she slipped the tape in.

The tape began to play. Ben felt vomit in his mouth. It was a video of the night he spent with Liddy. Ryan told him she liked to tape their sessions and critique them afterwards. He was going to kill the bitch for recording what they did. He tried to close his mind to the sight and sound. The moans, the looks of pleasure, the terms of endearment. He wanted to rip her head off right there.

"You want to kill me, don't you?" Liddy laughed as she bent to give him a patronizing kiss on the mouth. " Unfortunately for you, you're the one who's going to die."

As if on cue, Allyson was on the other side of the bed. Ben's horrified stare seemed to give her greater pleasure than orgasm.

The look on her face was utter bliss.

"She's enjoying this," Ben suddenly realized to himself. Aloud he asked," Is this a new type of foreplay?"

Both women looked at each other and laughed. " It is for us," Liddy drawled. "Hold his head steady," she instructed Allyson.

Liddy picked up the long, thin tube while Allyson held Ben's head with his chin against his chest. Liddy dipped the tube in a gel and brought it towards Ben. He tried to move his head but was so weak, he gave little resistance. Liddy slid the tube into his left nostril. He could feel it slide down his throat. Liddy took one of the syringes and attached it to the tube. She pulled back on the plunger until stomach contents could be seen in the barrel.

"Gotta make sure it's in the right spot. Can't overdose if it's not in your stomach now can you?"

Liddy picked up the other syringe and filled it with the liquid from the glass. "It's just aspirin, about fifty or so, and a tiny dash of foxglove for insurance. So, if the aspirin doesn't work fast enough, you'll have a heart attack. Best of all, it'll look like you did it yourself."

"The cuffs are padded," she continued, "so if you struggle there will be little or no marks. The tape and a note from Allyson telling you she's leaving will be with you."

Liddy attached the syringe to the tube and pushed the liquid through. Ben could feel a cold sensation starting at his nose, flowing through his throat and hitting his stomach. Liddy waited several minutes, then removed the tube. She wiped around his nose and lips. She dipped a spoon into the liquid and placed it in his mouth. The taste was bitter, as bitter as he felt now. He still couldn't believe this was true. At any minute, he expected they would tell him it was a joke to teach him a lesson for pulling this type of thing on other people.

He felt his lips move, but nothing came out. "It's a joke," he kept repeating to himself.

Allyson's face was getting fuzzy. He could see her lips move but the words sounded thick and foreign. "...and I'll be collecting your insurance. Almost a million. I should've done something like this sooner. Thank God for Liddy. She showed me the way."

Ben felt Allyson place something in his hand. It was a crumpled piece of paper. She bent close to his ear; "Here's your note. Hang on to it tight. I wouldn't want you to lose it."

"This wasn't supposed to happen," Ben felt his body begin to go numb. "I don't deserve this!" he screamed to himself. His lips wouldn't move.

Everything became darker as he watched the girls wipe knobs and tables free of prints. They chatted and hummed gleefully as they worked, totally oblivious to Ben. They put the tube and syringes into a plastic bag. Using a cloth, Liddy picked up the glass and pressed it to Ben's lips. They removed the cuffs and rubbed his wrists and ankles to make sure the circulation was good, then circled his fingers around the glass.

Liddy and Allyson smiled at each other and kissed Ben on each cheek. Ben heard them walk away. He could no longer see. The blackness had swallowed him.

Ben listened to their faint footsteps on the stairs. The front door slammed with finality. Then, Ben screamed and realized that it was all in his mind.

A Survivor of Nanking
David Lu

Excerpt from the private journal of Lau Ho Yip

Sept 18, 1982
It has been some forty-five years since the Nanking Massacre, also known as The Rape of Nanking. I write this because I have just heard that the Japanese government has begun to rewrite history—to make the massacre not exist. This is wrong, it dishonors the memories of all those who died, and it opens the way for it to happen again. There is a saying in the West that all those who forget history are forever doomed to repeat it. I will not allow the world and my family to forget all those who died; all those whose lives were destroyed must be willing to pass on this knowledge so that it is never forgotten and never repeated.

My story begins not in China, but in America. I was born and raised here. I was educated in the U.S. and eventually went to medical school. In 1936, I received my license to practice medicine. Like most children of emigrants, I faced my share of prejudice. But, it was not enough to stop me from living my life and succeeding in American society. I owe much to my parents. Their support and guidance was invaluable, so it was with a heavy heart that I left them to go to China to help in the beleaguered home of my ancestors. Those of you who have studied history will know that in the early 1930's, Japan invaded China and succeeded in establishing several beachheads on the mainland. I traveled to China to heal the sick and injured. I settled in Nanking in the first week of October 1937 and obtained a position as a staff doctor at the Episcopal mission.

The first few weeks of my work involved treating staff members for headaches, and the occasional cold or bruise. I felt useful despite the small number of people I treated. I even had time to sightsee and meet new friends. Among them was a young couple by the name of Yin Song Min and his wife Yin Tau Long. They owned a small bakery on the East Side of Nanking and I would often visit when I had free time. I had thought that I could live in China a few more years and return to the U.S. with a feeling of accomplishment. Sadly, with growing concern, we received daily reports and rumors about the momentum of the Japanese invasion of China. They seemed bent on the complete destruction of the nation. The Japanese pushed at the borders and killed countless troops and civilians in the name of war. In November 1937, the few foreigners living in Nanking created an international rescue committee whose purpose was to establish a safety zone within the city for refugees and soldiers. This safety zone was set up around the missions. I knew that my life as a simple healer was nearing an end. Soon I would be a doctor tending to the atrocities of war-injured soldiers and civilians.

On November 11, 1937, the Japanese Army took over Shanghai, with their sights set on Nanking. The Japanese Army fought a running battle against Chinese soldiers and on December 9th, they demanded that the defenders of Nanking surrender. When the Chinese Army refused, the Japanese Army attacked. I remember the fear I felt as people began flooding into the safety zone and the hospitals were overwhelmed with injured. I volunteered my services on the East Side of the city near the Yin's bakery. There I saw the clinic receive soldiers brought there by a rapidly dwindling army. I saw and heard the battle as the Japanese Army tightened their viselike grip around the city. The explosions, gunfire, and the screams of frightened citizens still haunt my dreams. The images transfixed my mind; of all the sights I saw at the clinic, the one that remains with me is the first time I saw a soldier die.

He was brought in by a group of civilians. They told me that the soldier was a truck driver transporting reserves to the front lines. The truck had flipped over and the survivors were brought to the clinic. The driver appeared to be no more than twenty, with sweat and blood covering his face.

"How long was he out there before you found him?" I asked an elderly woman who had brought the soldier inside.

"I do not know. When we found him he was trapped in the cab of his truck," she told me.

"Thank you, please go so that I can attend to him."

I said that as I looked over the mangled body of the human being before me. The lights in the clinic were low to conserve power and the windows were open to let in the sun's rays. In the light of day, I saw my first casualty of war. His uniform was stuck to his body by dried blood. His face was a mask of pain and bruises. I could tell that his arm was broken by its odd angle. My first job was to get his clothes off to examine him further. As I reached for a pair of scissors to cut off the side of his shirt, I heard him utter a dull moan, but in an urgent voice. When I leaned over to hear what he said, I didn't know to be happy or sad that my parents insisted I learn Mandarin Chinese when I was young.

"Please kill me, I can't take the pain, the pain, the pain," he moaned in a low, barely breathing voice.

I realized that even with treatment he did not stand much chance of living through the night. I touched him with my white-gloved hands and noticed that he was bleeding through the side of his uniform. His ribs were poking into his skin and probably into his lungs. His internal injuries were more severe than I had originally guessed. The soldier gave me a wide-eyed look as I bent low over him; his eyes expressed great suffering. Then, he spied the scissors in my hands. They were small and silver in color and intended to cut bandages. Yet, to him, they looked a godsend. He closed his eyes and shuddered once just before he died from his internal injuries and loss of blood. I knew though that he had expected me to stab him to death. Perhaps, he had closed his eyes to prepare himself. Perhaps, he died thinking that I had done it. A surge of mixed emotions welled inside me. I felt sick. I felt like crying. Yet I also felt like screaming, "I DID NOT KILL YOU!" but it was too late. Perhaps, I did kill him, unintentionally, as I slipped the scissors into my white coat pocket. If only I had acted faster to stop the bleeding. If only I had gotten more help. But, I was alone in the treatment room, and the soldier died on December 13, 1937, the day Nanking was finally taken by the Japanese.

I left the clinic to get some air when I saw the Japanese Army march into the city. The streets were alive with frightened people running for cover into buildings. I was torn between running away to safety or staying in the clinic to help the injured. Then I heard the guns; a steady and deafening blast of nonstop bombardment. I ran as hard and as fast as my legs would carry me. I looked back to see swarms of Japanese soldiers firing relentlessly at anything that moved. They killed survivors of the Chinese Army, and many more civilians; men, women, and children all cut down in a hail of bullets. The soldiers only stopped to reload or to beat and stab anyone that was still moving. I was horrified. For the first time in my life, I wanted to kill someone. My earlier experience with the soldier had sickened me and I wanted revenge! For the soldiers killed, and for the scores of innocent human beings killed by these monsters. I wanted revenge against these soulless monsters that masqueraded as people. "Damn the Hippocratic Oath," I thought. I screamed for them to stop, but, like many others, I simply ran with my white doctor's coat flapping about me. The clinic was all but forgotten in my selfish desire to live. Humans are odd that way. We hold onto our morals as if they give us life; but when crisis comes, how many people wear their convictions like armor and storm into battle?

I remember wanting only to live, to live to curse these killers and to help those in need. I hoped that the Yin's were all right and I wanted desperately to see them. Yin Song Min always talked about how he made his bread and his wife constantly chattered about how many children they would have.

As I ran with the screaming and dying crowd, I could smell the coppery tang of blood in the air. I saw bodies being mowed down around me, and I ran low to make a smaller target. I realized that if I stayed out much longer I would be killed. My ability to reach the safety zone depended solely on my survival. As I turned down another street, a sign in blockish Chinese characters beckoned. I silently thanked my parents for making me learn to read Chinese characters. Now, I was only a few blocks from one of the streets that led straight to the safety zone. With realizing it, I had run nearly a mile and a half. My chances of reaching the zone were minimal, with the crowd on the streets. I had to find a place to hide, until the sun went down, and then make my way under cover of darkness. Nearby was a row of shops. Entering would be a risk since the Japanese would probably be searching buildings. However, I had no other choice. I fought through the masses and into the doorway of a bookstore. Fortunately enough, no one followed me. The owner did not appear to be inside, but the door was open. Perhaps, he had left when the shooting had started. Frantically, I searched for a place to hide, but there was no back room or storage area that I could see. The register at the rear of the store seemed as good a place as any to hide. I dove behind the counter, squeezed down, and sat with my knees held tight to my chest. Breathing loudly would possibly prove fatal, so I took quick, silent breaths to calm myself. Outside the screaming and firing continued, without any breaks in the rhythm of the stutter of the guns or the chilling screams of the dying. I do not know how long I hid in the shop. My broken watch's hands stood frozen at three o'clock. I peered over the edge of the counter and continued to hear firing in the distance. The street was clear but it was still light out so I stayed hidden. I mulled over the fact that I might die in this store.

My body ached from running. I was hungry and thirsty, and my bladder was near the bursting point. Afraid to move, I held it and held it, as I waited. The sun dropped slowly down outside and it grew dark inside the bookstore. The lights in the store were either off or broken. I did not care, as long as this meant that people outside could not see me. More gunfire racked against stone, but as I prayed that my building would be missed, the glass window in the shop exploded. In an instant I heard Japanese voices nearby. My only recourse to keep from screaming was to bite my hand. The noise soon dissipated and as the interminable waiting continued, I felt my right hand wet with saliva and blood. The awful wails began again as nightfall embraced Nanking.

This was my chance to run for the safety zone. Upon my departure, I relieved myself under the counter and then crawled along the floor towards the shop front door. After taking a deep breath, I raced several yards across the street before stopping in the shadow of one of the buildings. In the darkness I observed mounds of people. Clumps of two or three bodies lay on the streets and sidewalks. Careful not to step on anyone and trip, I made my way to the safety zone. My own fear paralyzed me to the dead all around me. Many streetlights were broken which aided me in my escape, but smoke was rising in the distance. Nanking was on fire. Alternately running and then hiding, I darted through the city, noticing the blood-curdling screams punctuated by the sounds of gunfire. I raced through corners and blocks. When I finally reached my street, I knew that the safety zone loomed straight ahead.

Like a fly, I swerved seemingly aimless across whole blocks that still had streetlights. Three times I had to walk around blocks to avoid patrols of soldiers. I did not know whether the soldiers that passed by were Japanese or Chinese, but I could not take any chances. Several times I hid among the dead in the streets, piling bodies over me for protection, ignoring the putrid stench of rotting flesh. Very few people alive were on the streets. All of the lights in the surrounding buildings were off, and most of the windows were shattered, a mute testament to the devastation of Nanking.

The sounds of the slaughter did not abate. A woman wailed in Mandarin Chinese, "No, NOOOOOOOO, NOOO, Don't touch me, NOOO NOOOOOooo." This was the long drawn-out cry of desperation, so primal and animalistic in nature that anything with a soul would have responded. I heard another muffled yell for help, cut off by two Japanese voices. Then came the meaty slap of flesh on flesh. Down the street from me, two soldiers grappled with a screaming woman, tearing off her clothes. A white-hot rage burned inside me as I saw what they were doing. For the first time since the carnage had begun, I witnessed firsthand the perversity of the invaders. Even if I died in the process, I could not let this continue. Panicky, I searched for some sort of weapon to protect the woman. There was nothing nearby, until I felt in my pockets the scissors I had absentmindedly place there. One of the soldiers struggled with the woman on the ground. His friend stood guard laughing and yelling words of encouragement. My eyes narrowed with rage. Grabbing the scissors firmly in one hand, and my anger burning within lending me strength, I ran at them, attacking, and yelling for them to stop. In an instant, I plunged the scissors into the one standing guard before he even knew who I was. He screamed and gurgled as the blood left his body. I pulled out quickly and stabbed him again in his left eye. He wailed again, but this time the blood in his throat muffled his dying sounds. Before the rapist could react to my fervor, I kicked him between his legs. His pants were around his ankles and he toppled quickly. With his neck exposed, I stabbed him where the skull joins the neck. As he slammed to the ground, his body writhed in torment. The girl reeled in a daze, too frightened to realize what had just transpired. I jammed the bloody scissors back into my pocket and bent down to see if the girl was still alive. In the dim light I observed her vacant eyes. She was breathing so I could not leave her. The rapist partners now dead, I grabbed the girl and carried her three blocks towards the zone before I stopped to catch my breath. She remained in a daze so I took off my doctor's coat and wrapped her. My reassurances came hard.

"I will not hurt you. I am not like them. I will not hurt you," I told her over and over again.

I do not know if she understood. When we stopped to rest, I saw that she was only a teenager, no more than sixteen or seventeen, with her long hair in a tangled braid. Her trauma would likely stay with her for the rest of her life. I was just glad to have rescued her. I checked the streets and no other soldiers were converging on the area. The safety zone was probably only a half-mile away. I placed my hands around the young woman and we trudged onward. Thankfully, we crossed paths with only one other patrol. To escape notice, we lay on the ground by one of the buildings, pretending to be dead bodies. The soldiers passed right by us without stopping.

Toward dawn, we finally reached the safety zone. I was surprised to find the area unguarded and raced into it near exhaustion. We were met by several people, all Chinese, and I relayed to them my harrowing story.

It was a full week after the invasion and my arrival in the international safety zone before I was able to return to the Episcopal mission. By that time, the young woman I had saved was beginning to show signs of regaining her health. She had started to talk again, but still reverted to that dreadful night on occasion. When this happened, she could scarcely be calmed down. She never told us her real name, preferring to be known as Kuei, or "ghost" in Chinese. I guess we all had a piece of us die when Nanking fell to hostile invaders. I left the girl in the care of one of the families who met us when we entered. I never saw the Yin's in the safety zone, yet I never saw them killed. To this day, I hold onto hope that they escaped unharmed.

I returned to my work as doctor within the mission, but now I was treating refugees, victims of the horrors I had witnessed. We all bore the scars of those awful weeks of devastation. The scars remain both physical and psychological, but in times of crisis one does what one has to in order to survive. I am not sorry I killed to save the young woman. Yet, I still feel the pangs of guilt when I think of running away from the clinic. I do not lie to myself by saying that I should have died. I wanted to live. I was not a coward, no more so than the others. In a war, there are no heroes, or villains--only survivors.

A Good Name
Lisa Klassen

Sunlight falls through the kitchen window, tinted the faintly reddish hue only seen on a late afternoon in summer. The sunlight lies pooled on the immaculate, stone tiled floor, out of place in a room filled with gleaming steel, sterile blue walls, and a lingering odor of antiseptic. The woman paces the kitchen, unconsciously avoiding the puddle of sunlight. Her shoes rapping sharply against the tile, there is an agitated look in her eyes. She stops, leaning on the marble counter, tapping manicured nails while she thinks. The youthful prettiness she once possessed is transforming to the well-groomed look of a spoiled pet. Her hair is masterfully cut in the latest style; flawless makeup masks the heavy frown lines that are beginning to form. Her expensive clothes are perfectly tailored to hide the places on her body where fat is starting to intrude.

She pushes off the counter, and throws open a cupboard opposite her. Nothing inside but a few dusty bottles of wine. A bitter laugh escapes her reddened lips. She rolls swearwords silently over her tongue, afraid her husband may overhear. He does not approve of women swearing, he says it is unladylike. Every second and fourth weekend for a year in this damned place, and this is a first. They have no food. The grocery bags are sitting in their garage at home, the pate spoiling and the hand made ice cream melting. Her husband said they were in the trunk, not paying attention to what she asked, as usual. Now she doesn't know what to do. Her husband wants a smoothly run household; he won't take well to the lack of dinner. Though she knows it's his fault, the verbal blows she'd earn by saying so persuade her to find a scapegoat. He hates to make mistakes, vehemently denying them when he can. Someone on the kitchen staff at home will have to pay, instead.

At first she couldn't rebuke the staff, no matter how he raged at her. It wasn't in her nature, at least not until her husband said the employees all laughed at her for being so weak. She still remembers how terribly hurt she was. She tore furiously into them after that. She often suspects her husband told her a lie from the betrayed looks she received that first time. She had been a friend to many of them, lonely in her new place as the rich wife. The original help are long replaced, only her husband knows how she used to be. Now it's too late to relinquish her petty power, she's become dependent on it as the only control she has left in the life she leads under her husband's critical tongue. The present help are more afraid of her than him, a fact she finds both ironic and sad. This little mishap gives her another chance to exert that power. She rehearses what to say, and whom to select for punishment. She'll need the small release after the weekend is over. They are paid so well, scapegoat should be a job requirement, or so she tries to tell herself.

She roots vainly through the pantry in search of salvation. There isn't much of a personal nature at their island home, much less food. What lasts two weeks that her husband would actually eat? His snobbery extends to everything, including his tastebuds. These twice-monthly visits are a perfect example. According to him, wealthy people ALWAYS own a country home. All his friends and family own ostentatious second homes, huge country dwellings they refer to as "cottages". So they bought this extravagantly priced island "cottage" and barely use it. Her husband is excited, this Christmas it's his turn to have his family over. Every Christmas his family battles over where they'll spend next year. This year, he won. Another year with no chance of her going home for Christmas. Her family doesn't buy the feeble excuses she serves up each year. She always asks to go, he gets angry, accuses her of trying to make him look bad in front of his family, and says maybe next year. Every year she hopes it's time, but it never is. She sighs, and closes the pantry door.

She glances at the refrigerator hopefully. Maybe there's something leftover from last time. She pulls open the door, her fingers crossed. Ah, the horn of plenty overflows. Three measly items to choose from. A container of cream cheese, some molding kiwis and…a squeeze bottle of French's Mustard? She didn't buy this, did she? Her husband would sooner swallow bleach then use the cheap yellow liquid. So how did this get here? Wondering, she unscrews the lurid yellow top, and empties it into the sink. However it got here, she has to get rid of it before her husband sees the container. He would accuse her of buying it, and make fun of her 'roots'. She scoops out a tiny dollop with her finger, and puts it in her mouth. The taste reminds her of a younger, happier time, when she had believed that anything was possible. Belief is a sort of magic, transforming whoever is lucky enough to possess it. Loss of that belief has left her stranded in a once unimaginable place. She's tried drugs, alcohol, ski trips in Aspen, and hour long massages at her spa. None of it brings back that easy feeling of well being. It is beyond her, now, except in memories.

She breathes in one last whiff of the container, then throws it into the garbage. She has to make a decision about dinner, quickly. At home, the hired help make the decisions and take the responsibility off her shoulders. Out here she's on her own. All tasks become hers, including cooking meals. God, she just dreads the meals. It isn't that she minds cooking, in fact she used to love cooking for friends and family. But her recipes were mostly simple meals, not up to her husband's exacting standards. That first weekend out here had been absolute hell. Everything she cooked, her husband hated, and spared no effort to make her aware of it. After meals she'd hear him stalking about his den, muttering. Since then she's made sure to be prepared. She subscribes to every gourmet-cooking magazine and raids the finest stores for supplies before these country weekends. Still, she feels her stomach tense and her breath begin to shorten every time he picks up his fork for that first bite. Of course, if he has had a rough week, he'll start in on her no matter how good the food is.

Frustrated, she slams every cupboard and drawer in the kitchen. There really isn't a damn thing to eat in this house. She'll have to go into town and find something her husband will eat. In all their island visits she's never been to town. Her stomach sinks as she remembers jeering at the local supermarkets' tiny size as they drove by. Her husband always makes some local yokel joke, and they both laugh. She winces at the thought of shopping there. Her doubts on the stores' contents aside, they'll know she's a city dweller. She's conscious of the looks their brand new truck gets as they drive through town. She's heard the curses as her husband drives by a hitchhiker in the pouring rain on an island where hitchhiking is public transit. She quails at walking among them, her body laid bare to their curious glances. And she's painfully aware that people just don't like her anymore. Years of her husband's sharp tongue have corroded her self-confidence. Anything she says now is echoed back inside her head in his mocking tones, making it sound moronic. She never used to be this way, and it frightens her. When she was younger she always had plenty of friends, she was very easygoing with people. Now social contact with strangers has become loathsome to her, and she tends to spend most of her time inside. She's avoided all encounters for weeks and she's not prepared for one now. She must, though. Her husband won't go. The way he always scoffs at the locals makes her think he might be scared of them as well. He'll get angry with her for asking, and she'll end up going, anyway. Resigned, she plays with the key rack, trying to decide which car to take. She's definitely not taking the Durango. The shining newness of the truck bespeaks wealth playacting at being a regular Joe. She's embarrassed for her husband every time he gets into it. The truck doesn't suit him. She grabs the keys to the Mercedes, and lets the old feeling of superiority settles around her like a well-worn suit of armor. Feeling much braver, she leaves.

The ordeal nearly over, she waits impatiently in the checkout line. The selection wasn't as bad as she'd feared; now she just wants to get out of here. She taps her fingers against the steel rail, and looks disgruntled. There's only one teenage cashier working, and she's busy chatting to a customer buying cigarettes. Christ. She checks her watch three times, sighing audibly between each glance. This, at least, gets the cashier's attention, who rings her groceries through while talking with the local clodhopper. He eventually wanders off, and the cashier gives her the total. Presenting her credit card with a flourish, she watches the cashier's face to see if she looks impressed. The cashier (with a hint of condensation?) asks her for ID, as she isn't a "regular". Right. This is small town nosiness or small town distrust, one of the two. Anyway, just what she expected. Out to give her a hard time, punishment for not being local. She snorts and rolls her eyes, hoping the cashier notices. She scrambles to think up some indignant retorts as the cashier looks searchingly at her.

"Hey, are you any relation to the Bergers that live here? Natalie and John?"

Taken aback, she giggles at this unexpected turn in the conversation. Another couple on this tiny island with the same name as her husband? He would HAVE to find this amusing. Unexpectedly, she's happy. She has a story to break the tension of dinner. Okay, but she must play this out in full, so she can have a good tale to tell. With a flash of innovation, she replies.

"Why yes, I am related. John is my husband's brother."

"I knew it," the cashier bubbles happily. "I didn't think you and Natalie were related, you look a fair bit older than she is. She and John are a very happy couple, and such good people, don't you think?"

"Sure," she replies, rather roughly, her good mood vanished. She's highly sensitive about her apparent age. Only thirty-four, new acquaintances often mistake her for a women in her forties, much to their mutual chagrin. Spending life under the kind of stress she lives with will age a person immeasurably. To rub salt in her wounds, her husband doesn't look a day older than when they were first married. The cashier babbles on about the wonderful deeds of the alternate Bergers, blissfully unaware of the sudden mood change. She wonders when this torture will end. She used to volunteer her time constantly, and no one sung her praises. Of course, she hasn't done anything since she married; her husband disapproves. He never donates money for any other reason than a tax deduction. He thinks all that stuff about the homeless and needy is drivel, a scam to get money out of suckers. As far as he's concerned, anyone who gets fooled by that bit is soft and weak minded. She didn't want to give him a chance to heap that same scorn upon her head, so she gave it up. But she misses helping people, she misses it terribly. This is when she actually hates her husband. Not for the choices he forced her to make, but for the choices she made voluntarily, to protect herself. She has given up a career, children and various little things, like the chance to do community work, and for what? She's miserable. Ugh, why does she even waste energy thinking about things it's too late to change? She just has to live her life, such that it is. She is furious with the cashier for her part in this ordeal, and with the stupid Bergers as well. She reaches for her groceries, determined to flee, when something the cashier says catches her attention.

"Of course, if you are picking up groceries for the Bergers, why don't you put it on their tab sheet?"

Hmm. A pleasing ending to the story, one her husband would heartily approve of.

"I AM picking up some things for them, actually. They must have forgotten to tell me to put it on their tab."

"No problem, ma'am. Say hi to them for me, will you?"

"I'll make a point of it, don't worry." She scurries out of the store, feeling a little guilty for such a mean act. She throws her ill-gotten gains into the Mercedes, and speeds off.

She relates her story at dinner, but her husband merely shrugs indifferently and continues eating. He gets up and leaves without a word when he's done. Damn Bergers. Not only did they ruin her afternoon, but they don't even make good story material. She vows to go back to the store tomorrow and put the most expensive items she can find on their tab. Even better, she'll throw it all away as soon as she's out the door. Feeling worn, she goes up to her bedroom. Warm colors, comfy furniture, and the beautiful art in her room are a marked contrast to the icy blues walls and dark, heavy furniture in her husband's bedroom. She feels safe in here; it's a room of a happy little girl, or a lover's cozy nest. She designed it herself, with the help of a decorator. She wanted to decorate the rest of the house, breathe a little life into the impersonal space, but her husband wouldn't let her. The only personal touch in the rest of the house is a teal and cream colored Persian rug that she picked out for their living room. She crosses the deep plush carpet in her bare feet and hunkers down in front of her dresser. She opens the bottom drawer, searching for a comfy nightgown to wear to bed. One catches her eye, particularly soft and lacy. She runs her fingers over it, enjoying the feel of the soft fabric. Something crackles under her fingers. A piece of folded paper is in one of the pockets. She pulls it out. On the outside is a drawing of a bed, with a naked girl perched on it, knees tucked modestly up under her chin. With a creeping sense of unease, she realizes the bed looks exactly like hers. She reads the words inside.

"I love you with all my heart, my sweetest one. When I breathe, I smell your hair, when I close my eyes, your image burns there. Your voice in my ears is the night cries of sleeping birds. Every night I pray we will be together, forever. Your Love."

She sits on the bed with a heavy thump. Her jaw clenches as she crushes the card between bunched fists. Damn him, damn him. In here, of all places. Does his mistress sleep in her bed, too? She was half expecting this, but expecting and knowing are two different things. Furious tears stream down her face and fall into the folds of the nightgown. The passion infused in the card poises a mortal blow to her self-esteem. She's managed to keep herself intact all these years with the knowledge that her husband is incapable of being any other way. She's taken the jibes knowing any other woman he married would have to do the same. Has some woman seen a quality in her husband she's ignored? Has she been in the wrong all this time? She runs probing fingers over soft, doughy flesh that was once lean. With her body looking like this, its no wonder he doesn't touch her anymore. She swears she'll go to the gym more often. She's rationalizing, and hates herself for it. Any women's magazine would say confront him, but she isn't sure she's strong enough. She smoothes the crumpled card, trying to find a hint towards whether she's failed as a wife in the lovely lines, when she realizes this card isn't written by her husband. His sentences fall like a boy dropping rocks off a bridge. Chunk. There is one sentence. Thunk. There goes another. The verses in the card are light and flowing. And she knows he doesn't draw. This card is sketched with great love and a skilled hand. So who wrote it? His mistress? The words seem … masculine, though. Questions nagging at her, she stares at the ceiling late into the night before finally dropping into uneasy rest on the floor, beside a bed she is unsure has been desecrated.

The sound of the car leaving wakes her. Good, she won't have to face him with the question in her eyes. She assembles her breakfast of grapefruit and unbuttered toast while waiting for the coffee to brew, the repast of suffering dieters everywhere. Seating herself in the breakfast nook, she closes her eyes and lets the sunlight play over her face. While enjoying the warmth, an unforeseen revelation occurs. She isn't putting herself on a diet for her husband's sake, but for her own. In fact, she doesn't care what he thinks of her looks, or what he has been up to. Sometime in the night it ceased to matter. She laughs at how brave she sounds, at least in her head. The discovery does wonders, making her stronger in places she desperately needs strength. She's even going to confront him about his mistress, no matter what he says to her. After all, they're just words. She's the one who gives them the power to wound, and she isn't going to anymore. She smiles, a peaceful, easy smile. It's her first in a long, long time. The smile transforms her. She's achingly lovely in the warm sun, and doesn't even realize it. No one's around to gaze upon her in her fleeting moment of beauty. With the ring of the doorbell it's gone, as so many beautiful things are, unwitnessed. She gets up to answer it, carrying her untouched cup of coffee with her.

An older woman, graying hair pulled down her back in a long French braid, stands on her doorstep.

"Uh, hi there. Are you a relative of the Bergers?"

Oh, no. Has this woman spoken to the cashier? She's forced to renew a lie begun to impress her indifferent husband. Guiltily, she replies "Yes. Why?"

"Well, I was hoping to speak with Natalie or John. Are either of them here?"

She's being drawn into lying in detail. "No, they are not. Can I help you?" she reluctantly asks with increasing discomfort.

"Sure, just give them this envelope, will you? It's the notes on last weeks town meeting."

As she reaches for the envelope the coffee spills, splashing the pristine white rug. The smear of brown glares up at her, shocking against the snowy white rug. The woman looks as stunned as she does.

"You better put something on that spill, Natalie will freak out if she sees that, since this isn't her house."

Not Natalie's house? Of course this wasn't Natalie's house. She peers at the woman, searching for signs of senility.

"The one time Natalie and John had me over, they were fanatical about using coasters, and eyed my wineglass when I walked over the Persian rug. They are usually so easygoing, I was surprised to feel uncomfortable. They housesit for a rich couple, and worry about the house. Anyway, I'm sure you have seen that gorgeous teal blue and cream Persian rug in the living room. I wouldn't want anything to happen to that, whether it was mine or not ! Don't worry, I'm sure Natalie has some stain remover lying around."

With an almost audible click, the pieces all fall together. There's no other woman. There are only other Bergers. They live here. They LIVE here. The woman says something to her and leaves. She barely notices. The betrayal by her husband has transformed into a far stranger reality than she could ever dream. Unbelievable. Why would they do such a thing? They must have watched the house for weeks to make sure it was safe. A deep blush spreads across her cheeks. How routine their life must have looked to the hidden watchers. Humiliated that they decided breaking and entering was a safe risk, her shock melts into anger. How dare they? They haven't just subverted the car and house, either. Some girl has taken her life and lived it better than she could. They have fulfilling, helpful lives, while she has nothing. Her husband will be enraged, he'll prosecute the "Bergers" to the fullest extent and make sure they spend a long time in jail. The sweet words in the love letter spring to her mind, and she feels a pang of pity for the young imposters. Anyone so in love will find jail a waking nightmare. She admits to herself that the real reason she's incensed is because she's jealous of the love the young couple has. She actually admires the gutsiness of these two, become upstanding members of a small community without suspicion, knowing the secluded habits of their counterparts. They have certainly taken care of her home! They must have lived here for quite some time, and she certainly never suspected a thing until this weekend. The humor of the situation strikes her, and she begins chuckling. There is an appealing irony at having a counterpart who is doing good works and living happily under the same name that has caused her so much misery. The fact is, she'd love to meet these young ruffians. Her face falls at the circumstances she will probably meet them under. Her husband won't see the humor in this, nor will he recognize that there was no harm done. As far as he goes, the "Bergers" picked the worst home possible to pull this stunt in. Speak of the devil, his car's pulling in. Those poor kids.

All their leftover groceries are loaded into the car. It is the end of the second weekend of the month. She fusses around the counters, postponing the moment of departure. Her husband glares restlessly about him.

"Move it, let's get going," he snaps at her.

She levels a long, hard look at him, saying nothing. He tries to meet her stare, fidgeting, his eyebrows raised in surprise at this unexpected confrontation. Finally he looks down, and walks out of the house, a shocked look on his face. He slams the door shut behind him. She takes a last look around, then puts an envelope on the kitchen table. She shuts off the lights, and closes the door gently. The envelope lies gleaming on the table, caught by the afternoon sunlight. The front of the envelope is marked with a looping, childish hand. It says "The Bergers." It is the envelope the older woman left behind. On the back is written, in the same childish hand, "Thanks for the good name. I hope to see you soon. Regards, Laura Berger."

She grins as the car churns up dust speeding down the country road. It seems a waste to have something so expensive so rarely used. Her husband won't catch on, he never notices anything. Besides, they're the first people she's wanted as friends in a very long time. Laura Berger takes a deep breath, and begins to sing.

Hot Totem
H. H. Morris

Natalie Atropos had the personality of a porcupine on a bad quill day, greasy black hair styled by the Medusa Unisex Salon, and a rarely bathed body. If she owned more than one pair of jeans, she rotated them instead of doing laundry. She topped her jeans with a frayed seaman's jersey, a faded Broncos sweat shirt, or a tattered dungaree shirt. She'd cropped both sweat and dungaree to bare her convex belly. I easily envisioned Natalie as her namesake, the Fate who wielded the shears that cut a man's life short.

Not that she was currently Greek. She claimed to be Sioux. She needed certification as a descendant of Native Americans to direct the NeoPrimitive Players' production of Socrates Bald Eagle's *Our Glorious Heritage*. While all cast and crew were presumably tribal in at least one ancestral branch, outside contractors could be European, Asian, or African descent. She wanted me; German mixed with English, to supply security for a Pre-Columbian bison.

"Why?" I asked her.

"There's power in the artifact. It isn't a copy, Bill. It's genuine. The cast will feed on its aura."

Natalie and I met on a warm day, which meant I saw love handles hanging over her jeans and speculated whether the dungaree shirt's remaining two buttons could contain her large bosom. I also paid attention to her black hair, watching closely to make sure nothing jumped out of it.

"You're offering how much?" I asked.

She said, "Six hundred a week for the final three weeks of rehearsal—seven nights per week, some of them beginning at one in the afternoon, none ending before midnight. Six hundred for each Thursday through Sunday set of performances. The show should run at least six weeks."

That meant $1800 for working for no other client for the next three weeks, plus $3600 for giving the NeoPrimitive Players half a dozen more consecutive weekends. When she took out 30 green photos of Andrew Jackson—30 views of The Hermitage, if I turned the money over—Natalie had a private investigator and I had a client.

I assumed her bison a fake. I got paid to lend an element of authority to her claims. A couple of previous jobs had taken me into theaters. It's a world where overstatement is a religious obligation.

Natalie lived with the crew. She said that director and cast should never share quarters. I studied her housemates, two males with long hair, one female with braids, and thought they looked far more Indian than Natalie.

She led me to her room. It contained a battered chest of drawers, an unmade bed with dirty sheets and pillowcases, and a safe. Natalie opened the safe and examined the stone bison reverentially. Then she stood aside and told me to remove it and to carry it to my car.

The theater had formerly been a dive that smart men and women avoided. One fight too many, or else another underage drinker using the parking lot, had closed it down. The bar remained in place. Black curtains stretched from the ceiling to below the wood to separate the area behind the bar from the main section of the building. Metal chairs faced a small stage.

Seven men and seven women, five of the latter wearing leg warmers, stretched out. They stopped moving as Natalie and I entered.

"Ken, " she ordered an actor, "get the table for the bison."

I hoped the table was sturdy. It's amazing how heavy stone is.

A guy who looked about as Native American as I did ran to the curtained area and came out with a rickety table. Escorted by Natalie, I lugged the bison up two steps to the stage and set it down. I stepped back quickly as the table creaked.

Natalie said, "This is Bill Steam. He's providing security for our totem during rehearsals and during the run. His fee is part of the grant, a condition of our borrowing the sacred bison. Feel it."

I tottered out of the way as they crowded around the table.

"Yeah."

"This is the real article."

"I see my past."

I smelled psychology. I'd lugged that hunk of rock farther than I liked and felt nothing but pain.

While the cast found their roots, Natalie led me behind the curtain. The nearest end of the bar contained drums, rattles, flutes, feathers, and other objects.

"This is our props table, Bill," she said. "The bison stays here except when it's on stage. One of the actors will carry it on and off. The rest of the time, it's your responsibility."

"What am I protecting it from, Natalie? Do you expect art thieves among the audience?"

"You're protecting it from the cast, Bill. They might not have my strength of character, and when I touch that totem, I want to keep it rather than return it to its owner."

Natalie had a husky, sexy contralto voice that suggested too many cigarettes and glasses of whiskey in her past. It grated during rehearsal, when she yelled and swore at the cast constantly. She especially disliked the performance of a buxom actress named Monica Running Waters.

Socrates Bald Eagle, the creator of *Our Glorious Heritage*, was apparently tone deaf. There has never been a culture that confused such a cacophony with music, although a couple of local rock bands come close. Natalie claimed Monica couldn't sing. I wondered how anyone could tell.

On my fifth night of work, during a break, Monica leaned against the bar and asked, "What tribe do you claim descent from?"

"Angles, Saxons, and Teutons."

"You don't feel any power in the totem?"

I said, "I don't believe inanimate objects have power."

"You're the most honest person here, Bill. Do you care if it's a fake?"

"No."

"It's real," Monica said. "Despite what Natalie said, I don't think she feels much when she touches it. If I told her that, she'd smile at me and say a full-blooded Pawnee can never feel the same as a Sioux. We're traditional enemies."

Outside of shuddering at the music and being unable to make sense out of the show, which seemed a series of too many skits featuring various traditions, I found the first week easy. The bison wasn't getting any lighter, but neither was I growing weaker. At the start of the second week, Natalie had 30 more portraits of Old Hickory for me.

I toted the totem to the props table and put my chair in place. I did a double take. From the table to the front of the building the area behind the bar looked like a thrift shop.

"We're mounting a costume show, Bill," Natalie said. "For most productions, two or three dress rehearsals are sufficient. *Our Glorious Heritage* requires cast members to make changes rapidly."

"Some of these look like women's clothes."

"And others look like men's clothes, because that's what they are. This is the only area big enough to serve as a dressing room. There's no modesty in theater, Bill."

This theater had modesty. It belonged to Bill Steam, private investigator, and security guard for a hunk of stone that looked to have been tortured instead of sculpted.

Authenticity of dress meant no lingerie. Natalie's insistence on pace had the cast stripping the moment they got offstage. The bison and I frequently found ourselves surrounded by naked men and women, and because the show demanded lots of dancing, jumping around, pounding on drums, and yodeling, their mingled perspiration soon gave the area the aroma of a locker room.

If Natalie and Socrates Bald Eagle were correct, eastern Indians and some from southern climates ran around either nude or close to it. I lowered my income projection from $5400 to $2400, three weeks of rehearsal and one weekend, after which the show would fold, with or without the assistance of the law. I live in a suburban area. *Our Glorious Heritage* belonged in a metropolitan theater, where the audiences are more sophisticated about flesh.

After a few days of costume changes, Monica developed a new ritual. Every time she went by us, she'd rub the bison, then me, usually stroking my cheek or tousling my hair.

"Why?" I asked her one night.

"I stroke the bison for power and you for integrity. I think he feels cleaner after being in your company."

Don't stroke back, I told myself.

As if reading my mind, Monica said, "Natalie has fixed it so you can't meet the cast, hasn't she?"

"We set my schedule up front."

"Are you part of the crew?"

"No," I said. "I'm an outside contractor."

Natalie yelled for act two to begin. I relaxed as the area partially emptied. I couldn't be a member of the crew because I didn't carry a gun.

"I haven't heard of any museum thefts, Bill," said Mike Andrews. "I'll check. Heavy weapons make me nervous, too. Thanks."

Mike, a state police corporal, and I have a mutually profitable relationship. I occasionally come across evidence of lawbreaking. I play snitch for Mike. This makes him look smart, since I desire no credit for assisting the law. Cops don't run security checks. They take missing persons reports, but give them no priority unless there's evidence a felony is involved. Mike sends me citizens who want more services than his force can provide.

We reached week three, the last rehearsals. Natalie handed me my twenties after she opened the safe and before I took the bison out. It was another hot night and the buttons on her shirt failed to survive handing a man an envelope. I saw new areas of dirt.

As I drove to the theater, she said, "I'm not really a bitch, Bill."

"I don't care if you are. You pay your bills on time."

"I'll relax once the run opens."

"Your job must be stressful," I said.

"I want to get to know you better."

I didn't want to know Natalie better if it entailed what I suspected. Maybe I have a hygiene fetish, but I prefer my women to have showered within the past 60 days or so.

"You alleviate my stress," she said. "The actors see you watching the totem. The crew sees you take it from my safe and put it back. Neither group can steal it."

Wrong. The crew had automatic persuaders. The cast had numbers on their side.

Three nights later, Monica came offstage and caught her breath. Act two had just begun. All but six of the cast were performing. Monica wore a breechcloth that didn't always stay where it belonged, bands of feathers around her wrists and ankles, a necklace of bones, make up, and sweat.

She stopped by the bison and gave it a good rub. Then she cupped my face in both hands, tilted my head back, and kissed me.

"Right about now," she said, "I feel the need for a lot of luck."

I heard the door crash open, a male voice yell FBI, and the chatter of automatic weapons. I grabbed Monica so that she fell with me and rolled under the bar.

"Pray no one shoots low," I said.

The curtain over the bar danced. Several bullets hit the wood, always above us or we wouldn't have survived to hear them. I suppose the shootout lasted about a minute. It seemed longer.

Then there was silence, broken by loud orders to lie face down on the floor. Monica and I stayed in place. She kissed me again.

"You saved my life, Bill," she said.

Before I could respond, three armed agents came around the corner. They marched the other five cast members out with their hands making like bonnets. Then they let us get up.

"The guardian of the bison?" one asked me.

"Yes."

"You and Pocahontas come with me. Drew, confiscate the statue."

Monica said, "May I get my shirt?"

"Not your shirt, not your purse, not your toothbrush, Pocahontas. If you go on stage dressed that way, you can answer questions in the same clothing."

They herded us into an unmarked car. Drew, carrying the bison with far more ease than I'd managed, rode in the front passenger's seat. Our escort drove. When I realized they hadn't handcuffed or searched us, I knew what was up.

Drew turned around and said, "Steam and Waters. You acted independently of one another?"

"Yes," we said, almost together.

The driver said, "Miss Waters, I apologize for calling you Pocahontas. I'll find something for you to cover yourself with when we reach our headquarters."

"No blankets," Monica told him. "That would be an illegal ethnic joke."

I took off my knit shirt and gave it to her. She pulled it over her head. It looked better on her than it ever had on me.

Monica had contacted the FBI when she first saw the bison. My report moved me from potential suspect to cooperating citizen. If there was a cash award, Monica had first claim.

"Are any members of the cast involved?" they asked us.

I said probably not. Natalie had hired me to guard the bison from the cast. Later, she added the crew to those I was to watch. It had made no sense. Why live with people who might rob you? Why let them bring guns to rehearsal? None of the cast was armed. Their costumes couldn't hide a needle.

Monica said they lived together in a large house, several to a room. All had felt--or claimed to feel--the bison's power. The segregation of cast from crew was unnatural for a small theater. The composer and writer serving as a lighting technician was equally unusual.

"There really is a Socrates Bald Eagle?" I asked.

"The one with the longest hair."

"I wonder if he's tone deaf."

She said, "The way he was leaking blood, Bill, it probably no longer matters."

Outside of saying I'd initially thought the bison a fake and my hiring an expensive publicity stunt, I had nothing to add. Monica was an actress with several legitimate theatrical productions, a stint on a soap, and six films on her resume. She performed as Monica Waters. Her name really was Running Waters, but this production was the first time she'd used it.

"It's our bones we want back," she said. "They have a spiritual meaning. If this totem is genuine, it's from a time before our people met your people when you came to North America. Natalie's original theft of it from the Tulsa museum proves nothing. She's as fake as the entire show."

Drew said, "Native Americans…"

"Hold it," Monica told him. "I prefer Indians. The effort to change our name is a smoke screen, Mr. Drew. It's the same thing you've done to another race—from colored to black to African-American. It's easier to change the label than offer fair treatment."

Her sermon ended the interview. The Feds drove us to the theater and let Monica get her street clothes and retrieve her purse. An agent offered to drive her home.

"Bill can do it," she said. "I'm going his way."

"Thank you again for your timely help, Miss Waters. And, Mr. Steam, even though your tip to Corporal Andews told us nothing new, we'd rather have two witnesses than one."

I started the engine.

"The usual way, Bill."

I headed north on the highway, then turned east on another one.

"You weren't Natalie's lover, were you?" she asked.

"No, I like my women clean."

"I'm sweaty and dirty right now."

I said, "Honest sweat from a night of hard work capped by terror and the necessary application of intellect. I'm talking about the dirt of the ages and hair that may shelter mice."

"I don't want to go back to the house tonight, Bill. We might be wrong about the cast. I'm sure you know how to mix both of us a strong drink."

I almost joked about firewater, but wisely turned the remark into a cough.

"You're surprised?"

I said, "Yes, Monica."

"You'll be more surprised before daybreak. The agents didn't care if we survived the shootout or not. Two witnesses may be better than one, but none is needed when the criminals are dead."

"I got the same notion."

"You saved my life, Bill. Don't you dare have a guest bed."

Violation By the Highest Order
Milton Kerr

The night was clear and the stars were quite visible. Maybe that was what fueled me. It was the same kind of night when they took me.

Yeah, the memories. That's what kept me so pissed.

My 4x4 was parked outside the city limits. I wanted to be undetectable from prying eyes, human or otherwise. It was important to me that my vision wasn't obscured. It was necessary to see them when they arrived. Their landing was my sole purpose for my being out in the desert.

Assembling the stainless steel rifle posed no problem, not even in the dark. I had practiced so often that I knew every friggin' part by touch. There was no rush, or at least so I told myself. They were going to show and when they did, I'd kill them.

The Barrett 50 caliber was the closest thing to manmade thunder. From the outskirts of Phoenix, it would sound like a mountain storm. That was my intention.

Revenge isn't...

My mind kept reminding me how revenge wouldn't solve anything. Inwardly, at other times, I screamed my rage. I couldn't help it.

No, not after what they did to me. If they hadn't taken me, raped me, if the abduction had never happened, then I wouldn't be out here in the cold desert night, assembling a murder weapon.

Remembering what happened was easy. A major part of my mind simply could not forget. About three years ago I was riding around in my old truck. Nothing special, just killing time. It was the same night a "V" formation of lights was spotted over the city.

"No, it wasn't," I corrected myself out loud. "They were closer to the outskirts."

Oh, whatever. I was just driving around; never knew they were there.

"That's because the city lights just about hid them at sidewalk level. You had to be several floors up from the street to see anything. Besides, you were driving."

I didn't answer right away. The rifle was assembled. Looking for the finger-long rounds, I saw my other weapon; my 9-mm caliber Glock pistol and two clips. After slipping one seventeen-round magazine into the handgun, I tucked the other in my back pocket. The pistol was my back up. If things really went sour, well, no more me.

"It's not too late, you know. You can still stop this," was what I said to myself.

The hell I will.

My reply voice was louder than it should have been, but I didn't give a damn. Once they approached, I knew it wouldn't matter if they knew I was waiting or not.

The bastards had already implanted something inside me. Exactly where I didn't know. Could be I just don't want to remember.

One of those little tracking gizmo things might have been planted behind my right eye. There had to be a reason for them pulling my eye out by the strings.

"It was resting on your cheekbone, wasn't it? All warm and wet."

I know it. Shut up!

I lied to myself. I'd never forget and I was doomed to my memories. Just like I'd never forget those pale skinned heads, shaped like a reverse teardrop.

Sure as hell, my tears ran. I was scared shitless. They knew it and didn't give a shit. Was there any mercy in those big, dark, liquid eyes?

Hell, no.

So, that's why I'm here by the Estrella Mountains. Waiting, loaded for bear, with murder in my heart.

After what they did to me, you bet your ass.

My hands began to hurt. I had been gripping the Glock so hard, as if my hands could have crushed it. Lucky for me, the safety was in place. Once I secured the pistol on my person, I took up the rifle and spent about twenty minutes scouting out a good, solid, prone position. I scouted out a good position. It wasn't hard to find one.

"Really. You've been back and forth here, everyday for a week."

"I need a good set up place," I replied. "This damn cannon is gonna kick like a bastard."

"Oh, sure. Check this place out. It's a waste of time, just like all those UFO abduction survivor clinics you attended."

Not caring who heard what, I said, "Screw you. I'm tired of listening to you. You've been on my ass ever since I planned this thing. Where were you when I was strapped to that metal table?"

No answer.

I continued. "Yeah, you remember the table in the room with the black floor, don'tcha? You didn't say shit when they pushed those needles up my nose."

No reply.

"When they shoved that flexible pipe up my ass, while begging them not to hurt me, that I wouldn't tell anyone about them, where were you? They raped me. A foot and a half of pipe went up my ass and nobody cared. Not those little bastards and not you.

"After they had their chucks with me, they left me a half mile away from my car. Yeah, once the fuckers pushed my eye back in the socket, I was left with a sore asshole and a long walk. So, whatcha say now?"

"Nobody knows their motivations."

I patted my rifle. "You want motivation; I'll show you mine."

"I'm not asking you to forgive, but-"

"Forgive what? Are you saying that it's okay for those little monsters to treat me like some kinda lab rat? I'm a man, goddammit, a fuckin' Homo Sapiens and, tonight, I'm going to deliver the message personally."

"Well, hopefully, all your chat room buddies don't bullshit you about the aliens coming back," was what my mind spoke.

Sightings had been reported just about everyday this week. Always the same arrowhead-shaped formation moving from Phoenix to Kingsman.

"What's to say they'll be back tonight?"

"Yeah, sure they've got enough soil samples, huh? Shut the hell up, willya? Jesus Christ, I'm at the end of my rope. I can't take it no more."

"Can't take what?"

I felt the tears in my eyes.

"Thinking about it, the whole thing. I still see it, in my head, clear as day. I relive it while I sleep. Dammit, it's been almost two years."

"Maybe, it's time…to get some help. Professional help."

"Nobody can help me because nobody can take it away. It happened and it happened to me. And real soon, they're gonna be scared, too."

"Hope this doesn't start a war or something."

"I hope it does. It'll show them what happens when they screw with any of us."

The Barrett had a damn good range on it. I wondered if the seven hundred-grain bullet could hit their ship. Probably wouldn't do much more than a pebble-sized meteorite.

"Why waste time?" came the answer. Besides, they've probably got some sort of force field or protective ray that can stop rockets, far less bullets."

"No. What I want is a head shot on one of those little shits. I wanna see him fly apart."

"Just one?"

"I'll start with one, then try for a second. Yeah, don't tell me, I know they could shoot back and this baby is bolt action."

"Got it all figured out, huh?"

"Leave me the hell alone. I don't want to listen to you or anybody else."

My voice softened.

"They should be here around ten. Check the time."

Almost there.

According to my Internet contacts, the formation had been sighted just about the same time, like clockwork. No doubt, at least in my mind, they were going to land, looking for somebody, anybody. Maybe me.

While I was getting into a comfortable, prone position, getting the damn rifle balance in-between large rocks, my dream appeared in the skies. Although the five bright lights appeared to hover over the rooftops, I knew they were much higher. In fact, it was due to my position, which gave the appearance that they were directly over the city. Actually, they were outside the city limits.

Chambering a round, I looked through the scope. All I needed was one clear shot. A head would do, a chest, even an arm. Show me something.

Nothing.

I swept the rifle left to right, slowly trying to cover a full one eighty. Nothing.

Why don't they come down?

Looking up, I saw the arrow-headed, or call it a "V" formation, hold its place. No lights came from the ship. No smaller craft left it, either. I brought the rifle up to the lights. Then and there, I didn't care what I did. Maybe the seven hundred-grain slug would have really penetrated the hull.

Imagine me, knocking one of them out of the air with one shot.

It never happened.

The formation shifted. It wasn't a gradual move, but more like a sudden jerk. They moved as if they had all been fastened together and some unseen power moved them all at once. One minute, my scope was filled with light, the next; I was looking at black sky.

Realizing what happened, I lowered my rifle.

"Guess they showed you," I said to myself.

"Showed me what?"

The lights had gone east, then stopped again. Rough estimate was that they were at least a couple of miles away. At least.

"They showed you who has the right stuff…"

The rifle was down and I found my fingers brushing against the Glock. Either way, this was going to end.

"You thought they were just going to plop down, right here, right in front of your gun sights, didn'tcha?"

I didn't answer.

"Seems to me if they can go anywhere they want in outer space, there isn't anything saying they have to land in the same place twice when they come back to earth. Know what I mean?"

"Think they spotted me?"

"Oh sure, like you're that dangerous. Get with the program, huh? They don't care about you. They don't care about any of us. They go where they please and do whatever. Sure as hell we can't stop them. Never could; never will."

My hand closed about the pistol. All I had to do was bring it up and give the trigger a squeeze. No more nightmares or voices.

"You gonna say good night or will you just bag tonight?"

Tears ran down my face. I felt the barrel's cold metal kiss under my chin.

"Okay, call it a wrap."

Never fired the Glock at such close range. The damn thing was loud.

Flesh
H. Turnip Smith

Katie moseyed along the freshly black-topped lane that paralleled the rain-swollen creek while dust clouds billowed on the opposite hill where Roddy Bennet was helping bale hay.

"Who cares about him?" she muttered to herself, breaking off a smooth shaft of hawkweed and chewing on its resilient stem as she tried not to think about the note he'd passed her in the hallway. Bored, she tentatively tested a fresh tar bubble with her big toe. The squishy surface exploded with a splat, turning her toe black. It would be fun to be totally immersed in tar and bounce through the bull thistle and plantain right up the hill into Granny Houser's kitchen and plop down in the middle of the freshly-swept linoleum floor.

She abruptly pulled up short at the sight of a six foot long black snake, sunning itself on the warmth of the lane. She was not afraid. The scary things in life weren't nature's creatures; she'd been threading earthworms on fishhooks since she was three years old. The snake didn't even know she was there. Cautiously, Katie crept closer; the snake's black, shiny skin glittered like fire in the sunlight. Suddenly, Katie shouted "Hey!" so loud she scared herself. With a flash of luminous skin the blacksnake bolted, disappearing down a hole in the weeds. Dashing after the snake, Katie wondered how far the hole ran. Maybe it intersected with a whole series of huge tunnels that ran through the village under the gas station and up under the school house. There might be thousands of snakes coiled under the village. If she were tiny, she'd pursue the snake and discover the secret place where the eggs were kept.

But she wasn't that small. Sighing, she moped the rest of the lane into her backyard and plopped in the blue plastic pool that was too confining for her twelve-year-old body. The water was bathtub warm as Katie sprawled on her back, staring at the blinding sun. A wooly worm inched along the dark maple limb overhead as Katie closed her eyes. The pool suddenly lifted off the ground, higher than the tree line, slowly circling the village. From the sky Katie saw the unmade beds in Lucia Finley's bedroom, Grannie Houser staring at wrestling, Charlie Stump on the throne in his roofless outhouse. She laughed out loud and waved at Myrtle Bowman's three-year-old twins fighting over the tire swing in their backyard.

Suddenly Katie sat upright. Why she'd been asleep or daydreaming one! She scrambled out of the tepid water and gave her curly, blond hair a shake. "Too old for daydreams and a plastic pool," she muttered to herself.

Grabbing a threadbare towel, she rubbed at her hair and hollered onto the nearby screened porch where her mother was canning tomatoes, "I'm going up town now, Ma."

"Be sure and put on your shirt and shoes, Kathryn, " her mother hollered back. "You don't want to get cut and bleed yourself on all that alley glass."

Ignoring the sandals, the worn, plaid shirt, and her mother's advice, Katie took two dimes out of the shirt's breast pocket and ambled up the alley. The sun was warm and delicious on her skin, but she wrinkled her nose at rank odor from Cox's outhouse. She poked at a giant bagworm's web in Sunderland's back maple tree and stared at the bull's huge, rubbery looking testicles as it grazed
in Doc Woodley's cow lot.

When she got to the gas station, Addie Copas was listening to a cloth-faced, standup Philco radio, his yellow Studebaker parked outside, convertible-top down. She recognized the song on Addie's radio -- "You Belong to Me" by Jo Stafford. Such sentiments baffled her, but she liked the melancholy melody. Some day she'd be grown up and sing romantic songs. Addie was smoking and fiddling with a punch card, the kind where you took a key and discovered your fortune after punching out a slip for a dime. Because of his hunchback, he was barely visible behind the counter.

"And how's my little bathing beauty this morning?" Addie limped out from behind the glass candy case, spreading his gnarled, distinctive fingers on the counter.

"I'm fine, Addie," she said. "Can I try out that thing you got?"

"You can try my thing any old time," Addie said cheerfully, offering her the punch key. "Here, have a free one."

She punched, then unfolded a tiny fortune. "Something important will happen in your life today." She wondered what. Father said she was getting to be a big girl. Maybe it would be an invitation to a spin-the-bottle party.

"You believe in fortunes, Addie?"

"That depends," Addie said. "Well, been swimming I see. And barefoot again too. Little girl, I'll bet you're your momma's crucifix. She won't like you going around half-naked. But say, girl, aren't you afraid of snakes in that alley?"

"I ain't afraid of snakes," Katie blustered. "I figure this town is thick with snakes below ground. And anyways Momma don't care."

"Well if she doesn't care I don't," Addie raised his eyebrows. "So what can I do you for today, my young American beauty queen?"

Katie stared at the rows of box candy under glass and finally chose four paraffin soda pop bottles, the kind where you gnawed the top off and got one sip of colored syrup before you began chewing the soft goo that locked and held your teeth. Addie reached behind the counter and got the box.

"Lady's choice today," he handed her the box.

As she deliberated, finally choosing two red and two green, she became aware of Addie's hands on her still damp swimming suit. She looked down and saw how his fingernails were tobacco-stained and filthy, and she felt an ugly something suffusing her body. She backed away.

"That'll be twenty cents," Addie grinned.

"Here, take your old dimes!" she threw the coins on the counter, her face scarlet, turning on heel, remembering what Grannie Houser had warned her about men.

"Hey, you better not say anything," Addie said. "You know me. I'll be waiting in the dark."

"I ain't afraid of you, Addie!"

That evening as she stood gazing at herself naked in the full-length mirror, Katie felt a strange mixture of pleasure and remembered shame at Addie's touch. Her new breasts were pink buds barely opened and when she flattened her fish-white stomach; her pubic hair was as fine and golden as corn silk. She turned sideways to look from a different angle and suddenly saw something moving outside in the darkness. She turned out the light and flattened herself against her bedroom wall. By the light of fireflies she saw a hunch-backed shadow crouching by the corner oak in the dark. Cicadas fiddled crazily in the grass just as Father called up from the screened porch, "Lights out now, Katie. You've got to be ready for Sunday school."

"Sunday school," she thought. "Ugh! Place where they read lessons about dead people with funny names."

Two days later Katie found herself on the merry-go-round behind the Concord Elementary School, and Roddy Bennet was running furiously in the fine gravel, whirling her like crazy as fine dust blew to the east. Roddy was a year older in seventh grade and had pretty freckles disappearing up under his green tractor cap. On Sunday at church he looked scrubbed and innocent in a stiff white shirt, but she knew better. Now in his overalls and brogans he only looked fierce, grubby, and uncivilized like the boy who wrote her the nasty notes.

"Not so fast, Roddy," she panted as the merry-go-round whirled perilously and she laughed until she was out of breath.

"Chicken, Katie?" Roddy said.

"I'm not chicken a bit."

"Yes, you are," he said, leaping aboard and leering at her like a fun-house face.

"Aw, Roddy Bennet, you're a shithead," she said just like Janie Adams would have.

"Am not!"

"Are so!"

They wrestled in the grass and August dust, and he threw her down and rolled on top of her in a wrestler's pin so she could feel the length of his skinny electric body and smell his cigarette breath and feel his strong fingers with uncut nails just like Addie's.

"Why I ought to smack your smart mouth, Katie," he breathed as she squirmed free from under him until he tripped her back down again in a flurry of sweaty wrestling.

"Try it you think you can," she taunted. No stupid boy was going to whip her.

"You'll find out what I can do soon enough," he said.

She suddenly glimpsed Addie Copas limping along the nearby sidewalk, pretending not to look. Why was Addie always sneaking about? There were so many things to try to understand.

The next day he was found dead. Addie had slit his own throat with a broken Coke bottle in the little shanty behind the gas station where he lived. Katie's father went with the village men to investigate the death.

"I guess the poor son-of-a-bitch didn't have anything to live for," Katie overheard her father say to one of the men. "Hell, he had all kinds of money lying around that shack."

"What good's money to a hunchback," the other man said.

Katie's father shrugged.

Two days later Katie watched the adults march to the graveyard and bury Addie. A sullen rain fell all that day, and Katie tried to think of nothing. It was hard to think of nothing. Mostly she thought of the giant network of snake tunnels under the village and wondered if one of the tunnels exited into Addie's shack. The shack would be hot and close with a fetid, ugly smell like the yellow places on Addie's teeth.

That autumn the horses stood steaming in Adams' barn as Katie and Janie, whose mother was church organist, saddled the geldings. Old Bob patiently lapped a sugar cube from Katie's palm, and she delighted as his clean, pink tongue curled delicate to the touch as she slowly released the cube. How she envied his sure way of knowing. Knowing was the hard thing.

Early October frost caressed the corn stubble as they swung up to ride, first pushing the old plugs hard across the field at a gallop then walking them to the top of Mullet Hill, dodging the tangled brush traps left by old storms. She could see the horse's breath and her own chilled hands red on the reins. As they came back down off the hill, Katie gaily cried, "Race you!" and Janie shouted back, "No fair, you little cheat, you got a head start."

Old Bob out-galloped Janie's horse to the barn by two lengths. When the horses reached the tack lot, Katie and Janie walked the plugs twice around the barn to cool them down, horses' breath dissolving to smoke in the chill air. The plugs were breathing hard, snorting, and pawing the barn-floor straw as Katie began to unsaddle, leaning over and reaching under Old Bob's smooth, heaving belly to un-cinch the straps. Pressing her face against Bob's sweaty flanks she could smell urine in the straw and longingly feel the sweet slickness of his flesh and the powerful beat of his heart. And then she felt Janie behind her, leaning against her, cupping her newness in each hand.

Katie froze silently, standing patient as a saddle mare, feeling Janie's cold fingers and hands pressing against her flesh, experiencing the moment, feeling the thing she didn't know whether she liked. Katie thought of Roddy Bennet, waiting for what would come next, awaiting the beginning of some more real form of life, and then finally she burst out, "Janie Adams, leave me be or I swear I'll get Addie Copas to kill you some night."

"You are such a little kid, Katie," Janie said. "How you think some dead hunchback's going to hurt anybody?"

"Well, why does everybody want to touch me?" she sputtered.

"Cause that's what grownups do. You know what Roddy Bennet did to me once?"

"Shut up!" Katie cried. "I don't want to hear."

"You are so immature!" Janie said. "Well you'll find out what's it's all about soon enough."

That same evening Katie broke the rules and went to the deserted shanty. The moon dangled like a sad, confused face in the frozen, white sky. The padlocked door swung carelessly open in the pale darkness of the October chill. Hesitantly, Katie tiptoed onto the cracked, linoleum floor. On the wall of the sour-smelling living-room hung one of Addie's lopsided paintings. The creek and the old mill near Katie's house that he'd painted glittered with snow and ice. It was so beautiful it made

Katie wonder how such a lovely thing could have come from such an ugly, twisted body.

Working fast, she fumbled through Addie's scattered belongings filled with the bitterness of cigarette smoke. Finally, she made her way into the dark little room where Addie had slept. Eager with curiosity, Katie rummaged through what was left of Addie's clothes. In one of Addie's dirty woolen shirts she snatched a note from the breast pocket and stuffed it in her own pocket.

Hurrying on, she found what she was looking for in a yellowing envelope that she recognized under the crinkled newspapers on the bottom drawer of his dresser. Hypnotized as if by the flicker of a serpent's tongue, Katie stood in the dark and slowly opened the envelope, staring at the nasty photos that Addie had once showed her. Her stomach turned over.

"What the hell you think you're doing?" a cold voice crackled in the silence. Katie swung around and threw her arms up to protect herself.

"I wasn't doing nothing," she said, remembering the time the principal had caught her writing the forbidden note. She knew she was blushing.

Roddy Bennet stepped out of the shadows. "I heard you was really hung up on Addie Copas," he said.

"People didn't understand him was all," Katie said, thinking of the huge hump in the middle of Addie's back. Was it made of bone or was it full of hair? How would it have felt to touch? Could there have been a baby hidden in there?

"I 'spose you did then?" Roddy said.

"I didn't say that."

"Well I'm going to tell on you being here," Roddy said.

"Don't, Roddy," Katie suddenly pleaded, terrified of what her mother and father would say.

"What'll you give me I don't?" Even in the darkness she could feel Roddy's red, nasty eyes.

"I got some gum and stuff."

"Don't want no gum," Roddy said, stepping closer. In the dark his face was an ugly blur and his breath stunk like Addie's.

"What do you want?"

"Don't act so stupid. Like some immature kid."

Immature! Oh was she? Now she felt angry. "I'm not. I'm not," she said, battering at Roddy's face while he grabbed at her wrists and forced her to her knees.

"You little hellcat," he snarled.

When it was over, Roddy ran and Katie stepped out of the cabin into the darkness of a night where the moon had disappeared. As she stumbled along, her skin felt as foul as the peeling wallpaper in Addie's shack. She wanted to go underground and live in the snake tunnels that criss-crossed the village. However, she refused to cry, knowing that whether she did or not -- it could never be the same again. Never!

Then, as she fumbled in the direction of the creek, she thought of the scrap of paper she'd found in Addie's shirt. Pausing under a street lamp, she read the crumpled note.

"You're too young to understand this, Katie Conway, but I loved you, child! I really did! Like this note there'll be much in life you'll never understand, but don't be a coward like me. Keep your head up, kid, and always be brave- even when you're going in the dark and can't understand. Love always, Addie."

Tenderly, Katie re-folded the note and stumbled on, now crooning low and mournfully to herself as she walked in the shadows "You belong to me," she sang, thinking of the summer voices over Addie's radio, Grannie Houser's eyes gleaming as she watched the naked wrestler's glistening bodies, and the secret tunnels underneath the village peopled by writhing snakes. Above Katie's head, dark maples with desiccated leaves rustled in the faint October breeze, and Katie suddenly looked up, and then strode on, reaching ahead with hopeful steps.

Lights in the Barn
Ron L. Dixon

Eleven-year old Josh Handle lay awake in his bed. He watched the tree shadows dance on his wall. The bright October moon outside cast the shadows through the window at the head of his bed.

It had been a busy weekend. Josh and his parents had spent most of it trying to get settled in. They had just moved from the city to their "Dream farm out in the country." That's what his mom and dad called it.

He was tired from all the work. Yet he couldn't sleep because he was so excited. He had not had time to properly explore his new world. And boy, was there ever a lot to explore. He was trying to form an agenda in his mind of what he wanted to see and do, and in what order. Of course, all that had to be worked around his starting at his new school the next day.

That was excitement on top of excitement. Josh loved meeting new people. He made friends easily and was sure he would like the kids at his new school. Also, tomorrow he would ride a school bus for the first time in his life. How on earth was he ever going to get to sleep?

He forced his mind back to think about his schedule of exploration around his new home. There was the creek, and the cave the Real Estate guy had told him about. Josh loved caves. Also, there was the pond, all the animals, wild and tame, and the barn...

He had turned to look out his bedroom window at the old barn. There was a light out there. At first he thought maybe his dad had left a light on. Then he remembered his father talking about running wires out to the barn for lights and a workshop. There were no electric lights in the barn.

But there was some kind of light glowing through the cracks of the barn. It didn't look like any light he had ever seen before. It was an eerie blue light. He finally decided it must be some kind of lantern. He guessed he should wake his dad. He eased out of his bed, flinching as his feet touched the cold floor. Padding quietly across the hall, he was just about to wake his father when he glanced over his shoulder, and stopped dead in his tracks... The light was gone.

He returned to his room, and with his nose so close to the window he could feel the cold of the glass, he squinted, looking at the dark shape of the barn. The light was gone all right. Why would anyone be in the barn in the middle of the night? Maybe he had dreamed it. No, it wasn't a dream. There had been a light out there.

After a short time the chill of the autumn night reminded him of his warm bed. He climbed in under the warm blankets. Josh lay there thinking about the light, and his cold feet.

As fatigue finally forced sleep on him, his mind was filled with one conscious thought... the light had been moving. Moving back and forth from one side of the barn to the other. Back and forth... back and forth... like some kind of caged wild animal.

He had meant to talk to his dad about the light, but the excitement of the next week had erased the incident from his mind. Besides, he had told himself, maybe I just dozed off a little bit and really did dream the whole thing.

Yes, that was what he had told himself. And now, almost a week later, there it was again, the light in the barn.

"OK, Josh baby," he said aloud to himself, "what do you say now? You're wide-awake. You're not dreaming this time. Let's see you make up some kind of excuse for this one."

He had gotten out of bed and crossed the hall, to his parent's room, as he talked. He woke his dad. His father sleepily listened as Josh breathlessly told his story.

His father rolled over and looked out the window. Josh followed his dad's gaze. He realized he had goofed, the light was gone.

Josh was gruffly sent back to bed. The next morning he was on the receiving end of a very stern lecture which ended with the promise that he might have trouble sitting for a while, if there was a repeat performance of the preceding night.

"You're too big a boy to come waking your mother and me just because you had a bad dream," his father had said.

Josh made up his mind to ignore any more lights in the barn. And, he had done a pretty good job. The third and fourth times he had watched the lights for a while, then rolled over, covered his head, and with some difficulty, gone to sleep.

However, he noted, he had been right, the light moved back and forth. Josh was also very much aware that the number of days between the times he saw the light was getting shorter with each sighting.

Now, just two days after his fourth sightings, came the fifth incident. He knew he had to go see what it was. The idea scared him. But in this eleven-year old, boy, curiosity was stronger than his fear.

He dressed quickly and quietly. A glance as he passed his parent's room assured him they were sleeping soundly. He tiptoed down the hall and through the kitchen, trying to remember the location of every piece of furniture, or anything else he might bump into. Josh managed to get out of the house with only a minor collision with an out-of-place chair. Rubbing his smarting knee, he eased the back door closed.

He made it to the barn without trouble. Well almost, he had tripped over some unseen something about halfway to his destination. Josh had come close to going flying on his face. But, he managed to grab a fence rail and maintain his balance, only to feel ridiculous when he realized he was looking to see if anyone had noticed his clumsiness. Chastising himself for his stupidity, while at the same time watching the moving light, the young boy reached for the door handle. His hand froze halfway to the door. Josh was petrified.

"Oh, come on you chicken. You've imagined everything from a glowing dragon to the ghost of Blue Beard is in there. Most likely it's something simple to explain. Maybe a hobo sneaking a warm place to sleep. Or something like that. There can't be anything worse than what you've already dreamed up. Go on, open the door, you wimp."

Of course, this stern lecture was all in his mind. He didn't dare speak out loud. He didn't want who, or whatever was in the barn to know he was there.

The lecture and his curiosity again won the battle over his fear. He eased the door open. There was definitely a bluish, glowing light of some kind up in the hayloft. It still moved back and forth across the width of the barn.

Closing the door as quietly as he could, Josh crossed the barn to the bottom of the long ladder leading up to the hayloft. He started up....

His young legs were weak from fear, but he had made up his mind. He kept going. It seemed such a long way. Up and up he went, hand over hand, one rung at a time. Josh counted the rungs left as he climbed. "Only four rungs to go," he whispered to himself. Soon he would see what was up there. Only three... two... he was there.

Calling upon every ounce of courage he had, he peeked over the edge. Letting out a gasp, he begun to lose his grasp on the ladder. Though his mind was boggled at what he had seen, his young reflexes served him well. He grabbed the ladder and somehow managed to keep from falling.

Josh hung there, gasping for air. Fighting an overpowering horror, he began to calm himself. He peeked again... His self-admonishment had been wrong. It was more frightening than anything he had imagined. It wasn't a hobo. It wasn't Blue Beard's ghost. And, it wasn't a glowing dragon.

It was a young boy... More exactly, it was the ghost of a young boy. He was dressed in what looked, to Josh, like old time clothes. And, he was almost transparent. But the most frightening thing about him was his face. The hideousness of that face was what had scared Josh so bad.

The boy's eyes bulged out so much; they looked as though they would pop right out of his face. And his lips were so swollen it was amazing they didn't burst, like a balloon. And worst of all was the coil of rope wrapped around the boy's neck. Some of the coils appeared to be so tight they cut into the boy's skin.

As Josh hung there on the ladder, frozen by horror and dread, the boy stretched out his arms in a pleading fashion.

"Will you help me?" The plea was a hoarse, whispering, cry. "Can you find the ladder for me? I can't get down. Please find the ladder."

"Th-th-the ladder?" asked Josh. He didn't understand. "I-I-I'm on the ladder. See, I'm standing on it." Josh was shaking so hard he could hardly talk.

"NO! NO!" screeched the ghostly boy. "I can't use that ladder. You must bring the ladder I used to climb up here." His glowing, ghostly, body shook with sobs as he whispered hoarsely. "I've been here so very long. Will you help me?" he asked again, mournfully.

"Yeah, sure, but I don't know where it is," replied Josh, some of his fear leaving him.

"Look around the pigs," the ghost said. "It's somewhere around the pigs."

Josh's mind raced trying to understand what the boy meant. "The pigs? Somewhere around the pigs… OH SURE! The pigpen. The ladder must be somewhere around the pigpen. Is that what you're trying to tell me?" asked Josh excitedly.

"Yes," was the only reply the ghost made.

The whole time Josh had been trying to decipher the ghostly message. The glowing specter had paced back and forth, back and forth, from one side of the hayloft to the other. He had not stopped, even while answering.

The fear Josh had first felt had swiftly, and strangely, gone away. He knew he should be afraid. He didn't pursue the thought however, because of the "zillion" questions he had for the blue apparition pacing before him.

"HEY!" Josh said, "What's your name? How'd you get here? Why's your face like that?"

Josh had more questions. But, with each question he asked, the ghost had paced faster and faster. And, he had begun to moan. The faster he moved the louder he moaned. The more he moaned the louder and more frightening it became. Until, finally, again very much afraid, Josh said, "OK, I'll go see if I can find the ladder." He quickly climbed back down to the floor of the barn.

His mind filled with more unanswered questions, Josh left the barn. He headed toward the pigpen, which was further from the house, and his warm bed.

"I knew things were going to be different out here in the country. But, boy, is it ever more different than anything I would have dreamed up," he mumbled as he walked.

A bright moon lit the clear, chilly, autumn night. Josh had no trouble seeing his way to the pigpen without the aid of the flashlight he had stuck in his pocket, before leaving the house. Now, he pulled it out as he neared the "Pork Pound," as his father had called the pigpen. The pigs began to grunt and squirm as he shined the light around the area. They did not like this intrusion into their sleep.

Their prize boar, a very big, and sometimes menacing hog named Silas, came out to see, and perhaps challenge, whoever was there.

"It's alright, Silas," Josh said to the big guy. The boar seemed to recognize the boy's voice. After a check of the slop trough, Silas gave a loud grunt and returned to the warmth of the shed and his harem.

"Where would a ladder be out here?" Josh asked aloud, as he shined his light around from place to place. Suddenly he stopped. He was looking at the ladder. He had not known, or thought of it as a ladder when he had seen it before. He had merely thought it a part of the fence, around the pigpen.

At some time, in the past, some of the boards along the fence had been knocked, or had fallen, off. Rather than mend the broken spot in the fence, someone had wired the old, handmade, ladder along the outside of the pen. They had, in effect, patched the fence, without a lot of hard work.

Josh did not stop to reason that the pigs would get out. Neither did he question his actions. He had a job to do, take this ladder to the barn, and help the ghost boy down from the loft. And that was what he was going to do. He was not aware of the foolishness of his plan.

Unfastening the wire at each end, he tried to lift the long ladder. However, it was nearly forty feet long in length. It had been made many years before of hand-honed oak and it was very strong and heavy. The ladder was far more than Josh could lift and carry.

Quickly, Josh developed an idea. Laying the ladder flat on the ground, he turned his back to it. Congratulating himself for his great intelligence, he reached behind him and lifted the ladder. Resting the end rung on his shoulders, he hooked his arms through the ladder and began dragging it.

He felt very smug. The ladder slid along easily, but it was still far from an easy job. Each rut or rock the heavy ladder hit sent a resounding jolt through his shoulders. And because it was so long, Josh was forced several times, to stop, lay the ladder down, and go to the other end and move it so it could clear a tree or some other obstacle.

Now he was peering up at the hayloft and his ghost friend. Josh was sweating from head to toe. It had been hard work getting the ladder here. As he looked up, he wondered how on earth he could possibly get the heavy ladder up to the loft. It was impossible to lift it by himself.

The glowing apparition in the loft seemed to know Josh's thoughts. He pointed to a new coil of rope hanging on a peg on the far wall of the barn.

"Throw it over this beam," the ghost boy called to Josh hoarsely, indicating a rafter high in the ceiling close to him. "Then tie the other end to the ladder. I will help you raise it," he added.

"OK," Josh said. "Yeah, that should work."

As he talked he had gotten the rope, and after four tries had managed to throw it over the high beam. He then fastened one end to the ladder. Grabbing the other end, Josh and his ghost friend began pulling. The ladder began to elevate. It was still a difficult job. Josh grunted and strained at the end of the rope. Up and up the ladder went, until at last, it rested, somewhat precariously, on the edge of the loft.

"AT LAST, AT LAST!" cried the ghost boy in his raspy voice. The shimmering specter let go of the rope and started to climb down the old ladder. It started to slide at the bottom.

"WATCH OUT!" cried Josh. He strained at the rope. But he could not stop the sliding ladder. Suddenly he had a thought. If he hurried, he could take a turn in the rope around a large peg on a post close in front of him. However, he would have to move fast. He grabbed the coils of rope at his feet, and ran toward the peg...

Josh would never know what he tripped over. His foot caught on something and he pitched forward. As he fell, he threw out his arms, letting go of the rope he carried. Somehow, the rope coiled around his neck, just as the ladder fell.

The ghost boy stood on the barn floor. A smile twisted his bloated face. Looking up at Josh's dead body swinging back and forth at the end of the rope, he said, "You'll need someone to get the ladder before you can get down." With a strangled, whispered laugh, he faded away...

Eleven-year old Michael Grantz lay awake in his bed. He watched the tree shadows dance on his bedroom wall. The bright October moon outside cast the shadows through the window at the head of his bed.

But there was something else. Yes. Out there in that old barn. There was some kind of eerie bluish light, high in the barn. And it seemed to move back and forth, back and forth, like some kind of caged wild animal...

The Statue
Gavin Benke

The rails clacked as the train pulled into the station and stopped with a sudden jerk. Dozens of people filed out of each car in an orderly queue, and then found themselves without direction. The platform rippled with waves of navy blue, gray, black, and occasional flecks of red ties. Wing tips, penny loafers, and pumps dodged each other to get to the turnstile as the sound of shoes moving with quick, determined steps reverberated through the tunnel.

Moving in tempo with the crowd, Arthur Pennyfickle shuffled into the nearest car, and grabbed onto the silver bar as bodies pressed themselves into him. Finally, with an airy hiss, the doors closed and someone yelled "Goddamnit!" as he watched the train pull away from him.

Arthur spilled out onto the platform at his stop, and took a moment to reorient himself, fumbling through his pockets for his token, amidst a barrage of irritated "excuse me's" and hundreds walking with authority into cars and onto escalators. Arthur Pennyfickle had grown accustomed to this scene, and met it each morning and evening with stalwart acceptance.

He emerged from the dark tunnel and stepped off the escalator into a pink sky. His office was only five blocks from the station, and, as he did every morning, Arthur bought a cup of coffee from a nearby convenience store. He stopped in a small park across the street from the store and sat on a bench to drink his steaming coffee, becoming more alert with each sip. His eyes eventually settled on a statue of a naked man in the center of the park. Everyday Arthur passed the structure on his way to work, but today he felt compelled to examine it more closely.

It must have been cleaned recently, he thought. The marble was a gleaming white and wholly without blemish. The work's white body was composed of muscles that waxed and waned in smooth curves and even arcs. The figure stood in a refined manner. It was not an arrogant or even brave pose, but one of relaxed elegance. Its chin was perfect, the jawbone bending at just the right point and angle. The lips neither smiled nor frowned, but, in unison with the rest of its face and body, held an expression of complete calm and confidence. Its white hair was untouched by gusts of wind. It was a beautiful statue.

Arthur marveled at the symmetry of the design, and the easy dignity of the form's stance, one leg slightly bent, the other erect. He had never imagined how beautiful the human body could be. Arthur noticed every muscle in harmony together, each line suggesting fluid, graceful motion should the statue ever take a step. "Absolutely wonderful," he thought as he tossed his empty paper cup into a trashcan.

The sky was now blue, and Arthur's briefcase swung lightly at his side as he walked towards his office. All around him, cars beeped and roared and stopped. The sidewalk was a mass of people moving in all directions. Arthur carefully noted each person that he passed. He imagined their bodies underneath their suits in various states of working towards the sculpture's physique, and of their minds with the power and will to realize such beauty. Arthur regarded his own potential, and was exhilarated. The quiet perfection the statue possessed seemed unquestionably within his grasp. The notion of achieving absolute consonance with every facet of his mind and body filled him with a peculiar confidence has he strode into the lobby of the office building. He greeted the receptionist warmly as he entered the elevator.

The doors opened onto his floor, and Arthur was bombarded with florescent light as he made his way towards his cubicle and sat down. The desk was littered with papers, which he immediately set about sorting and placing into the appropriate manila folders. Over the course of ten minutes, Arthur adjusted his desktop. He straightened the desk calendar, put caps onto the corresponding pens, and tossed out irrelevant papers and pencil stubs. Finally, an order to the surface was achieved, and Arthur took a moment to contemplate it. Every edge was either parallel or perpendicular to one another. There were no impurities in sight, the papers with coffee rings and stray pen marks having been ejected. Arthur felt a sense of satisfaction as he logged onto the network to check his email. He had none.

"Good morning." A man with brown hair and blue pinstripes said as he approached Arthur's undefiled cubicle, clutching a huge pile of papers.

"Good morning, Mr. Piedmont." Arthur smiled, half expecting a compliment for his desk.

Mr. Piedmont gave no sign of such recognition, and dropped the stack of paper on the middle of Arthur's desk. The wind of the action sent every line into slants and a pen rolled off the desk and onto the floor.

"I need this by noon. Enter it into the database and save it in my file on the network. It's very important. Thanks."

Mr. Piedmont turned and walked through the maze of cubicles and into his office, closing the door behind him.

Arthur picked up the pen and examined the stack. It was a list of numbers, abbreviated words, and initials without vowels. He clicked his mouse and began typing. Arthur had no idea what the numbers corresponded with or what the initials and abbreviations signified, but he worked with quick, mechanical precision, and allowed his mind to wander. The image of the statue filled his head. Never before had Arthur thought that a man could be so inspired and gifted that he could create such a thing.

By ten thirty his eyes were glazed, and the computer screen glowed into a blur. He leaned back in his chair and thought of how statue was just an imitation of humanity, and of his own capacity for greatness. Arthur then straightened his back, slurped his coffee, and resumed typing the list.

"Art," said Mr. Piedmont, who stood directly behind him. It was a sudden jolt, and Arthur bolted upright, not having noticed his approach. "How's it coming along?"

"Good. It's coming along well." Arthur said and leaned back in his chair looking up at Mr. Piedmont.

"Hmmm. Are you going to have this for me by noon? I need this by noon." His voice contained a quiet sense of urgency.

"Yes," Arthur replied with confidence. "I'll have this to you by noon."

Mr. Piedmont placed the tip of his pen on his lower lip and sighed deeply.

"Okay." He blurted out abruptly and walked quickly towards his office, tapping the pen along the edges of cubicles as he went.

Arthur stared out into the hallway and imagined himself blossoming into a specimen of perfection that the statue could only represent. He resumed typing with determination.

Arthur felt endowed with a new sense of purpose and worth as he knocked on the door to Mr. Piedmont's office.

"Come in," said the voice from inside. Arthur entered the room and announced the completion of his task. It was only eleven thirty.

"Good. Let's have a look," Mr. Piedmont said, taking a sip of coffee and clicking the button on his mouse. Arthur could see the reflection of his morning's work in the other man's glasses. "Hmmm. You didn't tally up the totals in these columns here."

"But you didn't ask...."

"And you didn't put in a key for these abbreviations." Mr. Piedmont clasped his hands together, rested them on his desk, and stared at the ceiling.

"I realize that it's Monday morning, but this is really, very important. I need you to finish doing this…. I guess you can't finish it by noon at this point. Don't go to lunch until you finish this up. Thanks."

Arthur felt a burning in his chest as he walked back to his cubicle and slumped into his chair. He stared blankly at his desk for a few seconds before the apparition of the statue appeared in his mind. Arthur then straightened his spine, clicked open a new file on his computer, and began typing a letter of resignation.

He left for lunch around one o'clock. The air was warm and the sun was shining. He now stood in line at a deli counter and ordered a salami sandwich. All the tables were filled, so Arthur decided he would eat his lunch in the park. Certainly, he began to think as he walked out the door; the work he was doing was of no importance. Although Arthur realized he had no obvious talents, he knew he was destined for greatness of some sort or another. He was also aware for the first time that he had never exerted the full extent of his potential. Arthur rounded a corner, his mind moving much faster than his feet. The thought of going back to his cubicle, to his desk, his computer, and an inevitable new stack of numbers and letters seemed as ridiculous as it did repulsive. He decided that he would submit his letter of resignation as soon as he finished eating. Immediately after that, Arthur would start onto something else. What it was, he didn't quite know, but it would be beautiful, and the product of his own masterly execution. A vague sense of pride swelled inside him.

He reached the park and took his seat at the same bench he had that morning. Arthur turned to look at the statue for reassurance. It seemed ever more glorious. The sun shone down on it, endowing it with sparkling grandeur. Arthur stared at the statue, waiting for it to somehow reaffirm his decision, but it did not. He looked all around him. None of the people were nearly as beautiful as the statue. A fat man lumbered through the park. A woman who was much too short stopped in front of him to sneeze loudly. Her eyes were as puffy and red as her nose. A man in rags rummaged through a trash can. Everyone appeared grotesque. Arthur Pennyfickle ran his fingers through his thinning hair and a spot of mayonnaise fell onto his pant leg. He took the neatly folded letter out of his coat pocket and crumpled it up with his napkin. Perhaps, he thought, he could ask for a raise in a month or two.

Der Fuhrer's Wedding Anniversary
Aidan Baker

"Remember what today is?" I ask.

It is early, quiet, cold. Pale winter sunlight just beginning to angle into our bedroom window. I don't know what woke me.

"What?" you groan, still half asleep.

I repeat my question.

"Of course I do," you say and smile and roll towards me. You pull me tight into your embrace. Sex springs to mind, to loins, but somehow we both drift off to sleep again before anything is initiated.

We wake again, later in the morning, more or less simultaneously, still entangled in embrace. You are still erect and although I'm not sure if it's dream or desire (or both), I kiss you, slip you into me. It becomes desire soon enough and we move together in morning languidity. Finished, we lie there, satiated, comfortable and content.

Eventually, you complain of a need to use the toilet so I let you escape, watch you pad naked across the room to the bathroom. I wrap my arms around myself, curl up beneath the blankets, a finger of cool air having slipped in and chilled me.

"Come back to bed," I say when you exit the bathroom.

"And why should I?" you ask facetiously.

"Because," I threaten, "if you don't, I'll never speak to you again."

You laugh and say, "If only," but then do, of course, return to the bed, and to me.

It is, this day, this morning spent lying in bed, our anniversary. Eight years of marriage and two of shared residence. Not a big number, but neither an insignificant one; an entire decade, including co-habitation. A lot of almost constantly shared time and shared space and shared self. It's almost incomprehensible, if one stops to really think about it, how people can so easily bind their lives together. Two completely separate entities through what is ultimately chance circumstance coming together to form one. Well, not totally one, but close. Wouldn't it be wonderful...

We finally remove ourselves from bed around noon and breakfast on croissants and perfectly ripe pears, fresh orange juice, and fragrant gourmet coffee. Our plans for the day are not elaborate. We have given ourselves a three-day weekend. This evening my parents are taking us out for dinner. We will, probably sooner than later, exchange gifts of some kind. Other than that— no plans.

And indeed, the presents begin coming sooner. You are not like one of those comic strip men who forget birthdays or anniversaries and such and are always running out madly at the last minute to buy some dorky and usually inappropriate gift for their poor neglected significant others. You, you have your Christmas shopping done well before mid-November and have never forgotten our anniversary or my birthday or any other days to which we attach importance. You seem to take an extraordinary pleasure in giving gifts.

And I, yes, like receiving presents though sometimes I feel guilty, or spoilt by you, or just the teentsiest bit annoyed because you don't always have to go to such lengths! But I shouldn't complain, should I (and then feel guilty about complaining)?

FIRST: (immediately after breakfast) a book I have been longing for ages but have been too cheap to buy because it hasn't come out in paperback yet and hardcovers are just too darn expensive.
SECOND: (mid-afternoon, sitting reading new book, you slip up behind me, slip this around my neck—) a beautifully simple, unadorned silver necklace. I will wear it this evening to dinner.
THIRD: (late-mid-afternoon— nearing time to get ready to leave) is simply and practically a new case for my reading glasses as the old one was disintegrating and I had been complaining for some time but doing nothing towards replacing it.
My turn:
FIRST: (post-breakfast) a gift-certificate for your favorite record store because I never know what to get you, especially musically, so it's always just easier to let you get it yourself.
SECOND: (post-necklace— half in jest) a tie which you will probably very seldom wear because you dislike ties, but you need a nice tie as all your few other ones are disgusting and this is silk, and a designer name too, after all.

"I'll wear it to this evening's dinner," you announce, following my pronounced intention to wear my new necklace.

"I've nothing to reciprocate," I say, sadly, post reading-glasses-case gift.

"Good," you smile. "Now I've got the moral advantage."

"Moral advantage?" I laugh. "Don't know about that."

"Well, material, anyway."

One mustn't assume that we are completely frivolous creatures just because we spend the entire day lying about, exchanging presents, and screwing. We do not do that everyday (it saddens me [part of me] to say). We, of course, have jobs and work to keep food on our table, a roof over our heads, clothes on our backs...

And we, of course, have our disagreements and arguments, just like any other couple, even if they are over stupid things, and we try to never stay mad at each other too long. And my mate, however considerate, can be quite thoughtless at times. As can I.

We're not perfect. We're just like everybody else.

Late afternoon rolls around and I shower so that I don't stink at the dinner table. You, uninvited but not unwelcome, join me. I kick you out after awhile so that we won't be late.

We dress: I have to help you with your new tie. We lock up and head downstairs and have a brief discussion on the sidewalk as to who will drive (I don't mind driving there but don't like driving at night—the discussion stems from the possibility that you might indulge yourself and one really shouldn't drive after drinking...). It is decided that I will drive there and you will take it easy on the drinks. "It is your parents, after all," you say, whatever that means.

It's about a half-hour's drive, depending on traffic, from our downtown residence to my parents' condo in one of those a-bit-too-cutesy-for-its-own-good kind of towns on the edge of the city. I'm not entirely sure why my parents decided to retire there. My father gets an idea in his head...

My mother greets us at the door with kisses and hugs. My father also hugs and kisses me; for you, though, a handshake and a pat on the back.

"Well, well," my father chuckles, shaking his head. "Eight years. Happy anniversary, you two."

"It just doesn't seem that long," my mother says, ushering us into the living room. "It seems like only yesterday..."

"Shall we have a cocktail before setting out?" my father asks. "Hmm? Gin and tonics all around?"

He mixes the drinks and you and I sit on the couch, mother opposite us in the armchair.

"And how did you spend your day?" my mother asks. "Did you do anything special?"

You and I share a look, a smile.

"No, not really," I tell them and I show off my new necklace and direct their attention to your new tie.

"I did notice you were wearing a tie," my mother says.

I laugh. You blush and devote your attention to your just received gin and tonic.

We go where we always go for dinner with my parents. It is a quite passable restaurant situated in a converted Victorian house, elegant and pleasant enough, not terribly expensive (for this too-cutesy town), a decent menu.

They know us there (at least my parents are known; we are known as the daughter and son-in-law), greet us by name, and show us to a table. The view from the window is pleasantly fairy-tale-esque; looking out onto the snow powdered main street with its antique and kitschy shops, streetlights and the occasional strand of anticipatory Christmas lights casting their respective glows across the scene.

"The special tonight," our waiter tells us, "is breast of chicken with capers and a white wine sauce, served with wild rice and assorted vegetables." Mother and I decide on that. You and my father choose entrees from the regular menu. The soupe du jour, cream of leek, is ordered all around as a first course. You and father debate over the wine list, ignored by mother and I who are indifferent— so long as it isn't horrid— to such matters.

We are joined mid-meal— the room previously empty but for us— by an elderly couple. The hostess seats them at a table at the far end of the room. And they are, well, and I don't mean to be unkind, odd looking. They must, I presume, be in their seventies. The woman is short and plump, the man short and thin. She is dressed in a shimmery grey dress, as glimpsed beneath a silvery-white fur coat, her tightly curled silver hair partially hidden beneath a silver hat knit from some unidentifiable material. She clutches a large white purse on her lap. She wears white gloves. She removes not a single item of clothing the entire evening, sitting there as if the room were freezing.

The man wears a tan overcoat— which he does remove, draping over the back of his chair— an old-fashioned cut suit of a brown that my grandmother would have referred to as 'dog mess brown,' a light-brown or off-white dress shirt with a thin, dark tie. His face is somewhat square, blockish, lined and heavily jowled. He sports a small neat mustache. His almost black hair is brushed forward onto his forehead.

"Well! It seems," my father says, leaning across the table and whispering, "that Hitler has joined us."

"Don't be mean," my mother says, but she's smiling.

"I've never seen him with his wife before," my father says, surreptitiously eyeing the couple. "Maybe," he grins, "maybe they're celebrating their anniversary too!"

Everyone chuckles and I force myself to chuckle along.

I didn't once catch them looking at each other. Occasionally they mutter something across the table at each other. They order and eat quickly, impassively, and leave before we've even ordered dessert.

"What's the matter with you?" you ask in the car on the way home. "You were pretty quiet all evening."

I am silent a moment before answering, staring out at the darkened, snow-laden buildings passing us by: "It was that guy that looked like Hitler."

"What about him?"

"Everything about him, both of them," I start and then the words just flow out: "Everything! Did you see them? They hardly ever spoke and she never took her coat off and they ate like their food was cardboard! And if that's what they do for fun what must their regular life be like? And you were making fun of them! And what if Dad was right— what if they were actually celebrating their anniversary like us and they've lived together for I don't know how many years never saying anything to each other, or touching each other, or enjoying themselves, or anything, and what if that's what happens to us, what if when we get old we won't be able to speak to each other, or touch or...or..."

When you're finally able to get a word in edgewise you say, "Hey, hey, it's okay. Relax," stroking my arm. "Why should anything like that happen to us?"

"I don't know. It could..."

"Your parents aren't like that."

"I know, it's just...I don't know. They got to me for some reason. They upset me."

I guess you don't know what to say because you say nothing.

We arrive home.

In the elevator you suggest that perhaps they're so attuned to each other, know each other so well, they don't need to speak anymore.

Maybe because they've been together so long they hardly ever have to actually say what's on their minds.

I admit there might be some truth to that but it doesn't console me any.

We enter our dark apartment and perform our respective bedtime rituals. We go to bed and, too tired for sex, fall asleep.

My sleep is thin and dreamless.

The next morning, I wake at about the same early hour as the day before. I shake you awake.

"What?" you groan, still half asleep.

"Promise me you'll never be like Hitler," I say. "Promise me."

"I promise."

"Do you mean it?" I ask.

"Of course I do."

"Good," and I snuggle down next to your warm body, generally consoled.

"And I," I say, "I'll never be like Eva Braun."

Luck
Niles Reddick

After we moved into our forty-year old Cotswald cottage, I decided to do some yard work and clipped my finger, instead of the boxwood, with the pruning shears. I scrambled into the house in search of a Band-Aid. My wife Lauryn would have known if there were any Band-Aids in the house, but she was spending my money getting her nails done at a salon. Quite frankly, I was glad she was out of my way because she had been flitting about the house, singing, and she couldn't carry a tune. I didn't know why she was so happy, but I resented it.

The white carpet with blood spots looked like Chicken Pox and reminded me of Lily Tomlin on *Laugh-In* when she connected the dots. I wrapped my finger with half a roll of paper towels, knowing if I would have bought the quicker picker-upper instead of the cheap brand, I would not need so many. I noticed the mailman's jeep at the mailbox and walked out the front door and down the sidewalk, cursing the pruning shears that still lay by the boxwood. I gathered the bundle of junk, but was intrigued by a letter from a doctor. I opened it first, and as an attention-getter to get newcomers' business, he had stapled a Band-Aid at the top.

I promptly used the bandage and thought for the first time in twenty-five years that my luck might be changing. I had always identified myself with the guys in coveralls on *Hee-Haw* who moaned, "If it weren't for bad luck, I'd have no luck at all," because of marijuana and losing the Florida lottery.

Before getting married and taking a sales job in Miami, where I had to learn Spanish before making any sales, I was in college at a university in Georgia. One drawback to being white and middle-class was that I was unable to get federal grant money for college. My parents made too much money, although I never knew it. I had to work full time to pay tuition and living expenses. When I left campus for the 3-11 shift at the Ramada in my '78 Buick Regal, I was embarrassed because the silver paint flaked and the tailpipe left clouds of choking smoke behind. I had bought the car because the electric windows and gray velvet seats made me feel like I was moving up in the world. Although the car was already ten years old and needed major engine work, it was as comfortable as a coffin, except for the lack of air conditioning. In the middle of dog days in South Georgia, no air conditioning can be a death sentence, but I was able to take extended cold showers in the dorm, which kept me from pouring sweat on the way to work.

Before the electric door opened at the motel, I caught a glimpse of myself in the glass: Hush Puppy loafers, Duckhead khakis, and a plaid shirt. I looked more like a golfer than a motel clerk. I dreaded talking to Sam, the day clerk and assistant manager who had formerly been a minister. That is, until he got caught with his hand in the Baptist church's cookie jar and in his secretary's blouse. He loved giving unsolicited advice.

"How're you, Logan?" Sam plopped on the counter, his imitation gold Rolex glittering under the recess lighting above the maroon counter.

"Pretty good," I said. "Sure is hot out there." I had learned early on in life the weather can be a great topic of discussion when you want to avoid talking.

"You know what?" he asked.

That was his favorite question because he knew any polite Southerner would respond, giving him the ammunition to ramble.

"What?"

"It's never been this hot before," Sam said. "I honestly believe it's getting worse. It's in Revelation. All this evil in the world is rotting us away. One day, there won't be nothing left."

Sam's eyes rolled in their sockets, focusing beyond the windows. I knew he had spaced-out because there was nothing to look at except the dumpster behind the Sewanne Swifty; I also knew that the evil he enjoyed talking about so much was within himself.

"You're probably right." I knew the best way to reach success was to agree with others even when you didn't. You never know when you might need a reference.

"I'm convinced that the root to it all is drugs. It's just so easy to get hooked, and they can destroy a person." Sam's hands trembled. I had often smelled alcohol on his breath when I came to work, and I figured he probably had a drinking problem. I also knew he could only help himself.

"Lot of drugs out there," I said, taking the cash drawer out and counting the money. Although it wasn't required that employees check the money when changing shifts, I had been told by the manager, a former Baptist follower, to check Sam's drawer every time. I did. Lord knows I couldn't have paid a shortage, which was company policy.

"You ever do drugs, Logan?" Sam's eyes were piercing, and I felt my face flush.

"No," I nervously laughed. It wasn't that I had done drugs and was lying, but I had been offered drugs at fraternity parties, and I had seriously considered it. No matter how innocent I was, I always felt guilty in the presence of one who claimed to know God better than me. I was too busy studying, working, and socializing. "But I did find a field of marijuana once."

"Whose was it?"

I wondered why he wanted to know. "That's the funny part," I said. "It didn't belong to nobody."

""What do you mean?" Sam grimaced, and I knew he didn't want to hear me talk.

"Well, me and Felton, my friend from childhood, went through this cornfield to fish in the woods, and we discovered all this marijuana. We ran home and called the police. We were told we'd get a reward, so we went to the hardware store and got new bikes. The police sent the marijuana off to the GBI lab in Atlanta, and about a week later, the chief came to tell us the marijuana wasn't marijuana. It was some wild weed that looks just like marijuana. Our parents made us return the bikes since we weren't going to get any reward money."

Sam chuckled, and his belly shimmied. "I better get on out of here. Money check out?"

"Yeah, perfect."

Sam nodded and gathered his newspaper. "Give me a call if you need anything."

I knew it would be a slow night because we didn't have many reservations: a regular Frito-Lay trucker, shampoo salesman, and three unknowns. The unknowns were booked by the central reservation system, and I could bet money they were either Yankees or Canadians on their way to Disney World. I could also bet money they would ask me to repeat myself, delighting in the cuteness of my Southern drawl and reinforcing their notion that Southerners are stupid. It was them, however, that had been suckered off the interstate and would pay prices too high for everything. My grandmother had been right in the sense that the South would rise again, at least in their ability to take Northerner's money for cholesterol-laced food, uncomfortable beds in cockroach infested rooms, and tourist attractions like mosquito-breeding alligator farms or chigger infested moss gardens.

I turned on the lobby TV to CNN and hoped I didn't need to call Sam since he never answered his phone and didn't have an answering machine. Sam did usually call back shortly after I would call though just to check on things. The evening passed slowly, and I found myself being amused by bugs hovering around the outside lights and the repetitive headlines. My eyes grew heavy, and each time a car pulled under the awning, my body, like a robot, managed to find the energy to lift itself up and check the weary traveler in only to shuffle back to its position in front of headline news. At 9:00 p.m., I got up, locked the door, and opened the venetian blinds covering the night check-in window. Although some desk clerks opted not to use the half-moon window, I did for fear of being robbed. I positioned myself in the desk chair, listened to the hum of the portable fan, and closed my eyes.

In the dream, a man dressed in a business suit stood at the counter and said, "3-2-2." The numbers echoed about the lobby, and I kept asking him what he meant. And he repeated them over and over, and they continued to echo. When I was pulled away by a banging noise, I jumped up and sprinted to the glass door to unlock it for the graveyard clerk, Bill. He looked half-asleep, and although I didn't know him well at all, I had heard he worked the audit shift because he got nervous around people.

"You been sleeping?" He poured day old coffee into a styrofoam cup.

"No, just resting my eyes." It was a lie and the response I learned from my Dad.

"Anything happening?" He began straightening folios in the tray and seemed bothered by the ones that were not perfectly aligned with the metal separators; then, Bill moved to the circular phone stand where last names and room numbers were alphabetized. He straightened those, too.

"Quiet night," I said. "You gonna count the money?"

"No," Bill said. "You can go on."

"Thanks." I headed out the door, looking back at Bill who was straightening the pen attached to the desk by a chain rope. He lifted the pen into the air and made the chains form a circular pattern like the lines on a conch shell.

I felt most people were screwed up in one way or another, and I looked forward to the day I was out of college with a real job, making lots of money. I sunk into the velvet seats, cranked the Regal, and watched the smoke roll out and upward into the lights, confusing the bugs. I pressed the button and the window came down, and I breathed in the humid night air. As I drove down the street, I thought about the dream and the man's echoing numbers. On one level, I knew the dream was important and intuitively felt the numbers were the key to the Florida lottery, which was up to sixty million.

I was off the next day, and after class, I sat in my room, scribbling 322 onto a note pad and thinking about my new BMW, beach house, and all the European trips I would take. I told my roommate, David, "You watch. These numbers are my ticket out of here."

He smirked and replied; "All that partying your freshman year has had an effect on you."

I knew David would be jealous when I won, and I drove the twenty miles down Interstate 75 to the Florida line and spent my last twenty dollars on tickets. I picked various numbers and included combinations from my dream numbers. That night, I couldn't sleep. I knew I did not have the right number combination. So, when I got paid on Friday, I cashed my check, and instead of making my car payment, I drove back to the Florida line, stood in line for two hours, and spent my entire week's pay on more tickets. I told others in line: "You're wasting your time; I've got the numbers." They politely smiled, but I could see fear in their eyes.

When 10:00 p.m. came on Saturday night, I used the courtesy phone in the lobby to call my parents to tell them I was going to win the lottery.

"That's nice," my mother said. "Don't forget about us." I knew she didn't believe me, and when she asked, "Are you okay?" I knew she thought I was crazy.

When 11:00 p.m. came, Bill was obsessively straightening, and I plopped down onto the sofa in front of the TV. I watched the painted ping-pong balls float upward in the plastic bubbles. My heart raced, and even though the air conditioning was on in the lobby, beads of sweat rolled down my side from my armpits. As the carnival music played, the blonde lottery woman with breasts bursting at the seams of her blue sequined dress said the numbers into the camera. My heart sank. Although I had over 150 tickets, I knew the winning numbers were not on my tickets. Still, I wrote them down and reassured myself.

I stayed up until 2 o'clock in the morning, checking and rechecking my tickets and wondering how I would ever make my car payment. On Sunday morning, I ate breakfast in the university cafe and read in the paper that a homeless woman in Tampa, living in her station wagon with three children, spent her last dollar on a lottery ticket and won. I laughed and rationalized she needed it more than I did. The BMW became a Regal, the beach house became my dorm room, and the European trips became trips to the Ramada.

When Lauryn came back from the beauty salon, I told her about cutting my finger, finding the Band-Aid in the doctor's marketing letter, and how I believed my luck might be changing.

"Sit down," she said, smiling.

I sat in the green wicker chair. "What is it? Did you win some money?"

"No," she laughed. "I'm pregnant. I didn't want to tell you first thing this morning because you were so busy in the yard."

I had the same sinking feeling I had the time I found out the marijuana wasn't real and the time I didn't win the lottery.

"Sure is hot in here," I said, wiping my forehead.

Boating
Michael Largo

I parked the rental car in a pool of liver-colored mud. Here was the makeshift pier of scrap plywood and uneven planks lashed to submerged fifty-five gallon drums. A fleet of repossessed cruisers, speed boats and skiffs were roped to this exposed spine of salvaged timber. The few remaining canvas tops were sun-split and torn, fluttering in the Caribbean heat like shredded surrender flags. A police guard with a rifle hanging over his shoulder pointed to my boat: there--a hundred feet from the pier, lying nearly sideways between algae-stained coral boulders and the shoreline.

I had to wade through pools of oil and suctioning sand to climb aboard. I almost couldn't recognize it. The chair on the bridge was missing. All electrical equipment was gone; a bird's nest of colored wires sticking out from where the control panels used to be. A metal column substituted where the teak steering wheel had been. The engines hoisted from their holds and just some cut hoses, filters and a battery turned on its side remained in the engine's housing, a puddle of stagnate water. Inside the cabin a hole was blown through the side of the specimen tank I had custom made from molded fiberglass for Caroline's work. The cabinet doors were hanging from single hinges and there were gaps in the counter top where the sink and stove range had been. A line of small holes punched into the paneling and ceiling. The compartment where I had kept my papers and maps was found. Boxes of food, books with broken bindings, and pages from documents covered the floor. I started to go through them but they felt sticky, coated with dried vomit and blood. There was a picture, a photo of Caroline, stuck to a spaghetti box. Large, languid flies were everywhere.

I took Caroline's picture out into the fresher air and looked out to the sea. It was a photo of her in the weekend cabin we had in the mountains. I took that photograph when she was asleep on the couch under a heavy quilt. After, I carried her to bed and she had kissed me in her sleep. I tried to wipe the trash from the picture off on my pants.

Now two rifle holding policemen stood on the beach signaling me to come down. They watched me climb off my boat and jump into the shallow water. My shoes filled with sand and my cuffs got wet. The policemen seemed to hold back from laughing. They followed me to a crumbling concrete slab that had been the loading dock for this furniture company building now converted into a prison.

"The Chief-of-Police is waiting for you. Right this way."

"I don't think I'll see the prisoner now. We'll do that tomorrow," I said. "I'll sign the forms and re-claim my boat then."

"You'll have to discuss that with the Chief. Right this way." The police guards blocked my path to the rental car.

Inside the building they ushered me through a long corridor: panels of broken glass, cinder block walls, chipped plaster ceiling. Pigeons sat on the ledges of the windows and piles of dried drippings caked below them. Muffled voices and shouts were coming from double iron doors at the end of the corridor. Two additional guards stood on either side of the door. The ones escorting spoke to those two in Patois. They told me to raise my hands and patted me down, before they slid the bolt open on the door. I saw the Chief, the one with the white shirt and medals, standing with his legs apart, tapping a leather covered club into the palm of his hand. This section of the building was where they held the prisoners. It was two hundred feet long with cells constructed of crudely laid block. Iron doors with small barred windows, about eight feet apart, were on both sides of the hall. Soiled straw lay on the floor. The Chief motioned for me to follow him. The two guards who trailed us yelled at prisoners showing their faces in the small windows. I turned and saw them smash, with the butt of the rifle, any fingers clinging to the bars. Half way down the line there was another corridor which led to a room with folding chairs. The interrogation & visitor room; a windowless, humid box.

"Here is the prisoner, the one responsible for the theft of your property," the Chief said. "We have his full confession." He spoke in Patois to the guards before he turned and left with the ones from outside.

I thought it was a skinny woman with long black hair there waiting in the foul heat; hands awkwardly handcuffed behind the chair-- until the guard stepped forward and whacked his shoulders with his leather blackjack.

"You have a visitor," the guard shouted. "Wake up."

Greg lifted his head, his long hair covering his face. He was barefoot and his toenails were extremely long. He had fresh bruises on his face. It took a moment for him to focus before he managed a smile.

"Jim, man, get me the fuck out of here."

I asked him to tell me what happened. He coughed after each sentence, almost lifting out of his seat and buckling over.

"We were doing pretty good there for awhile. We had made eight runs, all of them smooth, without a hitch. We ran mostly out of Bimini. We got a big deal set-up out of Jamaica, first time down here, would you believe it?"

He told me what happened, coughing, and twice for no apparent reason, getting whacked on the back by the guard. His clothes smelled of dried urine. On the night he left me at the dock on the Gulf, stealing my boat, he and Eric, the other deck hand, met a Peruvian salt tanker in the Stream. They caught the bails tossed to them and swung around to Port Everglades. They made $25,000 in twelve hours. According to Greg, they had some trouble getting
organized at first. Eric was partying too much and they weren't taking care of business.

"We then hooked up with some women and the money ran out fast again. I sent for my girlfriend I was seeing up there in York. You know, the cute one who worked in the marine hardware store where you kept an account."

"She's in prison in Peru," he continued. "She was caught with nine kilos of cocaine. In Peru the justice is simple; one year in jail for each kilo. No negotiations, no parole. We were making this Jamaican run to get a big score to try and bribe her out. It was a bad scene. She was getting raped regularly, being a blue-eyed girl in a land of darkness. Eric said that it wasn't such a bad way to do your time, laying on your back," Greg shook his head. "Eric didn't have much sympathy, man. We weren't getting along too good on that run."

"The police caught you?"

"No, that's the sad part." He started to cough so hard he spit blood on the floor. The guard struck him for that. "These idiots wouldn't have been smart enough to get us on their own. It was the pirates, man. It was Eric's watch that night. Another guy we brought in with us and Eric's girl and me were in the cabin. Eric forgot to put the tacks on the deck before he crashed out."

"The tacks?"

"Yeah, you know, thumb tacks. We spread them on the deck and when the pirates come aboard you hear them screaming. These pirates aren't organized; they're just barefoot pieces of trash. They're not even looking for the drugs. They just want some brass fittings, some equipment, whatever they can rip-off and run fast. They go right up to Eric and take his gun from him and shove it down his mouth. Boom. The other guy we hired runs out of the cabin, goes up on deck and boom, he gets thrown backwards. These bastards come shooting into the cabin, splinters and bullets flying everywhere. Eric's girlfriend tries to run away and she's clawing all over me, trying to get past me, but there was nowhere to go. She gets shot in the back of the head and she falls down dead on top of me. Her blood covered me and I just stayed motionless on the floor. I stayed like that for about six hours, playing dead, while these guys are having a party, drinking the booze, cooking food. Boiling a fucking pot of spaghetti. It really rattled my cage, let me tell you. I thought I was going to die any minute. I had to stay so still and the chick's blood in my mouth all that time. When they finally left, I puked. Then I just went up on the bridge and started to scream. I don't know why, I was just screaming and then these Jamaican gestapo idiots take me in. They found the dope and I've been here ever since."

"How long?"

"Don't know. Seems like a long time. They're trying to make me tell them where I got the stuff from, but I won't do that. This Chief here is a rich son-of-a bitch. And mean. You got to get me out of here, Jim." He looked at me, strands of hair covering his face. "And I'm sorry man, to hear about what happened to your old lady."

I didn't want to discuss Caroline's car accident with Greg. I should've been hating him for stealing my boat and nearly everything I owned. Two weeks after he took my boat I received fifty $500 money orders with a note: Thanks Dude. Greg had been my deck hand for six years. I looked at him and said: "Just tell them what they want to know. It would be better to cooperate."

"Hell no." Greg started to cough so long and so loud, it sounded like he was choking. He was gagging and trying to sip his drooling blood back. The guard came from behind him and was about to strike his shoulder again, but Greg leaned back suddenly from a repercussion of a heavy cough and was caught on the side of the head with the blackjack. He was knocked to the floor, chair and all. I jumped up in the commotion. I hadn't noticed that the Chief and his men had come back into the room.

"I believe the interview is over, Mr. Key."

"What's his sentence?" I asked the Chief, watching Greg motionless on the floor.

"He killed one of the guards the day we brought him in. His sentence is life in prison. But it will be a short life. In fact, he was scheduled to hang himself a week ago, but then you called wanting to reclaim your property." He turned and spoke to the guards. They dragged Greg away.

I was led out of the room and down the straw strewn hallway past the cinder block cells toward the main steel doors. I waited for the doors to open, but they didn't. When I turned to see where the guards were, I saw the Chief with his flushed smile standing near an opened cell door.

He was tapping his blackjack in his palm again.

"If you don't mind waiting here for just a minute. In our guest chambers. We haven't been able to verify your registration documents." He grinned at a guard and said in that chip-chop Patois, slow enough for me to get the gist: "So, the rooster returns to find his lost chicken."

"I don't think you want to upset Mr. Mitchell," I said, immediately knowing I had made a mistake when I saw his smile vanish into a stern, expressionless look. Mitchell was an ex-partner of mine who had high government connections on the Island. I had known the boat was beyond salvage before I got here. I just wanted to see if any personal belongings were left, things of Caroline's, maybe one of the few photos I had of her.

"I am the boss man here, Mr. Key. Procedures will be followed by the mandate."

He motioned for me to go into the cell.

I went inside, ready to feel the blackjack against my skull.

On The Outside Looking In
Grady Hanrahan

As I emerged from the guesthouse, she declared herself in earnest, but I was determined not to give. Her frame was like a matchstick, about as thin, and her skin brown and aged. She had eyes as dark as coal that gave off the occasional mysterious and entrancing beam of hope.

"*Bakseesh*," she voiced, lowering her head in desperation. She lifted her calloused hands to brush back the thinning hair from her eyes and noticed me staring. She smiled at my curiosity, beckoning to me. I wanted to go to her, comfort her, but I shook my head as if to say no and continued into the dirt-laden streets of Delhi's largest bazaar. Giving only adds to the problem, say the brochures, "donate to local charities instead." Words of wisdom from inexperienced souls, I thought, those unaware of India's ever-growing problems. She was an untouchable, unable to climb the social ladder of India's caste system.

I left the bazaar to follow a side road that ran parallel to the railway station, connecting a string of shops where merchants sold their precious goods. A young mother with child in tow explored the selection of odoriferous spices; an old man sat sipping his morning cup of *chai'*. A rickshaw loaded with eager school children quickly passed; a mule driven cart with goods, and, high above on the rooftop, I could see an old woman hanging the daily washing. Orange and yellow flowers offered to the gods for luck, prosperity and a long life hung above her doorway - securely placed and changed on a daily basis.

My mood quickly soured as I continued along the narrow passageway that many call home. The signs of ill health greeted me: leprosy, goiters the size of golf balls, and the occasional corpse waiting for cremation. I came to this land confidently knowing that my senses would be assaulted, from the bright traditional dress of local people to the everlasting smells of Indian spices cooking on an open fire. However, I didn't expect my emotions to be breached, a frontal attack on all moral and ethical grounds. Was I, a man of Western standards and ideas, in a position to understand Indian life as it existed before me? Were these desperate people in search of a better life?

A man carrying a heavy load plodded towards me, his head hanging like a repentant monk. "*Namaste*," he said, reaching into his shoulder pack.

"Hello," I replied, and began to step away. He followed me, tugging gently on my shirt collar.

"Buy postcards?"

"No, thank you."

"Cheap price ... only fifty *rupees*!"

"Thirty!"

"OK!"

I walked away knowing that I paid double the price compared to Indian tourists. An extra twenty *rupees* means nothing to a Westerner. We *are* rich after all. I felt ashamed, stricken by a sense of uneasiness. I had just argued over the equivalent of fifty cents, an amount that would feed the man for days. I wanted to return to my room and bury my thoughts for the evening.

I hailed a cycle-rickshaw for the short journey across town. I couldn't be asked to walk. The driver took my backpack and flung it across the metal cage loosely attached to the rear of the pedal-powered machine. "Market?"

"No," I said, abruptly. "Blue Penny guesthouse near the railway station."

He gave a quick nod and began to peddle. You had to admire his energy. He, with the job of carting around the "elite" members of society, worked hard on his task. And still he had the stamina to talk, barefoot on the petals, smiling continuously. "What is your name?"

"Anthony," I said. "And..."

"Chandrashakar," he replied anxiously. "But please...call me Shakar."

His English was quite good, considering, and there was an air of enthusiasm about him. He wore a long, one-piece garment with tattered edges and sweat-stained patches along the back. His neck and bare arms were black from the summer sun, and his head kept cool by a wet cloth tightly wrapped into place.

"Where do you come from?"

"America."

"Ah...America! Land of opportunity."

"I guess so. Look, I would really just like to be left alone."

In reality, I was a bit embarrassed, ashamed of the fact that I had come from such a country. Opportunity does exist, more so than in India. Or maybe I was naïve, unaware of what the lower caste members actually felt about their situation. I reached and lightly tapped him on the shoulder.

"Shakar?"

"Yes, how may I help you?"

"May I ask you a personal question?"

"Please go on."

"Are you happy?"

"I do not understand the question."

"Are you happy with the way you are treated by society? What I am trying to say…"

"We are untouchables, but prefer to be called *Dalits*. We have been oppressed for many years, but remain happy and content with our lives."

"Even though…"

"Listen my friend! We accept our position within society. It may not be exactly fair, especially from an outside view, but this is our life."

This became obvious to me while traveling further into the heart of the city. Members of the community performed their particular roles with earnest, no matter how simple or complicated the position. Evidence of such work could be seen in the detailed latticework jacketing the buildings and the handcrafted goods displayed in corner market stalls. Individuals performing the most humble of tasks, at least humble in the Western sense of the word, did so with pride and complete determination. Society seemed interconnected, lower and upper caste alike, into one working unit. A daily system of buying and selling dominated the market stalls and roadside shops with sounds of friendly bartering echoing through the streets. It was a game I never managed to win, despite good-hearted attempts.

We reached the guesthouse much quicker than I anticipated. I noticed the same woman approaching an unsuspecting tourist who had just flown in from suburbia. He ignored her, in about the same manner as I had, and carried on his merry way. I reached into my pocket as Shakar unloaded my bags. "How much?"

"Pay me what you like. If you were satisfied, the price is no option."

"Please take this and keep the change. I enjoyed your company and your wisdom."

"Thank you my friend."

He kissed the note and pressed it against his forehead to give thanks and peddled away searching for the next customer.

It was a long, but mentally productive flight home. I had time to reflect upon my travels: the people, the landscape and the culture. It was the essence of Indian life, a place of daily meals and the occasional story or two. No one raised an eye as I strolled through this existence, taking in and learning as much as possible. The mood was up beat and a sense of optimism lingered in the air. Children freely roamed the streets unharmed while parents concentrated on daily tasks. I enjoyed this life and its unpretentious and unassuming ways. It was the India I never imagined.

A Return to Beasley Manor
Jackie R. Gates, II

The leaves had changed colors and the landscape was taking on the look of Mother Nature at rest. A chilly wind whipped across the meadow and along the large lake, which lay at the base of a forgotten valley. A car meandered along the narrow road.

Greg Beasley scanned his surroundings as he made his way toward the mansion. The trip from Baltimore had taxed him more than he had thought, and he was growing tired from the five-hour drive.

His '89 Saab started up the graded incline with a grunting effort. Trees were in a line along the road, an expansive lawn on either side. He could see the rusty iron gates at the top of the hill.

The incident leading to this trip had begun only three months ago. Greg understood what the letter in his mailbox was all about before he had ever opened it. It had a return address of Godson, Phillips and Mankewitz Law Offices in Alexandria. He knew his Uncle Clay had been ill for many years; this letter would confirm what he knew had probably happened.

Clay Beasley's last will and testament was read a week later in Jason Phillips' office. Greg, being the only living heir to the estate, was there to hear the solemn speaker.

Clay Beasley had made millions of dollars during the First World War. He had a plan, found a wealthy advocate, and he built the second largest steel factory in Virginia. During the war, Clay supplied America with a plentiful portion of the steel necessary to build her war machine.

After the war, the Depression had an effect on Beasley Steel but it still made a manageable profit. Fortunately, at least for Clay Beasley, World War II brought it back to the industrial power it had once been 20 years before. The company was up and running again at full strength and wouldn't stop for another 45 years, when it was purchased by the much larger Allied Steel Company.

Jason Phillips, Clay's attorney for the last 28 years, was an older man with a square jaw and piercing eyes. He read from the will like he was reading from an obituary: slow, methodical, and with little facial expression. Though it took an hour to read it in its entirety, the result was that Greg would inherit the mansion and nearly forty million dollars. While there was some excitement in becoming a millionaire, Greg was saddened by the loss. He had only met Uncle Clay one time, but it was a meeting he would never forget.

Phillips assured Greg that the money could be transferred to an account of his choosing within a month's time. The mansion, an antebellum-era domicile, was sitting on 135 acres of mostly wooded property. The attorney told Greg that the property had recently been appraised at two million dollars, and an interested party had offered $1.8 million not long before Mr. Beasley's death. Phillips went on to say that most of the furnishings in the residence were priceless and could take many years to sell, if Greg so wished.

Greg pulled up to the gates and stepped out of the car to get a better look. He hadn't been there since his childhood in 1974. His father, who had passed away several years before from cancer, brought him there, at the request of Clay Beasley, to meet the old man.

He could see the mansion from the wrought-iron gates. It was sunk back into a grassy, flat terrain with a distinctive pine tree wood-line behind it. The home, with large white pillars in the front, was redbrick with a large French-style window facing the gates.

The visit to the mansion, at the age of 12, had been frightening for Greg. He remembered he and his father being led through a myriad of hallways by a large black man in an immaculately white tuxedo. After several twists and turns, they ended up in front of two huge black doors that seemed to dwarf anyone standing by them. The black man, whom his uncle called 'Cyrus,' opened the doors and gestured for them to enter.

Greg pushed the gates open and drove slowly toward the house. The driveway was paved from the gates to the residence and was lined with small lights that activated at nighttime; he could see small sensors on top of each light. As he neared the mansion, it had an ominous, dreary, dark shadow around it. In the distant horizon, he could see the obscured forms of storm clouds. This was not unlike his first visit here.

There were no trees in front, or on the side, and the ivy was clinging to the bricks like parasites. Greg glanced at his watch and noted that it was almost 5:00 p.m. It would be dark soon and he had no intentions of staying the night there.

After Cyrus had opened the doors, young Greg could see a large room filled with books, furniture, and paintings of all kinds on the walls. He and his father walked into the room and Greg stared at the extravagant decorations, expensively mounted animal heads from Clay's safaris in South Africa, and stacks of classic books piled along the wall. A shiny chandelier dangled high from the ceiling, and the lights from within it illuminated the entire room with a splendid radiance. He saw a chair, its back toward him, near the far corner. A small wisp of swirling smoke drifted into view from the front of the chair.

Greg parked the car near the front door. He stared in wonder at the massive pillars holding up the front portion of the house like Atlas with the world on his shoulders. The mansion stretched out forever on either side and was two stories tall; it seemed even bigger than he had remembered. He walked to the front door and stared in awe at the workmanship of the craftsmen who worked ever so precisely to achieve perfection in each and every detail they carved into the woodwork.

He fished a key from his pocket. The key was attached to a medallion key chain with the initials 'CB' inscribed on it. The attorney had given him the keys to the home after the will was read. He inserted the key into the keyhole and gave it a quick twist. The door swung open, perfectly balanced on the handcrafted brass hinges that could handle the incredible weight.

The mansion was dark and smelled musty. The furniture had been covered in plastic sheets that were now sprinkled with a topping of settled dust. With the exception of the covered furniture, it seemed no different from the first time he had visited. Greg stepped back inside the spacious room. A large fireplace was to his right; the spiraling staircases directly in front of him and several hallways leading in numerous directions were off to his left.

The old man stood up. Young Greg could see his backside, covered in a red wool sweater, black trousers and a patch of thick gray hair curling about the back of his head. The smoke still drifted upward as he turned around and eyed Greg curiously. A note of recognition appeared in his eyes as he glanced at his much younger brother, Henry.

He approached them slowly, deliberately, and all the while with a dark-wood pipe inserted between his thin lips. He had a goatee hanging from his chin, nearly touching his chest. His face was distinct with a large nose and eyebrows so thick that they overshadowed his eyes. The edges of his mouth curved upward slightly as he stepped next to young Greg and placed an ancient hand on his shoulder.

Greg walked up the stairs and admired the quality of the workmanship. Not a board creaked as he made his way to the rooms above. Clay Beasley was notorious for making sure that all work done in his home was above and beyond the average. He had been a man of impeccable tastes for quality, regardless of the cost.

Henry glanced at his brother, nodded, then glanced down at his son. "This is your Uncle Clay." He said with hesitation. "Say hello to him."

Young Greg glanced up at the intimidating man and smiled.
"Hello, Uncle Clay."

Clay patted him on the shoulder and glanced at his brother. "You
did well with him, Henry. Very well indeed."

The upstairs was carpeted in hand-sewn Persian rug blocks. Greg
marveled at the amount of money it must have cost, even 50 years ago.
He lingered in the hallway for a moment then moved onto a bedroom to
his right. He entered the room and saw a large bed, canopied with a silk
cloth, and a bedspread made of red felt. The decorations in the room
were that of Greek art: small sculptures, paintings and handcrafts that
had lasted through the centuries of changes of ownership.

"He's a good boy, Clay." Henry said, with his eyes to the ground.

"I can see that." Clay answered solemnly as he knelt down and
hugged Greg with his two thin arms wrapped tightly around him. "How
do you like school?" Clay asked, a smile spreading across his face.

"Fine, Uncle." Greg said, unable to grasp the totality of the
circumstances unfolding around him.

"Have you heard anything about me before today?" Clay asked
suddenly.

Young Greg shrugged, glancing at his father for some type of visual
support. "I know that you made a lot of money in business."

"That's true," Clay agreed. "But there is more to me than just
money."

Greg nodded. "I know that. I'm just a little nervous, Uncle."

Clay hugged the boy again and chuckled softly. "I know, son."

Greg drifted in and out of the other six bedrooms. They were each
respectively of different themes: Greek, Roman, French Renaissance,
Empirical Russian, Victorian, Early American and African. Some of the
objects in those rooms were undoubtedly of museum quality.

He went downstairs and began walking through the hallways,
checking out all of the other rooms. Greg ended up at the den; this was
where Clay Beasley spent most of his life. It was where Greg first met
him.

"You want to see something extraordinary?" Clay asked the jittery
boy standing in front of him.

Young Greg nodded; he really wasn't sure if he wanted to or not,
but he dared not refuse.

"All right, then. Come with me." Clay said as he led Greg toward
the far end of the room, hand in hand.

They stopped at the edge of a large Mahogany desk. On the desk,
among many small brass trinkets, strewn paperwork, a pipe tray, and a

lavish quill pen made from a peacock feather, was a small statue made from wood. It stood about ten inches tall and was so dark in color that Greg had to step closer to make out the details of its features.

It was a long-faced, human shaped creature holding a spear at its side. It had only a loincloth and a headband with unique designs carved into it. The base was a crude circular chunk of wood with green stones spaced evenly around the edge. The statue's wood must've been very old, as it had long since cracked in places and had become pitted with age.

"I like it, Uncle." Young Greg said as he reached out to touch it.

"Don't touch . . ., " Henry said as he stepped toward Greg in a moment of excitement. Greg jerked his hand back and his mouth flung open, thinking he had nearly committed a cardinal sin.

Clay turned and held the father back with only a gesture. "It's quite all right, Henry."

Clay leaned down, took the pipe from his dry lips and held it away from Greg. He glanced at the boy and smiled as warmly as he ever had. "Go ahead, Gregory—touch it."

Young Greg reached out and took the heavy statue into his small hand. "What is it, Uncle Clay?" The curious boy asked as he carefully examined it like a practiced appraiser.

Clay stood up again, placed his hands on his hips and sucked from the pipe. He blew the smoke out and thought quietly to himself for a moment before answering. "It came from Botswana. Have you ever heard of that country?"

Greg nodded, still eyeballing the statue attentively. "It's in Africa."

Clay smiled, patting Greg on the back with delight. "That's impressive, Gregory. You are a very smart young man. How do you know about Botswana?"

Greg glanced up at his uncle and smiled proudly. "We studied Africa in school last month."

The old man walked around his desk and sat down heavily into the plush captain-style chair. He paused, then gestured toward the statue in the boy's hands. "There's a legend associated with that idol."

Young Greg placed the statue back on the desk and stood at attention, looking at his only living relative aside from his father. "What kind of legend?"

Greg entered the room and glanced down. He could still picture his uncle sitting behind the large desk. The room still appeared, amazingly, the same as he had remembered it. The decorations, paintings, and wall mounts had been left unchanged for many years. He looked up and smiled as he saw the chandelier, still hanging from the ceiling. He reached for the switch on the wall and turned the lights on. The many bulbs inside the chandelier came on with their usual brilliance.

He approached the enormous desk and stared at the items on it. He remembered the statue and where it had been sitting the first time he saw it. He glanced to his left and spotted a large gun cabinet filled with several high caliber rifles. He knew that they were the guns his uncle had taken with him to Africa over the many years he hunted big game. Clay was famous in hunting circles throughout the world.

Greg picked up a bell-shaped brass paperweight and turned it over in his hand. It was engraved with the words, 'To Clay Beasley, in remembrance of things done for his country... Gen. Pershing.' He set the paperweight down and walked around the room, touching this and picking up that.

"The people who made the idol thought it had a lot of magical power because it was made from a tree that was believed to have been blessed by spirits." Clay said as he emphasized the mood with a gesture and facial expression. "They believed that whomever possessed it could become wealthy and powerful."

Young Greg eyed the statue with a renewed respect. "Really? They believed that?"

Clay nodded. "They had reason to, according to the legend." He said as he puffed from his pipe again. A smile creased his face as he watched young Greg's curiosity grow.

"Why, Uncle Clay?" Young Greg asked.

"It seems that the first owner of the idol was a man who would later be King." Clay said with a nod of his head. "The next man to own it would discover the largest diamond mine ever found on the African continent."

Young Greg glanced at his father, who was not reacting in the least to the story. His face was impassive and Greg knew that he was only biding time.

"That could be a coincidence." Greg said with a shrug. Even at that age he was a realist.

Clay began laughing softly. "It could at that," He said. "But I haven't told you about the third man."

The mansion was quiet. Greg walked out of the large den and worked his way to the kitchen. It looked like the cooking area of a restaurant: two large ovens, a commercial-sized range, chopping blocks, and rows of pots and pans. In the center was an island, which held numerous drawers full of silverware. It had been built with the intention of hosting large dinner parties. A crew of ten cooks could easily work in the kitchen without worry of bumping into one another.

He stepped from the kitchen to the dining room. It was immense. The table was at least ten feet long and six feet wide. There were four chairs on each side, with a large red chair at one end.

Greg walked to the large window, adjacent to the table, and looked at the view outside. It faced the east side of the property. Some clouds were building in the sky and the sun was nearly gone for the day. It would be dark very soon.

Young Greg scratched his head and sat down in a chair near the desk. "What about the third man?" He asked curiously.

Clay tossed his head and shrugged. "He was a young man, not too many years older than you are now when he found the statue situated inside of an old hollowed-out tree on the African grassland. He was working for a company that sent him all over the world to look for natural resources that could be one day exploited. The man didn't agree with the ethics of his job, but he was paid well enough that he didn't complain."

Young Greg sat back in the chair. He was enthralled with the way his uncle was telling the story to him.

"Anyway, the man found the statue and was delighted by its antiquity and could only imagine its history." Clay said with a twinkle in his eye. "He found a local tribesman, whom he had met on previous trips into Africa, and asked about the idol. The tribesman told him about its legend. The man would never be the same after hearing about its magical qualities."

Henry glanced at his watch and approached Greg slowly, watching Clay for any dissension. He stood behind him and placed his hands on the back of the chair.

"What happened then?" Young Greg asked, his attention on the old man and his story. "Did something happen to him?"

Clay relit his pipe and nodded, flipping the match until the fire at its end was gone. "He went back to America and quit his job. He decided he would go into business for himself." He leaned back in his chair and paused, as if remembering a pleasant thought from long ago.

"In 1916, he found a wealthy financial backer to help him start a corporation that would rival J.P. Morgan himself." Clay leaned forward, his elbows on the desk. "He took steel from the earth and processed it for the approaching war. Within a year or so he was a millionaire."

Greg glanced up at his dad and smiled. "I think he's talking about himself." Greg glanced back at Clay and grinned widely.

Clay shrugged. "I can't get anything passed you, Gregory!" He chuckled and glanced at Henry, who had forced a smile on his face as well.

Greg smiled with a lot self-satisfaction. "I knew it was you, Uncle Clay!"

"I think it's about time we go, Clay." Henry said as he tapped Greg on the shoulder.

"So it is." Clay spat out as he stood up and approached Greg. "It's been a real pleasure meeting you, Gregory. I hope you will come back to visit again someday. Do you think you can do that?"

Young Greg nodded. He didn't know for sure because his father wasn't exactly happy about being here in the first place.

"Good," Clay said. "I want you to have something." He reached out and grabbed the statue, handing it to his nephew. "This is yours."

Greg held the statue in his hands and stared at it in wonder. He smiled and glanced back at Clay. "Thank you."

Henry stared down at the statue without expression or comment.

"I'm sure you don't mind, do you, Henry?" Clay asked with a daring glare.

Henry shook his head after only a moment's thought. "No, I don't mind."

Greg held the statue close to his chest and stood up, shaking hands with Clay. "I'll take care of it, Uncle Clay."

Clay nodded, taking his pipe from his mouth. "I know you will. Take care of yourself, young man."

Greg stood up and hesitated. He then lunged forward and hugged Clay, who was only too happy to receive the affection, tightly. "I'll never forget meeting you, Uncle Clay."

Henry placed his large hand on Greg's shoulder and escorted him toward the door. Clay followed them as they left the room and started down the long hallway. They finally made it to the main door, which Cyrus was holding open for them.

"Henry, you take good care of that boy, you hear?" Clay said with an admonishing tone.

"I'll take care of him fine, Clay." Henry said with a sigh.

Greg stopped at the door and glanced in one last time before he left. He remembered holding the statue as he left many years ago; now, through the years and after several moves from one place to another, he had misplaced it and hadn't seen the statue in six or seven years. He never was quite sure where he lost it at, but hopefully whoever found it would have as much luck as Uncle Clay.

Greg locked the door and got into his car. The visit had definitely been good for him. It brought back the memory of a lonely old man who took great delight in telling stories to an impressionable young boy.

He pulled his seatbelt over his torso and started the car with a puff of bluish smoke bursting from the tailpipe. The car sputtered for a moment, almost stalled, and then the engine resumed it vigorous purr. He put the car in gear and glanced down in the passenger seat as something caught his eye.

"What the...?" He asked aloud.

An object was in the passenger seat. The idol, which he had lost a long time ago, was laying in the seat next to him. He picked it up and stared at it for a few seconds. He could smell the aroma of cherry-vanilla pipe tobacco; the same smell that came from Clay's pipe. He pulled the statue to his nose and savored the smell that he had remembered from so many years ago.

Sometimes, he now understood, legends are more than just words.

"My Life as a Salesman"
Shane Mayer

I am vilified by the fact that in the land of good and plenty, I cannot separate myself from the pack. I cannot join the carefree, to willingly think of joy all day long, and to still have the night's rent. A parade of enjoyment passes by my eyes as the years pass through my head. It circles and pauses long enough to make me remember that I did something fun some time ago with someone that I have forgotten. I resolve to take comfort in the fact that the freedom dealt to the lucky few is a result of the confinement of the masses. She who plays in the park in the afternoon has a he who counts numbers until it is time to wake up and count more numbers the next day. He who sips Merlot to wash down his Poisson just before his cheesecake has a she who has laundered the laundry so often that gray looks yellow, yellow looks clean, and clean just means it is Thursday. My friends talk of the people who risked it to make it.

"Did you hear of what this guy did and he is only that old? Did you see her, she is worth that much?"

These success stories don't carve a path. I don't want to know how the famous became famed or how the rich became filthy. The stories that are important to me are never told. Those of the risk takers who risked it all and ended up with nothing. The explorers who traveled to the North Pole and were frozen in time and the entrepreneurs who are now among the working rank and file paying off insurmountable debt.

The fly that has entered my life has no idea of the kind of caged animal that lurks within this pale and gentle face. Quickly growing tired of my still life antics; the fly has taken his business to the lady in the next booth. I don't blame him after all. She hasn't checked her watch once since she has arrived. She hasn't turned to look for the goddam good-for-nothing waitress that hasn't brought the water she asked for. Her toes aren't tapping two beats faster than the Muzak that is playing in the background. Why are mine? Oddly enough, the fly has reversed course and is heading due north, directly for me. Buzzing up and then diving low, this fly has taken hostile action and is a dangerous threat to both my room temperature Monty Christo and me. Landing on my ear and then my arm, he has started the game, but we both know who will finish it. With one last distractionary fly by, he sights his target and goes for the kill. The target is my Monty Christo and this arrogant, free wheeling sonovabitch just entered enemy territory. He is obviously very confident; the quickness of a fly cannot be matched by many creatures anywhere. Taunting me with each sip of MY syrup, I am called to action. Like a karate master of the Noseeum Clan, I swiftly and efficiently end the life of the menacing fly. That is the price you pay for messing with the food I don't want.

The final ten minutes of my lunch are spent gazing at life. I have studied the world in this fashion for quite some time now. You would think that it takes more than ten minutes, but really, when you break it down, anything past that is just rehashing. Today's lesson was a simple lesson in the art of sales.

Walking back to the office my path crosses with the normal plethora of bums. The first bum is sitting on the corner holding up a sign that says, "homeless and HIV positive, please help." I don't break a stride. The next bum approaches me with a simple question; "Can you spare some change?" "Sorry Pal I'm empty," I say as my pocket jingles louder than I care for. The third bum approaches, "Sir. Hi, my name is Willie Freedmont. I have worked to support myself for 42 years. I have a cataract in one eye and this has caused my blindness. This is the most embarrassing thing I have ever had to do, but I am extremely hungry. I have recently become unemployed and this is my only option. Do you think you could spare anything?" I hand him two dollars, which, when translated into bum dollars on the hand-out market, is worth around two hundred bucks. He thanks me for the money and leaves. The story sold me and that is that.

I ride up the elevator and get off at the seventh floor; back to my throne of quiet insurgence. I hear some rustling from the conference room down the hall. I make my way patiently down to see that there is a company boys meeting being conducted over several deli sandwiches. There is only one prerequisite to joining this club and that is a penis. I take my seat which disturbingly is the same seat I have found myself slumped in for most lunches. I don't understand why each and every one of these robots takes the same seat day-in and day-out. Can't these clipped winged creatures of habit see that I am a hairy creature of unhabit? Can't they see that what they shave I want to scratch, that Monday morning is hell for them but it is a fucking weekly nightmare for me. Can't they see that I am just posing as one of them? I am a phony, but no matter what I do to expose myself, it just never happens. I never get called because these people are just too worried about being called themselves. I look at Steve McMartin. They call him McMartini around here because of his alleged drinking escapades. He is a tall version of a rat complete with buckteeth and a mustache. He is a middle manager in this God-forsaken widget company, has been for years and is destined to be for many more. Right now he is rattling off a ferociously untrue tale that involves strippers and him and some wood glue. I know it's untrue and it's a fact that isn't lost on anyone in the room. I don't even like to be in the same dimension with McMartin when he is eating. It's like watching a buzzard with poor manners.

"So I said to her…"

Without haste, I take the attention from him and turn it on him. "Hey Steve, why don't you switch seats with me?"

Shocked by the interruption of one of his classic stories, he gives me a look of puzzlement and then replies, "What? What is wrong with your seat?"

"Nothing is wrong with my seat. I sit here every frickin' day and now I want to sit there."

McMartin responds to what is obviously an insane request, "No way! Look, if you want this seat you can have it. TOMORROW! Now my ass is in it and it is going to stay that way."

"Look Steve, I don't want that chair tomorrow, I think I will take Deveroux's chair tomorrow. I want that chair you're in right now. You have monopolized it long enough. I bet you have your own official ass-prints in that chair."

Man does rat boy ever get riled up easy. Turning pitch red his voice rises, "You want the goddam chair then take it from me!"

McMartin leans forward and wiggles those whiskers as if to dare me into action. The challenge being noted, I devise an impromptu plan A and before ratface can even blink he has a half-eaten pickle on an inbound course for his forehead. Splat! Target located and destroyed. The pickle, defying gravity, rests motionless on his face for three to four seconds before dropping to his lap. McMartin stands up, grabs the rest of his lunch, and storms towards me. "You've got a bad attitude and you're an asshole. There's your fucking seat."

"On second thought, I think I will stay here." His only response was a final slamming of the door before he left.

Deveroux, sitting to the left of me, is my only real confidant in the place. The rest of the group just doesn't get it or they just don't get it the same way I do. Deveroux doesn't enjoy the work he does either; he is just more diligent about doing it than I am. He is still a cog in the wheel, but he just desires to be a cog in a different wheel. Above all else, he doesn't take me seriously which in this environment is the only way to take me.

"So Deveroux, what's your deal?

"No deal here, Krafty, I'm just hangin' and bangin'. You know what I mean? Day's almost over and I am almost out of here."

"Don't you ever get sick of that philosophy? The one-day-at-a-time bullshit that results in the daily time slowdown that gives us fifty-hour long workdays and three-minute long weekends. It's the only choice that suckers such as you and I have. If we were to look into the future thirty to forty years we would realize that we will have worked most of that time away. I want to fight time and not succumb to it. I want to wake up at a different time every day, shower only if I choose and decide myself when it is time to stop working. These shackles right here, are going to come off boy, believe me.

Today at 1:40 in the afternoon on January 20th, I, Jay Kraft, will begin to resurrect my soul. Conforming has done and will continue to do absolutely nothing but darken my soul. I have been traveling in a downward spiral right along with the collective conscious of the world. Right now, however, I am reaching my hand up for the seat to pull myself out of the toilet bowl of conformity. I will drip dry the main stream stench from my body and chart a new course to fulfillment."

As I looked up from my mid-afternoon rant, I noticed that the room was empty with the exception of Deveroux. He had a shit-eating grin on his face and was taking the last swig from his soda can.

Applauding as he stood, "Man that was inspirational. I got a few tears in my eyes and I think I soiled my pants. No, that was just a false alarm, but that speech was memorable."

"I'm serious, you bastard. I've got to find a way to jettison the rocket booster and simply orbit life at my speed."

"Well I don't know about you Krafty, but all I want is a shitload of money. I want money in the bank, money in my drawers, in my food, in my women, and I especially want money in my pockets."

As he says this he leans back on his chair and projects these visions onto the wall for me to see. "There is my house, you see I have 18 Mercedes, all black. Here is my girlfriend – pretty ain't she. Here is my maid – pretty ain't she. Here is my chauffeur – pretty ain't she. Oh, look at that. That is the viewing room. Full size movie screen complete with surround sound and vibrating leopard skin seats. Here is my fully stocked bar and behind that is another fully stocked bar, just in case. Upstairs is my master bedroom. My bed is 10 feet by 8 feet and I have twenty six pillows each with their own name."

As Deveroux fades into the depths of his fantasy, I return to my office wishing it were all so simple for me. Normally a good afternoon rant will hold me over for two to three weeks, but today was different.

At some point I have to decide what it is that I want. If it was just money, then I could just sell my soul to the devil. I am running the race of life and I cannot find the starting line. I thought I knew where it was but when I showed up there were just a bunch of fat women playing volleyball. I asked them if they knew where the race of life began, but they just asked me if I knew how to jump serve. I believed for a while that the key to life lies in experience. Experience would open doors and opportunities for me. All experience has to prove beneficial eventually, right? I thought the day would come when all of my challengers couldn't even compare to the wealth of experience that I would have to draw from thanks to years of sticking to my philosophy. Unfortunately I am realizing, even though I still refuse to believe it, that it isn't the way things really work. Thankfully, the buzz of the phone jolts me awake.

"Krafty, what do ya say to a little happy hour action."

"Sorry Deveroux, I have a meeting tonight. You know, gotta sell the company. Growth, growth, growth."

I find an afternoon of not doing work at work to be a refreshing and stimulating way to prepare for a sales meeting. It takes a lot of mind power to sell something that you don't believe in to a bunch of greasy money counters who only want to take from you, step on you, and accidentally spit on you as they steal your wallet. I say it takes a lot of mind power because you have to keep from using your brain for two hours. You have to find neat ways of saying nothing except more and better and then you have to buy these *business leaders* food and alcohol.

I don't even look at the crowd when I stroll in. I just plow ahead with my pitch. "So not only has our flagship line, The Imperial Widget, upped its market share a full 10 percent, but the technological possibilities of the new Fidgeting Widget are going to take us to the next level. On top of that we have just signed a deal to be the sole supplier of widgets for the entire defense department, so let's hope those A-rabs step out of line."

Giggles erupt from the crowd as do a large show of hands for the question segment.

"Jay, you stated that the fidgeting widget was the only product of its type, but I have heard that Mitsusushi has a product called the Itchy widget which outperforms yours."

Bob grins as he sits back down. Bob and I go way back. I have bought him a thousand lunches and he hasn't purchased one thing from me.

"Well Bob, Mitsusushi is coming out with the Itchy Widget, but don't believe the hype. This product has under-performed in all lab tests but you would have had to do some reading to know that. Anyway what do you care Bob, you're just here for a free dinner and an escape from the wildebeest you call a wife. I saw your son the other day and I decided to show him some mercy. So… I ran him down with my car."

With that a rapid-fire session of questions begins.

"Jay, are there any break points or discounts on certain quantities purchased?"

Finally, someone asks a legitimate question,

"Sorry Tim, the only breakpoints are on that chair your sitting in. When did you become such a fat bastard? Damn, you are swollen. I couldn't find your nose and I think you have a small animal in one of your chins."

"Jay, when will the Fidgeting Widget be fully integrated into your future forecasts?"

"Another excellent question, Chuck. If you would remove your head from your anus you would already know that I told you to shut the fuck up a half an hour ago."

"Jay, do you think this is really the most effective sales presentation?"

"Tom, no I don't, but I also didn't think that people grew hair from their foreheads."

"Jay, what time is it?

"It's time to get a lot of booze and a little food and it's all on me."

A wall rattling cheer echoes through the hall as I draw another successful sales meeting to a close.

Ajax the God
Brian Ames

"There ain't much to being a ballplayer, if you're a ballplayer."
— Honus Wagner, Pittsburgh Pirates, 1909

Pre-Game

Former baseball great Jackson Romero loaded four shells in the magazine of his Winchester Model 70, pushed the brass down against the springs, stuffed a fifth bullet in the chamber. He pushed the bolt home, snapped the safety lever on with his right thumb, shouldered the rifle with his left thumb and forefinger wrapped around the leather sling, and only then looked up to survey the Idaho forest around him.

It was cold, about nineteen degrees, barely past dawnbreak. Tall larch and tamarack pines reached up to a low, hard flannel, some of their tips lost in flat mist. It was quiet yet; the small forest creatures that make noise were not yet waking with their morning chorus of pips and squeaks.

Jack breathed in the clean air, drew it deep in himself, thought of the smell of *silver* – brisk, honed, paralyzing, diamond-bright. He looked around at the woods to the north side of the logging road – which ran here east and west – searching for the best entry point to the canyon that ran up the west flank of Pot Mountain. From next to his rig, standing on the tiptoes of his boots and craning his neck, he could see a shelf over the canyon through field glasses, a hideaway that promised to look back over and through the valley. He thought it might provide a promising vantage for grazing elk. Although he had hunted several times in this area, returned here with members of his Orofino Cement Company crew for two straight seasons, he'd never been up this draw before. But this site had beckoned to him inexplicably, driving this morning after dropping his crewmates up-road, big tires popping on gravel as he slowed for tight curves. He liked to pay attention to this sort of sixth sense; sometimes it paid off.

His eyes settled on an opening between two tall firs. Mind made up, he turned to retrieve wool gloves from the driver's seat, pulled them on, checked to make sure he had his keys, clicked the door locks and closed the door gently. Still, in the near-total silence of the Bitterroot morning, the engagement of the door's latch and lock seemed as loud as the smack of cured hickory on leather. Jack stood silent and waited long after the echo faded, blowing steam, the only movement his fingers inside the warm gloves. Then he stepped into the woods.

The First Inning

Somehow he'd gotten into his head, perhaps from the sharp report of the closing door of his Jeep, thoughts of baseball. This made some sense; he still constantly thought of The Game. Even though Jack had walked away from it twelve years ago, he had spent seventeen years playing. Most of his formative years.

As he stepped through the woods, over downed logs and through low groundcover that snagged at his trousers and bootlaces, he recalled his early love for the game, to play and play and play. His boots, moving through frozen grass and salal, small foot-level plants, made the sound of sandpaper circling on ash. It was not an unpleasant sound, but a racket elk would hear from hundreds of yards distant. The noise didn't much matter at this point, though. He'd have to make the vantage point he had spotted from the road and sit there, motionless, quietly, for more than an hour before he could trick the animals into believing – maybe – that he wasn't there.

As he climbed out of the hole, at perhaps a five-percent grade, his mind wandered over early ball games, the ALCOA Little League in Vancouver, Washington.

The springtimes and summertimes of southwest Washington state seemed, in his mind, to have been huge spans of time, entire eras in comparison with the lightning pace of life as a mature man. Summers had gone on forever, and he remembered the summer he was eleven years old, pitching for the Bevos – short for the Beavers, after the old Portland AAA semi-pro team.

As a boy, Jack threw the ball so hard the catcher would soak his mitt hand in a bucket of ice water between innings. Once that year he threw wild, the ball cratering into the left bicep of the opposing team's batter with an audible *WHULPPP* that made the small crowd of parents and siblings gasp from the bleachers. The ball arrived so hard its red stitches embossed a jagged line of hounds teeth on the batter's skin. As the unfortunate boy lay next to home plate, bat forgotten, squeezing and rubbing his muscle through tears, coaches ran from the dugouts to provide succor.

Jack had stood on the mound, unsure what to do with himself. He pulled his cap up, brushed his hair up under the bill, snugged it back on tight. Deciding a wild pitch was a risk every batter must assume, and no real fault of the pitcher's, he finally debarked the mound to check on the batter too. By the time he got to the plate, the unlucky kid was on his feet, still whimpering, and the small crowd was clapping its encouragement. Jack had extended his hand in a gesture of sportsmanship, meaning to apologize. But the batter ignored it, glaring through an ache that was not even close to subsiding, was, in fact, growing.

Jack shrugged, returned to the plate, and struck out the next two batters standing – six straight perfect fastballs – to retire the side.

That year, Jack started all ten games as pitcher, hit eleven home runs, had an earned-run average of less than two, and led his team to the league's first undefeated season for boys at that level.

The Second Inning

Jack shifted shoulders with the gun and picked up his pace, climbing harder now up the game trail. Here in the Clearwater unit, on the west side of the mountains, the temperature stayed below freezing for most of the morning – if it ever made it above 32 degrees all day. He was beginning to pass patches of snow left over from the first falls of autumn. The were places in the shadow of Pot Mountain where the sun never hit all day, down deep in ravines where drifts piled up and never melted until well into spring.

He'd been hiking about a half an hour, climbing all the way – he had achieved perhaps another eight hundred feet of elevation from the logging road. He believed he'd encounter the lookout point in just a few more minutes, and to his left the valley swept away below him. He could see the ground fall off steep, could look out at the tops of hundred-foot firs that seemed only feet away. The forest was dense here; so much so that the Jeep and road had been swallowed behind him within the first five minutes of the walk.

He heard the silky honk of a raven, its wings thumping against dense air, then saw the black form of the bird with its mate like two X's against the gray. He looked back up the game trail until it disappeared in trees, noted orange and white fungus underfoot, deer tracks, spoor – the sign of game animals everywhere here, but not quite fresh.

Another five minutes passed and the first sweat broke out beneath the brim of his hunter-orange ballcap. His back started to itch as perspiration seeped out there too, and the trail went steeper. In a couple of spots, the way was more like climbing than hiking. He went down on all fours, pulled himself over downed timber, grabbed frozen fern fronds to pull himself along.

At eye-level, he encountered squirrels, voles, the blue-gray backs and brown heads of common nuthatches. Friendly birds interested in his progress. He slipped on a scab of ice in the trail, went down on one knee hard, whispered *shit* more out of disappointment for the racket he'd made than any discomfort. He gathered and rose, adjusting the firearm, pushing higher, and suddenly the trail rounded up, evened off into a bluff of light, evenly spaced Ponderosa pine.

He walked slowly through the plateau, noting the jigsaw bark of the big, red trees, the long, thin green needles. Pressing on to the other side of the grove, he startled a wood grouse in an explosion of sound and feather. Jack couldn't tell when the frantic beat of its wings faded and the hammering of his own heart took over.

He was in the woods about an hour, and the small animals were fully engaged and, for certain, fully aware of his presence. Every time he would pause to rest, chipmunks would crowd around and scold him for intruding in their country. Hummingbirds would light among vine maple nearby for milliseconds, then take flight again, hover, jerk and dart on crazy, zagging courses through the low plants.

Jack heard the signature of beak against bark, one exploratory tap of a woodpecker. He knew it preceded, by only a few moments, a staccato rill of pops, a phalanx of drumbeats from the bird. But in the seconds between that first grub-seeking jab and the cacophony that was sure to follow, the single report echoed through the forest and down into the canyon, an exact tattoo of ball against bat. Jack smiled.

The Third Inning

One late spring day Jack Romero, batting cleanup for the Hudson's Bay Eagles, hit the ball so hard and so far, so *comprehensively*, no matter how hard they tried after the game, they couldn't find it. He had done this with the bases loaded and no outs, a *Grand Slam*, and he circled the bases whooping like a god, his arms pumping air.

A couple of weeks later Skylab fell out of orbit, and in the absence of evidence otherwise, Jack liked to tease that his home run ball had simply risen out of the Hudson's Bay High School ballpark, out of Vancouver, Washington, out of southwest Washington state at the northward bend of the Columbia River, and into the exosphere. There, still picking up momentum, it had pierced the aluminum hide of the world's first space station and sent the crippled ship – its orbit taking a few weeks to deteriorate – death-spiraling to final demise on the hardpan of Australia's Outback.

His girlfriend that night had allowed, on her parents' sofa, very heavy, very intense petting – more than she had ever given up. He went home afterward in the state of a young man who is simultaneously in two hemispheres: One foot was in the awed, frightened, curious, tiny-bit-guilty hemisphere of the slow comprehension of female mysteries; the other was in a complete state of rut, enhorned, manic for gratification. He went to bed early in the morning confused and thrilled, slept intermittently, and woke exhausted but with this knowledge: *Baseball is the key to everything.*

The next morning, a Sunday, he clipped the photo of himself jacking the ball out of the park from Page 1 of the *Columbian*'s Local Sports section. He slipped the clipping into the folios of a scrapbook his mother wanted him to assemble and caretake. *Not bad,* he thought, *the front of Local Sports.*

The next Friday afternoon, he stepped into the batter's box again out at Evergreen High, took the first pitch, then found the sweet spot with pitch number two, drilling it over the fence between the right and center fielders. When the hapless Plainsmen's pitcher finally was able to retire the side, it was already 5 to nothing, and Jack was taking the mound for the Eagles. He struck out the first five Plainsmen before one got a hit, a line drive that hit the tip of Jack's shortstop's mitt and caromed into left field.

But it was in the final game of his senior year, against the 8-1 Fort Vancouver Trappers at Kiggins Bowl, where Jack really earned his senior letter. It was there that he cemented a place in the Eagle baseball hall of fame, such as it was, an engraved honor-roll plaque in a glass case near the school office. Bay, also 8-1, and Fort were tied for first place in the Southwest Washington League, so the winner would be league champions.

The Trappers were the home team, so had last at bats. The score was 4 to 3, Hudson's Bay. Jack was exhausted, wrecked, still throwing in the ninth inning after more than eighty pitches. He'd struck out the first Trapper in the bottom of the ninth. The boy had gone down swinging so hard he lost his batter's helmet. Then Jack had momentarily lost it, walking batters number two and three. Now there were runners on first and second, and Jack threw his wildest pitch of the season, allowing both runners to steal bases. While the Eagle catcher scrambled around the backstop for the errant ball, the two Trapper runners arrived easily on the third and second bags.

Jack started to worry, but fired the next pitch a perfect, taken strike over the inside edge of home plate. The umpire howled an oath: *STEE-RIKE ONE!* and the Trapper batter stepped back out of the box, evaluating the ump as if he were blind. Shaking his head, he returned to the box, pounded the rubber plate with the bat, and made himself ready. Jack let fly another fastball, and the batter drilled it straight at third base, a bulleting line drive the third baseman squared up and caught as if it were a casual toss.

The Eagle students and parents in the stands roared approval, and Jack saluted his third bagger with a touch of his ballcap's brim. After the ball went around the horn and back to him, he squared off, with two outs, and runners still on second and third.

He threw two straight fastballs for two taken strikes. Then he reared back as if he were throwing another, but instead sent a change-up that left the helpless batter confused and cross-eyed for five years afterward; at least that's how the story was later told. The batter swung at nothing but air and the ball slapped the catcher's mitt with a puff of dust. The place erupted and Jack threw his glove into the air, the Eagles pouring out of the dugout led by Coach Ramsey, piling onto him on the mound. And the weight felt better than anything he had ever before encountered.

The Fourth Inning

When Jack arrived at the point he believed to be the vista he could see from the logging road, he turned around and looked back from the direction he had come. The clouds had lifted a little and he could see what he supposed was two-hundred square miles of the Clearwater system, the north fork wrapped around Pot Mountain like a bow wave.

He thought just at the horizon he could detect Dworshak Reservoir, and he recalled a Fourth of July at nearby Elk River Falls, jumping from high rocks. He'd come out with a group of Cougar baseball prospects after graduating from high school, and they'd skipped town, crossed the state line into Moscow, and headed into the mountains on a tear.

They'd spent the day drinking bourbon and cola, cans of beer, and eating pepperoni sticks and bags of chips, jumping off the forty-foot rock formations a mile above the falls. When they weren't swimming and leaping, they sat around an illegal campfire and swapped baseball stories from the previous season – the senior year in high school for each of them.

Jack had been quieter than some of the other boys, finding himself for the first time in company of his peers or betters – at least as far as sport went. He recalled countless strikeouts, pitches hit hard back at him, headed straight for his head at a hundred miles per hour and snagged in his glove an inch in front of his nose. He told the story of hitting a ball so hard it broke a windshield in the parking lot.

"The coach thought it was so cool he offered to pay for it," he remembered bragging.

Jack grinned on the hillside recalling his coach's kindness, his own inflated sense of power after having stroked the ball so well that day. He sat down on a huge felled log, down near the base just above the rootball, looked out again over the Clearwater valley. He turned around and looked back up the flank of Pot Mountain. When his gaze returned downhill, he could see the entire valley through which he had just climbed, could look across at several nice clear spaces where elk might wander through. He could even see some tight tangles of maple and aspen at the valley floor, places where the big bulls might be watering or resting. He'd wait here now, for hours if necessary, still, quiet, hardly moving, for game to show itself.

One of the boys had asked the group whether any of them had a no-hitter. They had all nodded no. The boy, from Mead High School in Spokane, had broken out in the grin of a grizzly with the blood of salmon on its teeth. "Well, I do," he had bragged, and the other boys had shouted *Bullshit* or *Oh, fuck you*, and then *Really?*, all trying to reconcile their beating desire for such an accomplishment, each wondering what the taste of ultimate fulfillment for a thrower would be.

The Spokane boy ran to retrieve his wallet from the glovebox of his car, returned fumbling in it, withdrawing an old clipping. He unfolded it like a treasure map, held it out as witness. A clipping from the *Spokesman-Review*'s Sports Section, Page 1: *Takeshita pitches Mead's first 'no-no'*. The boys passed the clipping around, holding it up to verify it was him, indeed, on the mound in the picture. Each boy hoped some of the luck would rub off the newsprint, just by having known, swam and drank with the lucky Spokane boy.

Jack looked out over the valley and remained motionless. A sort of hibernation descended upon him, the slowing of metabolism that allows an elk hunter to remain motionless and silent for vast stretches of time – two and three hours. Only his eyes would move or, periodically, one of his gloved fingers. His toes would curl and uncurl in his boots, enveloped in wool socks, to keep blood pumping through them and thus thwart frostbite. His ears remained on alert and one thumb near the rifle's safety as the weapon lay across his lap. He waited to hear the ungulate sounds of approaching elk – a snapped limb, a pulse like the footfall of a horse translated through the spongy earth at his feet.

The Fifth Inning

Jackson Romero loved the game of baseball. For instance the green expanses of the outfield, the freshly raked dirt of the infield, the rubber on the mound, chalklines etching the route for runners.

The shape of home plate, like an upside-down house, and how the eaves of the house pointed at first and third like the two stars in the ladle of the Big Dipper pointed at the North Star.

That baseball was a game purely of physics, actions and opposite reactions, ball mechanics, orbits and arcs.

The odor of mown grass and an infield freshly tended. The blast of his coach's whistle.

The slap of a well-thrown ball against leather, or the pulse of bats striking the leather spheres, and the competing cries of "I got it!" and "Mine" from outfielders in headstrong, sprinting pursuit of fly balls.

The sound of crowds, especially female fans, expressing collective appreciation for a ball crushed past the fence, or thrown perfectly down the pipe.

The fact that, in its barest incarnation, baseball was a game of wits, a mindgame. Chess with muscles.

Jackson Romero's head swam when he thought of all the ways he loved The Game. So when Jackson received a full five-year scholarship to attend Washington State University and play ball for the great Bobo Brayton in Cougar crimson and gray, he packed his '69 Chevelle, then kissed his mom goodbye and shook his dad's hand. "So long," he said, "I love you guys," and drove the six hours from Vancouver to Pullman without glancing even one time in his rear-view mirror.

He met up with his Elk River Falls buddies at Perham Hall, the athletic dorm, frequented the parties that the Cougar football jocks seemed to constantly throw and dominate. Most of the really beautiful girls seemed to go for them, but Jack and his teammates kept showing anyway, hoping the footballers would break some hearts early in the year and the baseball team could perform clean-up.

What they found instead is that no woman with any brains at all was having anything to do with football players. In fact, the smarter ones remained on the periphery of those parties, dragged there by their football-player-loving roommates. And when approached by a baseball player, these quiet wall-sitters very much appreciated the more elegant, more cerebral game of baseball, if the game were properly presented in that way by a properly behaving presenter.

Jack certainly had the gift to thus present his passion, and he did so, many times, until he hooked up with a grain-farmer's daughter named Ruth from the tiny eastern Washington town of Kahlotus, which was barely more than a silo at the bisection of two state highways. Ruth, biblically named, was in fact probably ten times as smart, from a straight I.Q. standpoint, as Jack. In spite of this they fell in together fast, dated and studied together, engaged in protected, but premarital sex, the first for both. This was, perhaps, Jack's most enormous leap to date into rebellion; both of his parents practiced strong Catholicism, his father Luzon-churched by severe priests, growing up in the humid, post-war squalor of the Philippines.

Jack assumed he and Ruth would marry after graduation five years hence; Ruth was a music major and would never make any money. He, on the other hand, was going to be a ball player and bring in plenty. They could enjoy a more-than-comfortable life together. He'd bankroll the whole thing; she could indulge her music. He kept calling her clarinet "that *horn*," no matter how often she corrected him: "Jack, Sweetie, it's a *reed* instrument, a clari*net*."

Around the beginning of his freshman baseball season, sitting with her at a table in the university's Compton Union Building, over cinnamon breakfast rolls and coffee, he disclosed his assumptions about their future. Then, as in the wake of a surprise slap, he sat humiliated and mystified by the outpouring of her wrath. She stood, her chair flying out from behind her. "How *DARE* you?" she shouted.

He poured the unexpected loss of Ruth's companionship into the baseball season, translated the abruptness of her departure into well-swung hickory. The raw ache of her absence, so fresh at the beginning of the season, fueled the velocity of every pitch he hurled at the catcher's mitt. And when he homered in his first college baseball game, as a freshman, her outrage faded like the aftermath of fingers retrieved from a pail of water. After a few successful games, it was as if she had never been there. The lessons she had tried to teach him through her outrage – there were other important matters beyond Jackson Romero's personal universe, other persons beyond the totality of baseball players, with aspirations and passions of their own – were lost on him.

The Cougars were champions of the Pacific-10 Conference's North Division that freshman year of Jack's, as they were the year he red-shirted (Anne), his sophomore year (Leesa) and his senior year (Sherry).

The one blemish on the series of championship seasons was during Jack's junior year (Linda), when he was benched for the last half of the season with ripped-up hamstrings. So it was no fault of his.

The Sixth Inning

An hour and seventeen minutes after he hove to on the timber downfall, just as clouds seemed to be thinning and strained sunlight washed patches of the valley face opposite him, Jack detected movement at the periphery of his vision. He turned slowly to where he thought he'd seen something, let his eyes still and focus, waited again for something to shift.

There. He saw it again, maybe. Cocked his head to the side, the movement barely perceptible. Tightened his gloved grip on the barrel and stock of his rifle. He sat as immovable as a column, facing, searching again for a visual disturbance. And then the core channel of his vision clicked like a shutter. From all the competing, in-rushing ocular stimulation emerged the full body of a bull elk, facing him head on, its rack high and beautiful. The animal was maybe two hundred and fifty yards away, in plain view but camouflaged against a backdrop of dirt and rock. The animal had probably been there for some time, even as Jack stared straight at it. His vision only resolved the big bull after a smallest movement of the animal's carriage.

Jack strained to count the branches of the elk's antlers. He fought the urge to lift his binoculars; the animal was still looking straight at him. Any movement might alarm the elk, sending it careening down the hillside to be lost in thickets at the base of the ravine, or up over the ridge in only a few seconds. As it stood now, if the animal turned away – if just for five seconds – Jack could click off the safety and lift the rifle in one fluid, arcing movement, find the bull in the scope, center the crosshairs slightly over the animal to compensate for the longish shot, exhale, and pull the trigger.

It was impossible to establish whether the animal detected Jack's presence. It simply stared in his direction, intermittently lowering its neck to graze on frozen mountain grass. Jack didn't see any cows near him, which made sense this time of year. Most of the big boys traveled alone in mid-fall, the rut having concluded a couple of months earlier. The bull turned its neck to look east, and its rack moved over a patch of snow behind the animal. Jack counted five points in silhouette, unless he counted the eye guards, which some hunters did, making it six. Making it a *Royal*. A Grand Slam.

After what seemed like hours but was probably only a couple of minutes, the bull turned lengthwise to Jack, bent to the earth to graze again, and presented a perfect target. Jack lifted the rifle, closed his left eye and squinted through the optics with his right, flicked the safety, and fired a 7-mm lead projectile at two-thousand feet per second across the air that separated the valley walls. The bullet pierced the bull's hide, shattering bone, ricocheting through guts, liquefying flesh and sinew in its mushrooming passage.

The bull fell to its front knees, haunches in the air, and bellowed as the rifle's sharp report faded. Jack, ears ringing from the gunblast and shoulder tender from the jump of the stock, could see the steam roll out of its muzzle as it cried once, then fell over.

"Yes!" he whispered, unable to restrain joy. "YES!" He rose from his seat, pulled the bolt back and discharged the spent shell, shoving the bolt home again to engage the next bullet. He watched the still bull for ten seconds, then lifted the binoculars to get a closer look.

The bull lay in the circle of the field lenses, its chest heaving. Jack could see blood on the ground next to the animal, thought he could see the entry wound, although he was a long way off for that.

Then, to his amazement, the bull gathered, found its feet, and leaped out of the circle into black.

Jack jerked the glasses down, struggled to find the fleeing animal again with naked eyes, raising the rifle, saw its hindquarters disappear into a stand of tamaracks. He fired again, working the bolt, and again, and again, and spent the magazine carelessly, firing into nothing or, if anything, the bull's tawny ass. "Fuck!" he shouted. "Shit!" They were the only words that seemed half-adequate, clipped off and spat.

He started to sprint toward where the bull first had fallen. Now he would have to track the animal until he found it. As he ran, stumbling, raising all kinds of ruckus through his traverse down to the ravine base and then up the other side of the hill, he began to feel optimistic. First, he was sure he had mortally wounded the animal. Second, the animal had gone uphill, so would tire faster. Third, it was bleeding profusely, and following a trail of fresh blood – there were gallons and gallons in a mature bull, certainly enough to track – would be easy. It would leave a red, gory signature everywhere it went.

"No where to run to, baby," Jack panted the song, as he climbed to the bloody spot. "No where to hide."

The Seventh Inning

Jack called Jaime Romero, his father, on the telephone with the good news. His mother answered, but after rushed pleasantries he asked for his dad, promising to get her back on the line in a minute. He wanted to honor the man first with this triumphant information.

He imagined the old Filipino would jump off the couch, where he was probably watching golf, leap into the yard and shout the news to neighbors. He thought his dad would probably drive his co-workers nuts the following morning running around at the phone company future-tripping about the new house his boy would buy for him.

"Dad, I've been drafted by the Angels," he stated.

"Maria!" His father gasped. "God's mother!"

Jack heard garbled articulation through the handset; his father had obviously covered the mouthpiece, more than three hundred miles to the west, and was shouting at his mother. Then she got on another line and they both chattered through their pride. His mother said she wished she could come through the telephone line and hug him.

It took a while for him to explain that although the Angels had drafted him, he would not be moving to southern California just yet. He had been assigned to the Boise farm team, a Single-A outfit called the Hawks. Just a year old, they played out next to the Western Idaho Fairgrounds, and he hoped they'd be able to come out next spring and watch some games in person. Meantime, he'd make sure he got them tickets to the graduation ceremonies, a couple of weeks hence. And yes, he *would* be graduating.

In spite of his batting prowess, Jack was selected by California mainly for his arm. He was a great hitter; he was one of the best right-handed pitchers scouts had seen come out of the Pac-10 for several years. They wanted him to work with the Hawks for a while, then maybe move him up to one of the AA or AAA franchises. If he proved himself there, he could expect a call to The Show. He looked up a map of California in an atlas at study hall, found Los Angeles, then Anaheim, where the Angels played. *Damned near next-door to Disneyland*, he thought, and laughed aloud in the quiet library.

Jack played almost two seasons for the Hawks in the hot, arid dust of central Idaho. The sun would beat down on Memorial Stadium during day games and, occasionally – especially on promotion nights – the stands would be filled to capacity.

He would watch, warming up in the bullpen, as forty-five hundred Hawks fans in a line of cars approached on I-84, turned off on Cole Road, parked on the hot asphalt, engine blocks ticking. Those scorching afternoons, he'd stand on the bullpen mound and stare down the chute, then grasshoppers would leap out of his way as he wound up, cranked his leg around, and stepped out into the urgent delivery of his pitch. High clouds would coalesce overhead, merging into thunderheads to the north, piling up against the Sawtooth Range. Sometimes there would be lightning displays during the games, and the players from Eugene or Portland or Everett would look around nervously.

Jack started as a relief pitcher, and by the end of his first season, enjoyed the most saved games in the league. This was no small feat, since the league comprised the Single-A teams from all three states of the Pacific Northwest – seven teams in all, each with a squadron of great throwers.

He was throwing the ball so well in training camp for his second season the manager made him a starter. To celebrate, he bought a used Chevy Blazer, put magnesium wheels on it, and rode around Boise with a cowboy hat, new boots and western wear. He developed a modest reputation for evoking an enthusiastic response from the cowgirls he dated, hung out mostly with two or three of them and some of the other pitching staff. He even introduced one of the women to his mother and father, in town on a visit. The pair smiled and nodded, went back to their hotel after a steak supper, and laid down some serious Hail Mary's for young Jackson.

Jack was a large part of the Hawks' championship season that year, with an ERA of 3.2 and a very aggressive fastball. He averaged 94 miles per hour clocking out, and his fastest pitch was an even 100, and dead on. The catcher would shake his mitt like a wounded paw, stand up from a crouch, slide his mask up to rest on the crown of his head for a moment and holler, "Jesus Christ, Jack. Take it *easy*!" before throwing the ball back. Fans started calling him Ajax, and in the promotion of these new phonemes he was complicit: he signed the balls admiring boys would hand him over the outfield fence '*Jaxon* Romero.'

Angels management loved this new talent, and when they called him to The Show three quarters of the way through his second season, they did so with a summons to his manager's office in the training facility at Boise State.

"Jackson," his manager said. "I got good news, damned good news."

"Yeah?" Jack knew what was coming.

"You're going to be a Major Leaguer, son."

"Yes, sir." Jack tried to sustain control.

"You're going up to The Show, Jack."

"Yes."

"Congratulations," his manager said, extending his hand. "We'll miss you."

Jack felt like a firework, fuse sparkling then spent, now going off.

"It's OK to holler, son – this is a big fuckin' deal."

Jack hollered, grabbed the manager in a full-bodied press and slapped the man's sunburned back a few times. The pair danced around the office, Jack leading, knocking chairs out of the way, smacking his legs against his manager's desk. "The Show, The Show!" he chanted. "I'm going up to The Show!"

Two days later, as he worked with a new agent to find an apartment in Anaheim, the Angels traded him and the Angel's current third bagger to the Mariners for Seattle's current right fielder – a fellow who wielded a seriously large stick – and future draft picks.

So long palm trees and bikinis, Jack thought. *Hello rain.* "That's the way it is in the Bigs," his agent said. "It's just that way. Better get used to it."

His mother and father could not possibly have been more pleased.

The Seventh-Inning Stretch

Jack arrived at the spot where he'd dropped the big bull with his lungs scorching from the aggressive climb. He'd just run, at near full gait, five-hundred feet down one side of a heavily wooded ravine, battled his way through a tangle of alder, vine maple and compacted ice at the base where a small creek ran, then up – practically vertically – another five hundred feet in elevation. The forest floor was awash with bright crimson, and the elk's cloven feet had torn the path up pretty good.

He could track the direction of the hoofprints by recognizing which were fresher, and by the fact that there were sporadic shade pockets – those areas which were never touched by sunlight all day – all along the trail. On the dirty white snow of these frozen patches he could detect splashes and drips of fresh carmine. He knew the wound would be draining the bull's strength with each step the big animal took. The faster it ran, the harder its heart would pump. The more blood on the ground, the easier to pursue.

Jack knew the ultimate ethic of hunting big game: Take everything you kill; use it all. Never waste an animal. Never take a stupid shot. Never take a shot you aren't sure of, and never, ever, shoot an animal you don't intend to track and finish – even if you're out all night and have to follow the beast for days in the wilderness. It is simply not done.

He reviewed these simple rules as he rested above the blood, gathering strength to resume tracking the dying bull. He felt relief wash over and through him; on the run over, he had let some doubt creep in as to whether he would, in fact, be able to successfully track the animal. Elk are fast creatures; if panicked, they can be two ridges distant in the time it takes a fat hunter to get off a stump and raise his gun. And there would be nothing like the initial adrenaline kick of a gut shot to get a big bull in a profuse state of panic.

But looking around, Jack knew. This animal was dropping blood at a rate it couldn't sustain. This animal, whether it leaped and caromed for a quarter of a mile then dropped, or five miles then dropped, was going to fall over dead soon. This animal was doomed.

And this pleased Jack, because then he knew he had shot well, and he had covered the hunter's sense of ethics well. Jack took on the confidence and countenance of Ajax again, a side of his personality that did not often emerge anymore, this past decade. He smiled, shouldered the rifle, breathed in deep, and took off in the direction of the fleeing animal, as evidenced by the deep signature of confused hooves and the unmistakable path of blood.

Soon the track of the animal's flight veered upward again, so that with each step Jack was gaining further elevation up the south face of the ravine. He crossed an area of open ground, scrabble stones that had sheered off from above and collected in a delta slide of scree. The way through was delicate, each step a process of evaluation for stability and selection for foundation. This slowed him up; against the light shale-colored rock, he could see the red afterimage of the elk's passage well enough, but a misstep meant a hard tumble that could go on for a painful while. So Jack made the way across carefully, sensing each step through his bootsoles.

At the other end the tracks, blood and game trail entered a stand of spruce and turned uphill yet again. Then it passed through a thick area of scrub trees, limbs scratching his face and knocking spent needles down the back of his neck. For the rest of the day, needles would jab into his sweaty neck and down his back like little harriers, but still he pressed on, higher.

Jack was no longer a jock, hadn't been for some years, but he wasn't soft either. His stamina was holding up, and once in another clear area, he stopped to catch his breath. His blood hammered in the wilderness; his temples sounded like they had helicopter rotors near them.

The he heard the sharp crack of a broken limb, the movement of an animal's chassis across dry wood, a snap. Then a rustle of leaves. He turned quickly to face the source of the sound, uphill, and saw the bull forty yards away.

Hunting is a pursuit one part skill and one part coincidence – being in the right place at the right time, with the right part of one's body facing in the right direction. All the planets must be in alignment for success. If, at the moment Jack saw the bull again, his body had been facing the animal slightly more, if the gun had been held in the hands at that point rather than slung over the back, if..., if..., if..., and so on. Jack would have been able to finish the elk there and then; from that range a kill shot was as sure as sunrise.

Instead the elk sensed his presence, and as Jack was fumbling with the rifle sling to pull it over and around off his back, the animal fled again.

The Eighth Inning

Ajax Romero stares at the batter as he approaches home plate. Ibanez is hitting .344 so far this season, his second with the Angels. Ibanez stares back with the insouciance of a caught, but recalcitrant, thief. The way he swings the bat as he approaches the box is unruly. He spits tobacco obstreperously. He glares balefully, brown eyes with pupils pinpoints in the Kingdome's ocean of halogen. He cuts the air a couple of times with the bat, a promise that he will rain down enormous disappointment. An oath: *I will rob you.*

Sixty-one thousand Mariners fans are shouting in crowd rhythm *A-JAX A-JAX A-JAX* and the organist, his key-tappings amplified in waves across the domed stadium, throws back his head and smiles while he plonks out his simple tune. Jackson Romero cannot hear any of it; he is in full bloom of perfect, zen-like concentration. His focus, his reason for being, his teleological purpose, is the strike zone, the catcher's glove and the pitch, which he has not yet selected.

Jackson is like a computer's motherboard: at this moment, he knows only data that has been input. There are no runners on base. The Mariners lead four to nothing. The Angels have two outs in the bottom of the ninth. Ibanez could be their last batter. The Angels' box score, winking in digital readout over the visiting team's dugout, has a 0 in the "hits" field. Jackson is one out away from pitching a no-hitter.

This delicious notion, like a sweet apple falling from an orchard tree into his outstretched palms, first occurred to him in the sixth inning. He ran it from his mind like a bad dog, *too early, too early,* he shouted inside. He didn't want to think about it and for sure screw it up.

In the seventh inning the notion surfaced again, and he could tell with each stance, windup and delivery, the crowd was now aware he had the potential to close in on it. While the Mariners were batting, no one came over to sit by him in the dugout, neither in the eighth inning nor just before now, the top of the ninth. A pitcher with a no-hitter in his grasp is like an anti-leper, but the effect is the same: utter abandonment. Solitude. One is alone, tormented by one's hard desire, left bargaining with God. A pitcher within spitting distance of a no-no is so potentially holy that no one wants to effervesce his rhythm, bollocks his luck, jinx his hoodoo. No one wants to fuck him up, to be the cause of all that.

So Jack had sat at the end of the bench, alone, watching the Mariners top of the order get one hit. But the side retired with a snagged fly, a strikeout, and a foul-tip snared in the mitt of the Angels' catcher.

Ibanez steps fully into the box and pumps the bat. Jack stands, the ball held in his right hand so it's visible to the outfielder, so the batter can't see the configuration of his fingers over the seams. Jack's catcher flashes signals under his mitt, and the umpire's mask towers over him like a gargoyle that could be friendly or malevolent. Jack pulls his glove over to his right side, reaching across his chest, the start of his windup. Turns with his right side facing the batter, pulls back rearing like a horse, lifts his left leg to pull the pitch forward and establish inertia, and flings his eighty-third pitch 93 miles per hour into the strike zone. Ibanez pulls the bat back slightly and cuts like he's going for glory, fans airspace a millimeter above the ball, and has one strike.

The crowd, on its feet, goes insane. The catcher returns the ball to Jack, who removes his glove, rubs the bill of his cap, returns his hand to the mitt and hoists his pants. Climbs the mound again, deaf, solitary.

Jack's second windup and delivery produce a ball Ibanez lets go by. It sure looks like a strike to Jack. The catcher wants to stand up and get in the ump's face, but refrains. No interference in this standoff. This is between Ajax and God, with the umpire in the dual role of adjudicator and advocate. The count is one and one.

Then he throws another ball, and the count is two and one. His fourth throw is a slider. To Ibanez, it appears the ball will arrive high and outside of the strike zone, but with a few feet to go its internal gyros swerve and the ball curves inward and down, penetrating the zone as Ibanez stands watching, bat still up. The umpire holds his fist up and howls *STTEEEE*, doesn't even finish the word; to do so would be vestigial.

A no-hitter beckons him. The count is two and two, and he must simply deliver a strike. Like a hundred-thousand strikes he has thrown over the past fifteen years: just one more. He is as serene as the Buddha. The crowd noise diminishes into the click of a metronome, metering out what he must do, what lies in front of him. It is as if he and Ibanez and the catcher's mitt and the strike zone are deep in the vacuum of outer space. It is the game of physics.

A drop of sweat that might make the difference escapes his cap-brim, slides down his forehead, stings in the corner of his eye. He winds up and throws for glory.

Ibanez swings at Jackson Romero's eighty-seventh pitch of the game, a 91 mile per hour fastball, and misses.

The 120-point headline on Page 1 of the next day's *Seattle Times* proclaims simply, as if all other words would be superfluous: *Romero: 'No!'* It hovers over a full-color, above-the-fold photo of Jack on the mound, still alone, his arms in the air, right hand bare fisted, left hand gloved, a champion. In the lower left hand corner of the frame is his catcher, just rushing the mound but not quite covered the distance from home plate yet. He had been the first of Jack's teammates to arrive, and they had en masse, and buried him at the bottom of a dogpile, in a joyous baseball celebration.

A local firm, whose chairman was one of the partial owners of the club, ran a congratulatory advertisement every day for the following week. It showed the same photo, **ROMEROOO OOO OOO!** over it in banner type, the **O**'s to replicate the Angels' box score, each a placeholder on the way to his defining moment.

Top of the Ninth

Jack climbed faster, and now his stamina *was* starting to fade. He ran around rock outcrops, climbed over huge felled logs driven over in windstorms that roared out of the Bitterroots, slipped on ice patches. Every step he took was taxing him more, and he was drenched, by now, in his own sweat.

Still, he was determined to track and finish the big bull. To concede would be unacceptable, anathema to his sense of fair play.

Up above him, another fifty yards, he could see that the hillside terminated in summit. He did not know what lay on the other side, another pleat in the chain of foothills, he guessed. But he would find that damned bull and show mercy. He would deliver the kill shot, come the end of the world or not.

Bottom of the Ninth

Ajax Romero was like Icarus or a supernova. Immediately after throwing the no-hitter, people had to shield their eyes from his effulgence. He exploded before them in carmine streaks, great gouts of bright flame. A Seattle-area celebrity, he was held in awe as one who had flown close to a sun rarely encountered. He appeared impervious to the surety of its burns.

But a nova flings its gases about in extraordinary display quickly, like the unfolding and stowing of a peacock's train, and then the light ebbs, and swirls in eddies that are only an echo of the explosion. The wax holding the feathers in the wings melts, and they fall away and, lift thus flummoxed, Icarus crashes like an asteroid into the Aegean Sea.

Jack threw two more seasons for the Mariners; halfway through the second year, they pulled him out of the starting rotation and put him back in the bullpen as a saver. When that didn't work out, they sent him back to the Tacoma AAA team for "rehabilitation," according to the M's front-office news releases.

Ajax Romero was waived by the Mariners organization in the early Spring of 1988, just as Cactus League play was starting up down in Arizona.

Jack lived in Seattle for more than a decade afterward, keeping a nice downtown apartment, living off savings and investments. He didn't have a regular job; although once in a while he was invited, for a speaker's fee, to deliver a homecoming or matriculation address at an area high school or junior high. His father, then his mother, died in Vancouver. Every once in a while he'd be asked to play in a celebrity golf tournament for charity, his partners and opponents washed-up jocks too. And he once got a gig doing a Jeep-Eagle commercial as a caricature of himself – *Zero Hits, Zero-Percent Financing!* No one got the tag line.

He started to haunt the Cloud Room, nine stories above Ninth Avenue in downtown Seattle next to the reconditioned Paramount Theater. He would hover over the bar there with Ansingh, the Indian barkeep, and drink gins and tonic. He liked the British guard on the Beefeater label, so that was "his" gin.

In time, Jack spent so much of his days in the mahogany and leather upholstery of the Cloud Room, he moved into the Camlin Hotel underneath it. Then he could take his breakfast, lunch and dinner there, and get his news from the television that hung over the bar like a barn owl. It was in the Cloud Room, for instance, that he first learned the Mariners' owners, dissatisfied with the earnings potential of the Kingdome, were threatening to move the team to another city if a new stadium wasn't constructed.

And the consequence of public approval for this notion was that the Kingdome would be razed and a new stadium erected, and where the Kingdome had stood would be the parking lot of the new structure. Jack rejected the notion, tossing back more gin: People would now throw their cigarette butts and leak oil from their untended crankcases and spew vomit from consuming too much beer onto the spot where the pitcher's mound had been. It was almost as if they would desecrate the only holy ground he knew.

He thought of Babe Ruth's famous words, dying of throat cancer: "The termites have got me." He felt the familiar friend of drunkenness settle in, convince him sickly, sweetly, that it doesn't matter. He belted back another shot, ordered another G&T from Ansingh, fell off the barstool in a stiff wind.

Another Cloud Room patron looked over at the wreck of Jack. "Ain't much of a man if he can't handle his mud," he pronounced. "Hey, isn't that Ajax Romero," his companion asked. "The pitcher?"

The Post-Game Show

"It is a statistical fact that the vast majority of no-hitters are achieved in the ninth inning."
— *Anonymous Wiseass*

Jack was nearly passed out from oxygen deprivation, from deep, hot breathing, from exhaustion, when he crested the last rise of the hill, slipped in another puddle of the bull's blood, and crashed onto both his knees. The rifle, falling forward from his shoulder, clattered on the ground.

His calves burned like they'd been poked with needles, and his thighs ached. He was wet clear through his clothes and breathing hard. It put him in mind of the wind sprints he used to run in spring training. Continuously they would sprint, fifty yards at a stretch, with only ten or fifteen seconds of rest in between, through the training grounds in

Vancouver, or the Palouse Country around Pullman, or in the dry scrub-dust of Boise, or in the high desert around Peoria, Arizona. Young then, they would gasp and laugh. Today, Jackson Romero was not laughing. He was now in no small amount of fear of a pending heart attack.

At this moment, the thought of letting the elk escape first entered his mind. It was an unwelcome, vagrant thought, which he immediately quelled, but which would not stay down. As he lay gasping on an alien hillside, he thought of the story he would tell the other members of his concrete crew. He'd just moved to Idaho two years ago, a geographical cure to all the depression and troubles that dogged him in Seattle. It had been a long, hard task, the winning of their respect. Giving up a wounded animal would, to a man, be a setback. And he couldn't hide it from them; they would have heard his shots. They would know he had hit something.

This realization drove him to his feet, and he lumbered slowly up, like he had life-draining wounds himself. The desire and obligation to locate and dispatch the animal from its pain surfaced again – more powerful than the selfish consideration of what his crewmates would think of him. Left unpursued, the beautiful bull would take one final step, crash to earth as its lungs filled with blood or its heart stopped, siphoning nothing but itself, a seizing, dry, sticky pump. Or it would lay bleeding to death, and the smell of it would attract coyotes. The wild dogs would eviscerate the bull without mercy, the pack feasting on its guts – the soft, unprotected parts of it – tossing bits of meat and fat in the air while the bull's vision grew dim, but it nevertheless watched.

Jack caught his breath, steadied himself. Climbed the final steps to the summit where he saw blood in hoof-stamped snow. And watched the world drop away.

Below him was a cliff face, and he stood on the rim of a steep cirque, a knife-edged ridge that plummeted a sheer two-hundred feet to an inaccessible floor. There was no human way down, in, up or out. The bull lay broken at the base of the cliff.

Jack Jackson Ajax Romero shouldered his rifle, turned and started the hike out. He began assembling his story.

Contributors

BRIAN AMES writes from the Puget Sound area of Washington state. He has had short stories and essays in *The South Dakota Review* and *Snow Monkey*, and has work forthcoming in *Glimmer Train Stories* and *Happy*. He is a former editor of *Wind Row*, Washington State University's 1983-1989 award-winning literary journal, and is at work on short story collections and a novel.

Hailing from Glasgow, Scotland, eighteen year old JASON ANDREAS enjoys writing and listening to music. He's a first year student at Glasgow Central College of Commerce.

AIDAN BAKER is a writer and musician based in Toronto who's had poetry and prose published internationally in various literary journals. Baker is also the author of two chapbooks, available through a website: www.yesic.com/~abaker/home.htm. A book of poetry and drawings follows early next year.

Primarily a science fiction writer, TERRI BARCZAK lives in Corvallis, Oregon. She has five finished short stories and is researching two novel-length stories. She enjoys hiking, golf, movies and water sports. Her motto: The Common is Never Ordinary.

GAVIN BENKE was born and raised in Maryland. He graduated from Georgetown University with a BA in English Literature in 1998. After graduating, he toured the country playing the saxophone in a band. He has just finished a stint in the Dulles Corridor, and currently lives in New York City. This is his first published piece.

PATTY COLOMBE, a thirty-five year old registered nurse, wants to explore the dark spot inside all of us. She counts Edgar Allan Poe, Alfred Hitchcock, and Rod Serling as her inspirations.

JACK De VRIES began his writing career in 1991 by winning Bloomfield College's George M. Jones Award for literary excellence. His first published work appeared in the 1991 Cleveland Indians Yearbook, and he has written for the Indians ever since. Jack has also written numerous stories for *USA Today Baseball Weekly*, *Beckett Tribune*, and *New Jersey Monthly Magazine*, and authors a weekly column on sports for New Jersey's *Herald & News*.

RON L. DIXON is a sixty-year old, lifelong writer. In 1986 he was named an Amherst Poet. Dixon holds seven Golden Poet Awards from the World Poetry Society along with many other awards. At present he has a Self Help book and a work of fiction being considered for publication.

BRYAN STEVEN FOLLINS has a background in sports and technical writing. He is currently working on his Microsoft Certified Engineering Degree (MCSE). Follins, a 1981 journalism graduate of Louisiana State University, currently lives in Atlanta, Georgia. He dedicates his story to Ray Bradbury.

SUE W. FUERST currently lives in Maryland and looks for beach glass on the Delaware coast. More stories about Aunt Daisy are promised; Sue is also working on a novel.

JACKIE R. GATES, II is a freelance writer and former law enforcement officer. He has been previously published in *Sapphire Magazine*, *Country Back Roads*, and one of his poems was included in the poetic anthology *Listen with your Heart*. Jackie resides in the Branson, Missouri area with his wife and daughter.

Originally from the United States, GRADY HANRAHAN recently moved to the beautiful Devon coast of England. He enjoys travelling and writing about his experiences.

Active as a writer, musician, and playwright, MILTON KERR graduated from Worcester State College with a BA in English in 1977. He's currently a musician and playwright for the Blackbird Radio Theatre and the Blackbird Video Theatre.

LISA KLASSEN is a twenty-five year old Canadian girl, desperately in love with both the smell of trees and life in the city. This conflict is never resolved, and she spends her life either in the city or in the forest, moving back and forth when the need for the opposite becomes too unbearable. She feels this conflict oftens reflects itself in her stories and poems.

MICHAEL LARGO has published a book of poetry, *Nails in Soft Wood* (Pikadilly), and two novels; *Southern Comfort* (New Earth Books) and most recently, *Lies Within* (Tropical Press). He resides in a remote region near the Everglades National Park.

DAVID LU is a junior at Hunter College in NYC. He's a Psychology major with a minor in English. He plans to attend law school following graduation.

SHANE MAYER is a twenty-six year old aspiring writer and marketing professional. Born and raised in Philadelphia, he graduated from Albright College in 1995. Shortly after, he moved to New York City where he still writes and resides.

This is a first effort for MARY McDONALD, who has the beginnings of a novel in the works. She was, for many years, an Executive Secretary in Ossining, New York. She is now retired and living with her husband in Boynton Beach, Florida.

H. H. MORRIS is a retired teacher of college English and Speech. He made his first short story sale in 1963 and over the years has written everything from op-ed pieces to contract novels. He currently has two books available electronically through ebooksonthe.net. Morris lives in Aberdeen, Maryland with his wife of 38 years, three dogs, and a variable number of cats, guinea pigs, and mice.

PAUL PERRY has been writing short fiction for thirty years with more than 150 stories published. For the last thirty-three years he's lived in San Antonio, Texas, and all of his more recent stories have Texas settings. When he was a teenager, Paul hitchhiked around the country for two years. He especially likes to write about street people, homeless people, and what he calls "dispossessed" people. He presently teaches English at San Antonio Community College.

NILES REDDICK teaches English at Motlow State Community College in Tennessee and lives in Murfreesboro with his wife Michelle and his dog Harper Lee (named for the author). He's editor of *The Distillery*, a literary journal, and has been published in several journals. Reddick is busy on a film script.
He drinks too much coffee.

STEVEN RIDDLE has written poetry, prose, and nonfiction for more than thirty years. His life bears absolutely no resemblance to his fiction and he is, therefore, reluctant to burden readers gracious enough to read his fiction with the details. He has earned degrees in English Literature, Geology, and Paleontology and has recently had work published in an anthology of Florida writers and in *The Oxford Companion to Crime and Mystery Writing*.

JESSICA SLATER was born in England, to an English mother and American father. She's studied Philosophy, Psychology, Physics, and everything else that began with "P." After graduating from Oxford, she lived in London. She currently resides in the Denver area.

H. TURNIP SMITH is a medium-sized vegetable living deep under the ground. A serious candidate for Ohio's most boring man, Turnip writes stories to ward off insects. For more, plug his name in at Dogpile.

MERRYN SPENCER is seventeen years of age completing her final school year at a country high school in Australia. She is a member of the Poets Union and has had writing featured in *The Sydney Morning Herald*. Merryn has won local writing competitions and has been published in online 'zines. She has been twice highly commended in the prestigious Young Writer of the Year Competition.

www.ingramcontent.com/pod-product-compliance
Lightning Source LLC
Chambersburg PA
CBHW060746180626
46818CB00002B/463